MW00617300

A·CRAVING FOR·WOMEN

A · CRAVING
FOR · WOMEN

· SYBIL CLAIBORNE ·

E. P. DUTTON  NEW YORK

Published in the United States by E. P. Dutton,
a division of NAL Penguin Inc.,
2 Park Avenue, New York, N.Y. 10016.

Published simultaneously in Canada by
Fitzhenry and Whiteside, Limited, Toronto.

Library of Congress Cataloging-in-Publication Data

Claiborne, Sybil.
A craving for women.

I. Title.
PR6053.L24C7   1988   823'.914   88-3909
ISBN 0-525-24682-7

DESIGNED BY EARL TIDWELL

1 3 5 7 9 10 8 6 4 2

First Edition

*This book is dedicated to my writing group,
Carol, Ingrid, Eva, Suzanne, Kate, Sue, and Vera,
whose dissection of it, chapter by chapter,
deepened my intentions and enlarged my vision.*

I want to thank the following: My husband, Bob, whose graceful writing style has enhanced my own; my friend Adele Bowers, for a serious reading of my work; my agent, Frances Goldin, for her appreciation and hard work; the Dorset Colony House for Writers for giving me sanctuary.

PART I

1

The trouble started on a Sunday. We were having a brunch to welcome Valery, Saul's new wife, into the fold. I think of that day as a milestone, an event that separates life into compartments, before and after the flood or fire. For us it was the end of an era.

I do not believe in predestination; each of us is responsible for our lives. Yet so often we seem doomed to act within a defined pattern, our choices circumscribed by traits—lust, self-indulgence, delusions—that leave little room to maneuver. Or so it was with Saul. Yet even if I had been aware of his intentions and had known where his cravings were leading, was there anything I might have done to prevent the catastrophe?

Probably not, but it is hard to accept one's helplessness, one's inability to change things. Anyway, I wish I had tried, even if the attempt was as futile as the effort of that heroic, doomed child standing at the dike, fingers pressed into an ever-growing gap to stop the flood. If I sound melodramatic or vain, that is not the impression I wish to give. For, in truth, I was more like a Greek chorus viewing

Saul's folly with sorrow and concern and yet at the same time distancing myself.

But all this is hindsight. Let us start at the beginning, on a sunny fall Sunday. It is a little after noon; we are gathered together to meet Valery, Saul's new wife. Each of us has something for her—a present to welcome her into our midst. We are excited, curious, eager to meet her, to see what kind of person Saul has chosen this time. "It is remarkable," we tell each other, "that we are so compatible; sheer luck that we are all so interesting and intelligent."

Evelyn says, "How do you buy something for someone you've never met? It's pure guesswork." Evelyn, a lawyer with a heavy schedule, is frequently short on sleep. "I need a vacation," she is always saying. She says it now. She has brought Valery a basket too bulky to wrap. "What a handsome basket. What a generous gift." We pass the basket from hand to hand, admire it, fondle it, scrutinize its interior, each of us reluctant to give it up.

The patriarch will soon be fifty. Is that why he took a new wife, to mark the occasion, reassure himself, prove his attractiveness, his sexual prowess, his hold on life? We discuss his motives among ourselves while he sits nearby listening. He enjoys the discussion, occasionally interjects a remark to set the record straight. "That's where you're wrong," he says. And, a little later, "You took my words out of context."

I am the oldest and the first, not that that matters anymore. These days, Saul is more like a business partner than a husband to me. I'm not without feeling toward him. He is a lovable man, so filled with error and doubt one wants to protect him, hold him close. His personality intoxicates people—the blend of self-indulgence and generosity makes women think they can change him, suppress the bad, bring out the good, mold him into a more acceptable form. "He is basically a sweet and sensitive man," the wives tell each other. Even when he is at his worst, boiling over with insecurity, shattering everyone's

4

sleep for strategy meetings or long encounters in dark rooms, one struggles to forgive him and overlook his flaws. There was a time I saw him as a big cuddly bear. I wanted to sleep with him, make love to him, more than I wanted to do anything else.

He tells me everything, his innermost thoughts, confesses, makes himself vulnerable. "You are the only one I really trust," he says. He tells me things he would not tell to another living soul, criticizes his other wives, discusses their shortcomings, all the things about them that disappoint or irritate him. "Evelyn is too career minded," he says. "She doesn't know how to relax. . . . Jen is going to kill herself one of these days if she isn't more careful." He confesses things: "I once wanted to be a girl. Picasso bores me. I have never been able to finish *The Inferno*."

His self-doubts appear and disappear like seasonal allergies. He can pinpoint the event that set them off. "My cousin, a nothing person, became the world champion yo-yo player. Everybody in the family treated him like a celebrity. I never won an archery contest after that." "There must be more to it than that," I say. "There is," Saul says.

"He has a weak ego," Connie, his fifth wife, says. She makes me promise not to tell Saul.

"I am a seeker after perfection," Saul says earlier that Sunday before the others have arrived. Each wife represents a different aspect of womanhood—beauty, brains, wit, charm, skills, insights. "I am the last romantic," he says; it is this belief in perfection that keeps him seeking and marrying. He is the opposite of cynical. His heart is open to experience. He believes in happiness, he believes in love. He is a knight, the last of the troubadours.

My own view is somewhat different. He is a sensualist, a lustful man. "Not so," Saul says. "My sexuality is a learning experience; erotic desire a longing for the beautiful. The elaboration of technique is a way of interpreting the world, extending the boundaries. What is pleasure,

5

what is lust? How can we explain these things without first experiencing them?"

Saul and I are setting the table. He is explaining to himself as well as me his motives for taking another wife. "What's she like?" I say.

"She has a dimple here," he says, pointing to the small of his back. "Her hair is the color of maple leaves in the late fall, at the height of the foliage season. Her lips are as inviting as damsons, her skin is like peaches."

"What kind of peaches?" I say.

Saul, a fruit lover, takes this question seriously. "White peaches," he says, "the Italian kind."

"Her breasts are like grapes," I say.

"Everything is a joke with you."

"I wish it were so," I say.

When we are gathered together we all fear levity, our situation taking on comic aspects, ourselves clowns, or fools. We discuss among ourselves whether we are serious people. "Helen is a serious person," they say about me. "She has her work, responsibilities. The happiness of all of us is in her hands." Evelyn is a serious person. She is a lawyer, a mother, a success.

Usually it turns out that only Saul and Beryl are not serious people: Saul with his craving for women, Beryl with her love of useless gadgets—the perpetual light bulb, the ever-sharp knife, a double-duty duster—each one some magical solution to a problem hitherto unnoticed. "You can cut both oranges and bagels with this knife," she says. "But who would want to?" we say. Saul is not a serious person because his mind is so restless, shifting from here to there like a compass needle out of control.

And Valery, will she be serious? I wonder.

Saul and I are setting eight places at the long table. He is folding the napkins, each with its own wooden ring. Jen and Kelly made the napkin rings. Jen works in wood; her craft is of a high order. Each ring has the name of a wife incised on it in Art Deco letters. Kelly painted the letters in a soft greenish blue. Whether Saul is willing to

6

acknowledge it or not, we owe much of our success in the construction business to their skills.

Saul slips a napkin into each ring and starts to place them next to the plates. Then his eye is caught by something across the room: a listing palm tree. He goes over and turns it toward the sun. He is always like this—jumping from one thing to another. "You are the most restless person I have ever encountered," I say, though today I feel tender, even tolerant of his restlessness. But often this trait drives me up the wall and I feel like roping him to a chair until he has finished the task at hand—going over a blueprint, or estimating the board feet we need for a particular job.

Now he has returned to the table, where he is studying the place arrangements. I watch him rearrange the napkins, move Kelly next to Evelyn, Beryl beside Connie. Then he changes his mind and relocates Beryl next to me. As soon as he looks away I move her to another place.

"Is the tofu fresh? Will there be enough tabouli for the girls?" he says. The "girls" are Jen and Kelly, vegetarians both. "Are you sure there'll be enough to go around?"

"Everybody is bringing something."

"Did you remember to tell Connie to go light on the salt?"

"I remembered," I say.

"I hope Kelly gets good apples."

"Of course she'll get good apples." He is fiddling with the silverware, lining up the knives and forks in perfect symmetry. "Saul, why don't you go for a walk?" I say. "Or take a long bath."

"What time is it?" he says. He stands before the full-length mirror studying himself. I glance around the loft to see if everything is in order. The coffee table is strewn with Sunday papers, and although I hate clutter, I leave them as they are, for Evelyn will want to read aloud from the News in Review, so that we can share her outrage at the latest perfidy from Washington, and Beryl will want

7

to scan the Arts and Leisure section for news of her former boyfriend.

Our loft is long and narrow. A couch stands between the high windows at one end, flanked on either side by dried grasses in tall vases. In front of another tall window a palm tree waves its fronds. The golden pine floor shines. The long table where we eat is parallel to a brick wall where ivy hangs. The room is austere, nearly empty, as if waiting for an occupant. But it is the way I like to live and I am constantly on guard against additions. When the other wives bring me presents, I give everything away, pretending not to remember when they ask me what became of this lamp, that pillow, the handsome cut-glass vase. "Pillow?" I say. "What pillow?" Saul comes to my rescue. "The space is in her custody," he says.

Saul is still fiddling with the silverware when the bell rings. "I bet it's Evelyn," I say. Saul presses the buzzer. As it turns out, they all arrive at once, all but Valery, the wife we have gathered here to meet. Saul kisses his wives one by one. I kiss them too and take their covered dishes from them.

Evelyn has brought a lentil salad garnished with two scallions in the form of a V for Valery. She herself has no time to cook; Josh, her thirteen-year-old son, loves to mess around in the kitchen, try new recipes, invent new ways of preparing a dish. He invented a new way of shaping hamburgers, which he is trying to get Evelyn to patent so he can offer it to McDonald's for big bucks. I admire the V and so does Saul. "Josh is a very creative person," I say.

"Did he finish *The Mill on the Floss*?" Saul says.

"Not yet," Evelyn says.

We set the presents inside Evelyn's basket and place it on the table at Valery's setting. Jen and Kelly have brought a wooden bowl they made together, unwrapped because "It has to breathe"; Connie, something bulky wrapped in trendy graffiti paper. Beryl has brought day-old flowers. She gets them at the Catholic church after the Sunday

8

service. We put the flowers in water and set the container next to the basket.

Valery is late. Saul moves around the room as if he is looking for something. He stands before the high windows staring at the Empire State Building. Then he moves among his wives, trying to make small talk until Valery arrives.

He fondles Jen's hand. A month ago she hit it with a hammer, blackening the nail. She had barely recovered from a broken toe she injured when she dropped a wrench on it. We have long discussions about the underlying reasons for these accidents. "Why is she punishing herself?" we ask each other.

Saul presses his lips to the injured hand. "It doesn't bother me anymore," Jen says. "Now it's my ankle. I twisted it a little jogging." She thrusts out a bandaged ankle.

"I told her to be careful," Kelly says. She and Saul exchange a meaningful look.

Saul bends over the ankle. "Have you had it X-rayed?" he says. "She shouldn't run," he tells Kelly. "You ought to make her stop."

Kelly snorts. "Try and make her do anything," she says. Or at least we think that's what she says. She has an Australian accent that is not readily understandable. Kelly and Jen live together. Saul fell in love with Jen's cabinetwork. "Have you ever seen such craftsmanship?" he said. Kelly needed a green card in order to become a resident alien. She had come here on a student visa to study pigmentation with a New World master, decided that she wanted to stay if only she could get the necessary status. "Marry an American," she was told. Saul married them both in a single weekend.

Kelly is a painter. Before emigrating from Australia she did eighty-five scenes of the Outback. Each of them now hangs in a provincial hotel. "I am searching for a New World landscape that will stimulate my creative juices the way the Outback did," she told us. In the meantime she works for the construction company. She oversees the finishing—the sanding and varnishing, the subtle blending of pigmentation. Like Jen she is a craftsman, a seeker after perfection. Once a week, Saul spends his allotted night with them, but whether they make love or something else, nobody knows. The other wives take me aside, ask questions, offer theories. "Perhaps they spend the evening building something," I say.

Saul has moved over to Beryl. He is studying her belt. In order for him to get a good look at it, she is removing it from the belt loops of her jeans. It is woven of many multicolored strips of plastic. "Isn't it gorgeous?" Beryl says.

"Yes," Saul says, though if anyone else wore such a belt he would say it was tacky. "Where'd it come from?" Saul says.

"I got it at the store. It's one of our new lines." Beryl works in the five-and-ten.

While Saul is greeting his wives, touching this one, talking to that one, let me linger over Beryl, since she is soon to occupy much of this space. She is the youngest of the wives, not quite twenty-three. Saul found her weeping on the street one rainy Sunday. She lives in a hovel, is frequently broke. Our money is doled out based on a complicated formula, but Beryl can never make hers last. She borrows from the rest of us and fritters it away on takeout food and gadgets. Saul loans her money too, which he tries to keep a secret from the rest of us. She brings us presents: ballpoint pens, cotton balls, Krazy Glue (I have warned her to stay away from the glue), the kind of small item a person might grab and make off with. "I have a discount," she says. "They let me have anything I want at cost."

I suspect, when she is down in the basement doing inventory, she pockets whatever takes her fancy. "You have a suspicious mind," Saul says. "You think everyone has bad intentions."

"Not everyone," I say.

Beryl is a basket case. We all feel sorry for her. When

10

Saul said he wanted to marry her, we encouraged him. Even Beryl's mother, who runs her own consulting firm in the West, thought it was a good idea. "That girl needs guidance," she said. Each of us felt we could set Beryl a good example, be a role model, perhaps help her find herself. I want to make this clear; none of us objected to the marriage. I know there are going to be distortions, stories that falsify what actually happened. We encouraged Saul to marry her, to take her in hand.

Her mother wanted Beryl to go back to school, get her BA, and then go on for a Master's. "There is money set aside," she said. "She's not dumb," she said. "Her problem is a lack of motivation." She wanted Saul to talk to Beryl, convince her that she should complete her education. "I'll see what I can do," Saul said. But his gloomy look, his voice filled with doubt, made us wonder if he really wanted to.

"He likes her the way she is," Jen said. Perhaps, but Jen's mind lacks a certain subtlety. "He needs someone he can feel superior to," Connie said. Her analysis seemed more on target at the time.

Saul is often moody when we are all gathered together. He doesn't know how to act, who to be. With each of us, he plays a different role. With Connie, he is both guide and playmate. They go to galleries, try on clothes, unearth trends, seeking not mere pleasure, as the rest of us seem to think, but self-definition, a deeper understanding of the meaning of life. With Evelyn, he has endless discussions about Josh, the boy's every act analyzed and dissected in an effort to allay Saul's fears that our family arrangement will stifle Josh's development. He also turns to Evelyn for legal advice. She draws up all the firm's contracts, makes sure our liability insurance is adequate, intervenes in disputes with clients.

With me, he is a business partner and friend. We discuss contracts and schedules, gossip about the bizarre tastes of our clients, their eccentric ways. We spend a lot of time going over the layouts I design.

My specialty is spaces. I designed an igloo on West Broadway, a huge domed room enclosed in fiberglass ice bricks. To create a sense of truthfulness, water from concealed pipes dripped from the ceiling, an old bear's head doubled as a planter, an open fire burned in the center of the room. Another of my spaces had holes in the walls, broken tile, exposed wires. "Playful and original"—that's what the critics said about my work. "Her spaces with their unfinished quality leave room for hope, for change and growth." Not everyone agreed. "Her work leaves one in a state of unrelenting despair," another said. You can't please everybody.

Saul moves around among his wives inquiring about their well-being. "Did the pipe stop leaking? Is your allergy under control? Did you call the exterminator?" Domestic things. Husbandly things. He has a kind and courteous air, like an elder statesman circulating among his followers. But once these inquiries are over, he doesn't know what to say. He paces, looking anxious and lost. He stacks the Sunday paper; then he alphabetizes the sections. He walks into the kitchen area, pauses before the calendar with his conjugal schedule marked on it, then walks out. He looks at his watch, compares it to the clock on a distant tower.

"Does she know it's today?" someone says, and someone else says, "She doesn't know this neighborhood. It's easy to get lost in SoHo."

"I bet her train got stuck."

"Maybe she met with foul play." Beryl says this, and it makes Saul groan.

He deplores foreboding, although he himself is a captive of dark thoughts, gloomy expectations. "It is better not to speak of misfortune," he says. He prefers happy themes—a family party, large sums of money flowing in, fame, acclamation in the marketplace. He likes others to be happy too. "The trouble will end," he tells his wives. "The cold spell will soon be over." When Jen broke her ankle skiing, we fell so far behind in our work that the

12

entire family anticipated business failure. "That's not the way to look at things," Saul said. "The ankle will mend. We will catch up on all our commitments." But when the clients threatened lawsuits—a man sat in his tub weeping, waiting for the plumbing to be installed; a woman stared out of holes where windows would ultimately go—then Saul stopped answering the phone.

We try to reassure Saul now. "She's not all that late," we say. "She probably took the wrong subway."

"I gave her explicit instructions," Saul says. "I drew her a map."

"Maybe she lost her nerve. It can't be easy meeting a whole bunch of strangers," Beryl says.

"What sort of person is she?" Connie says. She fiddles with her bag, fighting a desire to pull out her notebook and start writing.

"She's very nice," Saul says.

Everybody exchanges an exasperated look. "Nice, what does that mean?" Evelyn says.

"You know: quiet, sensible, sweet."

Beryl is sulking. Until recently the newest and therefore the most desired, she feels displaced. Saul puts his hands on her shoulders but she shrugs them off. "This has nothing to do with us," he says.

"How'd you meet her anyway?" Evelyn says.

Now it's Saul's turn to look exasperated. "You never listen to a thing I say. I met her at my symposium. She came to hear my lecture. I told you all about it." Saul often accuses Evelyn of being too immersed in the law.

"Somebody has to be," she says. She never gives an inch.

Jen and Kelly are having a separate conversation. They are discussing work. They are working on a complicated storage wall with cabinets, hidden recesses, turntables, drawers. I have not yet told Kelly that the client wants everything finished in a high-gloss navy. Gloss depresses her.

"Why do you hate gloss?" Connie once asked her. She

13

is always trying to help us get in touch with our hidden feelings.

"It isn't natural," Kelly said. "That's why. It's an assault against nature. Of course I hate gloss. What normal person would want to live with shine?"

"But nothing is natural," Connie said. "We wear clothes, we cook food. There is something deeper involved here. Is it possible that gloss represents your opposition to the power structure?"

Kelly told her to fuck off.

"I was on to something," Connie told us later. "The problem with Kelly is she doesn't want to face her unresolved conflicts. She fears her anger."

"She's not the only one," I said.

Connie was training to be a psychotherapist at the time. She sent Saul a bill.

Saul was furious. "How can you do that to your fellow wives?" he said.

"My fellow what?" Connie said. I had to step in and smooth things out.

"Connie just wants you to know her value," I said. "That she's not just anyone giving advice but a person who one of these days will be a professional. People in their own families don't always get the recognition they get elsewhere. It's a question of respect, isn't it, Connie?" Saul took her home and spent the night with her even though it wasn't scheduled.

Beryl keeps wandering over to the long table and stealing a piece of bread, a hunk of cheese. "Beryl, stop acting like a child," I say.

"I'm starving," she says.

"We're all starving."

"Why doesn't she come?"

Saul picks up the phone, listens for a dial tone, hangs up. Now she is nearly an hour late. "Try calling her," I say. Saul dials a number. He lets it ring and ring.

Evelyn rummages in the briefcase at her feet and pulls

14

out a brief. "Let me know when we're going to eat," she says.

Beryl moves her flowers from Valery's place to her own. "I may just take them home," she says. "I hate being kept waiting."

"We'll eat in fifteen minutes," I say. "It's unfair to keep everyone waiting." Saul looks pained, starts to say something, then changes his mind.

"Maybe someone pushed her onto the subway track," Beryl says. "There's an awful lot of that kind of thing going on these days."

Saul groans. "Oh, don't say that," he says.

"Or she could have been mugged walking up the subway steps." Connie is writing Beryl's words in her notebook; I think she is doing a paper on us for one of her courses, a close scrutiny and analysis of a polygamous marriage in the Industrial West: how we interact, what we eat, whether our vocabulary has increased or decreased as a result of our multiple marriage—that sort of thing.

The meal has been eaten and Valery still hasn't arrived. Now we are all worried. Nobody knows what to say. Saul paces up and down the length of the loft, pausing in front of the mirror to stare at himself as if his reflection might offer reassurance, advice. He rubs his face, twists and pulls at his curly hair. He sucks in his stomach, brushes a crumb or two from his sweater front, and continues on his nervous way. "Was I wrong?" he says aloud. "Did I make a mistake? Is my sense of people beginning to weaken, to fray?"

Eash of us murmurs a reassurance: Oh, sweetheart, oh, brother, oh, love of my life, oh, patriarch of the entire clan. You are never wrong. When have you ever made a mistake?

Actually what we say is somewhat different. "You are always plunging into things. You are very self-indulgent. You never think."

We are still criticizing when the bell rings. "It is she,"

Saul cries, and he runs to the intercom to explain the complicated way to get into the building.

"Am I late?" she says, bounding into the room.

"This is Valery," Saul says.

"Are you hungry?" I say. Saul introduces us one by one, beginning with me for I am the oldest, the first, the wisest, or so I am told.

"How nice to meet you," Valery says. She leans toward me and gives me a kiss, greets each of us that way.

"Where were you?" Saul says. "Were you stuck in traffic? Did you lose your way? What happened?"

"Would you believe it, I lost track of the time." She turns to the rest of us. "I'm a compulsive knitter," she says. "This sweater that I'm wearing, I just had to finish it before I came here."

I am blinded by the sweater. Almost as long as a coat, its front is adorned with flowers, grapevines, trees heavy with all manner of fruit. On the back, small animals partially hidden by vines and leaves and grasses encircle a giant unicorn, shapely, beautiful, strangely familiar. The unicorn is Saul. A rush of love sweeps over me, erotic longings. I remember my young self, long, arduous nights of love, impossible postures. I run my hand over the sweater. My heart pounds. I long to take Saul into some dark corner, some private cranny, and take off his pants. How long is it since we were together in that way? We sleep together still, but I mean something different, that almost forgotten ardor, the experimentation, the lust, the greed, the allure of another body, the insatiable need to know and touch.

"What a lovely sweater!" I say.

The other wives look dazed and flushed, as if they too have read erotic messages in its design. We cluster around Valery like bees around blossoms wanting to cling and nourish ourselves. Each wife feels the need to touch, to scrutinize, to study each flower, each living thing. The sweater is filled with historical curiosities, flowers that no

16

longer bloom, sweet-faced fauna long obsolete, other creatures unimagined or not yet evolved.

"Saul tells us you are a knitting designer," I say. "Your work is fantastic. This is the most beautiful sweater I've ever seen. You must be very successful." Gradually I begin to focus on her, to get a sense of what she looks like. She is tall and slender, wholesome and very pretty. A feeling of envy sweeps over me, so unexpected it leaves me desolate.

"I'm supposed to make things that the average knitter can copy. But the truth is my work grows too complex. The company I design for keeps telling me to simplify. I start a garment thinking I'll make something easy, but while I work on it it becomes something else."

"I used to be that way too," Connie says. "I'd start a paper and end up with a textbook. That's before I learned to structure. Maybe I can help you."

"I need help," Valery says.

"I want to make a sweater like that," Beryl says.

"But Beryl, you have difficulty threading a needle," I say.

Connie lectures Beryl for taking on projects beyond her skill. "This kind of thing only intensifies your sense of failure."

But Beryl isn't listening. She is squeezing the sweater, bringing her face up close as if contact might unlock its mysteries.

"And another thing," Connie says. "You are totally irresponsible. You never returned my handbook on creative marriage."

"Was that a loan?" Beryl says.

Saul suddenly intervenes. "The more you criticize, the harder it will be for her to realize her potential."

"What potential?" Kelly mutters.

"She doesn't even try," Connie says.

"She tries," Saul says.

What will Valery think of us? "We're not usually like this," I say.

17

"We're not like this because we suppress our feelings," Connie says. "We avoid saying what we really think. We are in danger of losing touch with ourselves."

"If we are all surface," Evelyn says, "it is the price one pays for being in a collective marriage."

"You mean polygamous?" Valery says.

"I wouldn't call it that," Saul says.

Evelyn has warned us never to use that word. "It is an admission of guilt, of breaking a precise law," she says. "The authorities could use it against Saul."

Saul now attempts to use his patriarchal prerogatives to impress Valery with his position of authority. "No more bickering," he says. "No more criticisms. Let us spend the rest of the afternoon in harmony."

Everybody ignores him. Connie continues to lecture us on our repressions; the rest of us deny her accusations while Valery examines her presents one by one. Can anything we give her compare to the beauty of her sweater? I wonder.

Saul stands before the mirror staring at himself, as if some magic power might arise out of him and turn him into the patriarch he longs to be. I feel sorry for him, start to go toward him to soothe his hurt feelings, give him the attention he craves. But before I can carry out my impulse, Beryl is by his side, running a hand down his sleeve, talking softly to him. Whatever she says seems to soothe him, to cheer him up. As I watch them, Beryl says something that makes him laugh. Then he says something that makes her laugh. Then she shows him her biceps. She has been lifting weights. As she bends her arm, he squeezes her muscle.

I turn away distracted by the others, the presents being opened, the comments, the explanations. Valery is telling us how great it is to be among us, her new family, her friends. Her warm response makes us feel good, makes us value ourselves. We pile her plate high with food and watch her eat. Evelyn asks her a political question, Jen invites her to jog, Kelly tells her about the slaughter of the kangaroos.

I think of that Sunday afternoon as our last happy time, our final sojourn in the garden of Eden. Oh, Saul, oh, foolish man, intemperate man.

I glance over at him and Beryl; they are still laughing. What in the world is so funny? I wonder.

2

He's spreading himself too thin," Evelyn says.

"He always does," I say.

"He's endangering not just himself but the entire family. I wish he had consulted us before taking this step. He just goes ahead and plunges into a new marriage without even discussing it."

"You know Saul. When he wants something—whether it's a new car or a new marriage—he can come up with a million reasons why it would be a benefit to all mankind. Face it, Evelyn. Even if he had consulted us, it would simply have been to validate his decision."

"He'll regret his impulsiveness one of these days," Evelyn says.

"I wouldn't count on it," I say.

Evelyn and I are having lunch at the Hunan Daisy. Saul is supposed to join us, but as usual he is late; we order lunch without waiting for him. "What logic did he offer this time?" she says.

"He felt sorry for her. She has a gloomy nature. He hoped marrying her would cheer her up."

"Valery gloomy? You've got to be kidding."

"I agree. But you know Saul. His assessments of people's characters are not always entirely accurate. Remember the way he described Connie before he brought her home? 'A poor, lonely widow.' "

" 'A pitiful soul.' " Evelyn giggles. "He certainly has a talent for twisting reality."

"Or, worse, he doesn't perceive it properly," I say.

"That's probably closer to the mark. And how does he account for Valery's gloom?"

"According to Saul, she is having vocational difficulties. Knitting is merely a sideline. She's an actress who can't get parts. Actually she's had parts, but nothing that leads anywhere. She had a wonderful part in an avantgarde play. Everybody in the play was dead. She got rave reviews. 'You truly believe she is dead,' the critics said. But when she tried to get a part after that, she was typecast."

"So she took up knitting?" Evelyn says.

"Among other things. You know what actors have to go through to keep themselves going. Valery's done her share. She's given out sausage samples at a supermarket, demonstrated carpet cleaners dressed as a clown, walked dogs, watered plants, conducted tours at a shopping mall. At least she's making money now. In addition to designing sweaters for pattern books, she knits custom-made sweaters. But Saul says she doesn't value her craft; as far as she's concerned it's just a sideline. She keeps going to auditions and getting depressed."

"She seems so uncomplicated," Evelyn says.

"So do I; so do we all until people get to know us."

"Believe me, Helen, I have nothing against her. It's the marriage that worries me. Sooner or later they're going to catch him."

"And then what?"

"We'll have to plead him not guilty by reason of insanity."

"How can we do that? He's not insane."

"There are ways. But we should start now; we should

get him to a shrink so we can start documenting his instability."

"It would make him nervous," I say.

"Prison would make him more nervous," Evelyn says.

Evelyn borrows trouble. She sees problems before they develop. "It may never happen," I say. I glance at my watch. "I wonder what's keeping him."

"He's always late."

"But never this late. Did he say what he was going to be doing this morning?"

"To me?"

"Didn't he spend last night with you, Evelyn?"

"No. I was going to ask you what's been happening to our schedule. He's missed several conjugal visits lately."

How strange, I think. On the wall in our kitchen space is a giant calendar, marked with the schedule of Saul's visits to his wives. Without this timetable he grows confused, forgets appointments, arrives at the wrong house on the wrong night. When this happens, he returns home disappointed or hurt. "Nobody was home," he says, or, "They were having a meeting and I was in the way." I try to visualize the calendar; could I have been mistaken? Was it somebody else's night?

"He's probably spending all his time with Valery," Evelyn says. "Nothing like a little novelty to spice up a person's life."

"Maybe," I say, and yet somehow I don't think it's that.

Evelyn and I are here to go over the contract with Saul for our current project. The client is a collector; his specialty, depression utensils: pots that flaked, knives that could not cut, spatulas that rusted, a roasting pan that leached foul chemicals and killed a family of twelve. Our client is president of the Depression Utensils Collectors Association of the U.S.A.

We are designing his space to set off his collection; a ridge edges all the shelving so that the utensils can stand on end. Special lighting will illuminate their defects. "They are of museum quality," he says. To heighten the period flavor, a frieze made of pink suede will encircle the wall; on it will be mounted photographs of some of the depression-utensil victims. "I am an unabashed nostalgic," the collector says.

"It's not easy to design spaces for people you don't like. The temptation is to put doors that lead nowhere, shelving that no one can reach, closets too shallow to hang anything in," I say.

Evelyn laughs. "You wouldn't," she says.

"You haven't heard all of it," I say. "The client wants a totally controlled environment. 'Think sanctuary,' he tells us. 'Think womb.' When he comes home, he wants to forget there is a street below, what year it is, and whether it is cold or hot or snowing or raining outside. By means of climate control, and window shades depicting various seasons, we will shut out the world. His wife calls him a benefactor. 'Our environment will make it possible for visitors to forget the state of the economy,' she says, 'unless there is an upturn.' Whenever she opens her mouth, the client tells her not to interrupt."

"He sounds like a love," Evelyn says.

"In some ways he's like Saul, one of the last of the romantics."

"At least Saul is never vulgar." She glances at her watch. "Damn that man, where the hell is he? I can't wait all day. He thinks nobody's time is important but his own. I have clients too: an office full, if I don't get back there soon."

Evelyn is edgy. She stabs a snow pea with a chopstick, assaults a piece of tofu. "What's the matter?" I say.

"It's Josh," she says. "He's really impossible." Josh, her son, is Saul's son too, his only offspring. Were it not for him, our multiple marriages might never have taken place. "I'm worried about his future," she says. "We've applied to five different high schools and they've all turned him down."

"But Josh is brilliant," I say.

23

"It's my fault," Evelyn says. "I am not a good mother."

"Just because you work twelve hours a day?"

"I never seem to have good time for him."

"He gets plenty of attention from everyone else," I say. Josh moves from wife to wife on extended visits. Each place has a corner where he lives, a futon or air mattress, a student lamp, shelving for his books, games, and equipment. He comes and goes as he pleases, like a cat. Nobody knows why he chooses this place or that, what his motives are or even his needs.

Saul and I had been married five years when we decided we wanted to have a child. For one reason or another, I did not conceive. "The worst thing is to get edgy," we told each other after a couple of months of trying. We made love in the morning, at night, on Sunday afternoons, hoping to encourage some lively, talented sperm to penetrate and fertilize an egg. We tried various postures, intricate holds. Each time we held each other, make it happen now, I would think.

I was thirty-two, Saul approaching forty at the time. After a while, making love became a chore, a burden. That's when we decided to consult a doctor. "Take your temperature," he said. "Relax." He told us to ration our sex. "Let the little sperms grow strong and restless."

This suited Saul. Half Italian Catholic, half Jewish, his sensuality had always been tempered with guilt, with a sense of error and blame. In this post-Christian era, Saul no longer believed in God, but he believed in sin; he believed that the nonexistent God was punishing him in some way for his love of sex and that this deprivation would therefore please Him.

We followed instructions. I didn't get pregnant. We consulted a nutritionist, a holistic healer, a psychiatrist. "Eat whole grains and goat cheese. . . . Sleep nine hours a night. . . . Take a bath together. . . . Analyze your dreams." We followed their directions, abstained from sex, exercised, sought other interests in life.

We were just getting started in our construction business; it was a time of tension and strain. Saul was absent from home a lot. "I have to see a client," he would say.

I spent all my spare time constructing a model space in the hope of winning an important contest. The space was a room. The walls were crumbling, the windows cracked. The floorboards were warped. In my vision of the future, nothing worked, and I was trying to invent ways of depicting ruin and decay. It took hours, days of my life. The more disappointed I felt at not conceiving, the more intense my labors grew. I developed cobwebs, artificial dust, cockroaches so tiny one had to view them through a magnifying glass to understand their perfection.

Somewhere in the geography of limbo her work is located. It lies between the post-modern and the proto-apocalyptic. Her idiom is her own, a blend of coziness and despair. One walks into one of her spaces and begins to feel dead. Or, if not dead, immobilized, longing for oblivion, for sleep. One wants to slough off all worldly things—vanity, women, ambition, chocolate. Her work is a metaphor for the exhaustion of contemporary ideology; bravado and despair mingle in her spaces like Siamese twins.

A critic wrote this in an art magazine—not then, but later; he called me one of the first of the proto-apocalypticals. "A visionary, a ruthless truthsayer," he said, "austere in her refusal to hope, totally unsentimental." How wrong he was. What could be more sentimental than pseudo-poverty, people able to come in out of the cold, to bathe, to sleep, to nourish themselves?

But even if I wanted to, it is too late to change my style. I am known for my bleak spaces. I started with a cube, a three-dimensional square. I put a window in the cube and then a door. I hung a bomb from the ceiling, a replica of a nuclear device; wired it for light. I could have continued adding things, a chair, a table. But they would have provided too much consolation.

At the time of our troubles, I was at the beginning of my career. Nobody knew what I was trying to do. I labored over my space day and night, determined to be noticed.

Meanwhile Saul was out a lot. "Business," he would mutter, as he crept into bed. The symptoms were all there—those late nights, the silences, the many small irritabilities. He found fault with everything. The bread was stale, the knife was dull. A button was missing from his favorite shirt. Somebody had thrown out his green sweater. He had looked for it everywhere. I could barely tear myself away from my constructions to look up and answer him.

He came home late one night. It was after two. I was sitting at my drafting table finishing my space. It was almost done. I wrenched myself away from my work and looked up at him. "Where've you been?" I said.

"There is a woman," he said.

"A what?"

"She's pregnant." He began to cry.

I crushed my structure. I smashed it into pieces.

Saul tried to stop me, to take me into his arms. "Just let me explain."

I pushed him away from me, tore at his clothes.

"I want this baby!" he cried.

"I know you do!" I yelled.

Evelyn was in her last year of law school. We met in a neutral place, on a bench in the park. Saul introduced us. She's dumpy, I thought. I made my face go wooden. My hands were cold. I had no intention of crying in front of her. "The problem is," she said, "if they find out I'm pregnant, they won't let me finish law school."

"Maybe you should sue them," I said. I wanted to tell her to get rid of it; she wouldn't be the first woman to have an abortion. But what would be the point? Saul wanted a baby, and our marriage was on the rocks. What would I

have if I separated them? Nothing. "You want a divorce?"
I said.

Saul covered his face. "No, I don't. I love you."

"I'd hate to think what would happen if you didn't," I
said.

Evelyn laughed. Then she apologized for laughing.

I took another look at her. Her face was open and
unadorned, attentive, intelligent; she had the look of a
woman eager to learn about life. Well, she was getting
plenty of opportunity, I thought. "How did a smart woman
like you get yourself into this mess?" I said.

Saul took my hand and hers. "I knew you two would
like each other."

Actually it was weeks before I agreed to meet her. But
each adulterous event is much like another: the anger, the
bitter denunciations concealing pain, misery, a sense of
inadequacy, of total failure. Only the details differ, the
outward form—tears in one person, gluttony in another,
little acts of vengeance.

It is the aftermath of suffering, the sifting through
the rubble in search of something salvageable—hands
touching in the night, a shared laugh, a memory—that
leads finally to the abandonment not of pain but of a sense
of doom, of hopelessness. *"I can't go on. I'll go on."* That is
the story that grips.

So when we finally met, the three of us discussed the
problem like mature people, or as we imagined mature
people would behave. We searched for alternatives, a solution that would cause the least amount of pain and disrup-
tion. "You want a divorce?" I said. Divorce was the only
option I could think of.

"I've been researching domestic law," Evelyn said.
"Bigamy is one of the least prosecuted crimes. For every
bigamist who comes to trial, it is estimated that hundreds,
possibly thousands, walk the city streets unscathed."

Saul looked at me. "I'll have two wives," he said. He
tried to keep his face serious, but his mouth twitched with

27

suppressed pleasure. I didn't know whether to kick him or to bury my head in his flesh.

"Okay," I said. I couldn't think of what else to do. And if he had to have two wives, he could have chosen someone a lot worse than Evelyn. "I think I can live with it," I said. "I'll try."

Saul kissed me. Then he kissed Evelyn. Then we had lunch.

Evelyn and I became friends. I helped her find an apartment. She had been sharing a place with two other law students. We shopped for furniture, baby clothes. I designed a floor plan: a work space, a place for the baby, a living area. After Josh was born, I baby-sat while she studied for her finals and prepared for her bar exam.

I gave up trying to have a baby. If it happens it will happen, I decided. Our business was prospering. We bought a loft in SoHo, divided it into living space and work space. I was very busy.

Now Josh is thirteen. The trouble with him and Evelyn is they are too much alike—hardworking, ambitious, competitive. Josh borrows his mother's lawbooks. He writes in the margins. "Plato said that two thousand years ago. Nothing is really new."

"I'll kill him if he doesn't leave my books alone," Evelyn says. She complains to me, she complains to Saul. Josh has decided to teach himself the law. He intends to bypass law school and simply take the bar exam when he is around fifteen or sixteen years old. This is typical of Josh. He thinks he can do things the quick and easy way. In that way he is like his father.

Fortunately for mother and son, Josh can always leave home and stay with someone else when he feels like it. He drifts from place to place, for an evening, a weekend, a month. Jen is teaching him the rudiments of carpentry. Kelly is showing him how to blend colors. He follows Beryl around in the five-and-dime, helping her do inventory. He organizes the merchandise, adds things up on his pocket calculator, and Beryl writes down the results. He spends more time with her than anyone else. "That's because they are closer in age," I say. Saul disputes this. "She is kind and patient. Nothing gets her goat."

Lately Josh has taken up video. We bought him a camera for his birthday. He is always dropping into the loft and shooting family scenes: the preparation of food, the watering of plants, Saul on the phone talking to a client.

Josh is very critical of his father, says cynical things to him. "You told them the cabinets were finished and they haven't even been nailed together," Josh says.

Saul is always trying to explain. "Daily reports make them nervous."

"Lying destroys more brain cells than alcohol," Josh says.

"That's absurd," Saul says.

"There was this long article about it in *National Geographic.*"

"Do you want us to be constantly enmeshed in lawsuits?" Saul says.

Saul longs to be close to Josh, but he dreads it when Josh stays with us. He worries about being a bad influence, a poor role model. He wonders if he is ruining his son's character by exposing him to his business affairs. "Forget it," I say. "He's only trying to get your goat."

I show Josh how to read a blueprint and construct a three-dimensional space. He builds a model darkroom, but when I look it over I see the walls tilt inward, the floor slopes. "Why didn't you follow the blueprint?" I say.

"I would rather improvise," he says.

This attitude gets him in trouble at school. He refuses to do the assignments, is too impatient to learn the basic skill. "He doesn't even know where Albania is," Evelyn says.

"Who does?" I say. "He'll change his attitude once he starts high school."

"Why are you always so positive?" Evelyn yells.

She's right. I practice being negative.

"He's never going to get into a decent school," she

29

says. "You should see his test results. His trouble is arrogance."

"I know," I say. When we beg him to work harder, take a remedial course, he says, "I already know what I'm going to be." Josh wants to be a famous director when he grows up. To prepare himself, he does close-ups of Jen nailing a board to another board, me bent over a blueprint, Saul lying to a client or a wife, Beryl stacking cartons in the five-and-ten, Evelyn correcting a brief. He calls these short takes "Moments of the Truth."

"He simply refuses to listen to me when I tell him there's more to life than operating a video camera," Evelyn says. " 'What if you want to be something else?' I tell him. 'You won't have any of the skills to be able to make choices.' We argue all the time."

"Maybe Connie should talk to him. She had to take all those remedial courses when she went back to school."

"He wouldn't talk to Connie. You know that. He doesn't respect her. He can't stand the way she handles her dogs."

"He's not the only one," I say.

Connie's dogs are delinquent. They lick people, jump on them, pee where they please, snatch food from the table, howl, chew shoes and other articles of clothing. But no matter how antisocial their behavior, Connie has an excuse. "They were traumatized as pups," she says. "Weaned too early. Frightened when the plumber came to change the pipes." If only she were as tolerant with the rest of us, for she cannot resist urging us to act better than we do and explaining all the ways that might make this possible.

"The problem isn't just Josh. Everyone spoils him, covers up his mistakes, excuses his arrogance. How can you raise a responsible person in such a permissive atmosphere?"

"Some of the worst children become splendid adults," I say.

"There you go again," Evelyn says.

"No, really, Evelyn, you're too close to the problem. I think you're overreacting."

"Just tell me this. What's the use of being brilliant when you can barely write your name?"

"Maybe Saul should talk to him," I say.

"Saul? You've got to be kidding. Saul's more pampered and spoiled than his son."

"That's true," I say.

We blame each other. They are always accusing me of pampering Saul, of sacrificing myself for his benefit. "You have no life of your own," they say. "You spend all your time designing spaces for him. He uses your talent for his own advantage. His reputation rests on your skills."

It's not so, I think. Evelyn is the one who has given up everything for him. A young woman when he got her pregnant, a mere girl, she has since that time lived the life of a monk. Between Josh and her job, there is little time for anything else. Her only social life is us. "If it weren't for Saul, you'd have a man of your own," I say, "a normal life."

"The last thing I want is a man of my own," Evelyn says. Her previous lovers were full of flaws. Abby would not open the door to deliverymen—"They may be someone else," he said; Jonathan ate an entire birthday cake without offering Evelyn a piece. "If you have to have a partial man it is better not to have him full time," she says.

Privately, I think the whole family is spoiled, waiting always for me to arrange matters, to see that Saul is where he is supposed to be, his clothes clean, his body bathed and sweet, his mind full of interesting things to tell them. I remember birthdays, keep track of allergies, likes, dislikes, family connections, dreams. I see myself as a juggler, keeping seven (eight now, with Valery) balls aloft. I know where to seat them when we are all together: Evelyn as far from Beryl as possible, Jen from Connie because the dog hairs clinging to Connie bring on Jen's allergies. I know better than to put meat on the table when Kelly is present. The sight of a roast or steak brings tears to her eyes. "I didn't come ten thousand miles to be with carnivores," she says.

Evelyn glances at her watch. "I can't wait much longer."

"Here he is now," I say, as Saul walks through the door. "Don't say anything about Josh. Not today, anyway. He has a lot on his mind. It will only upset him."

Evelyn laughs. "And you accuse the rest of us of being overprotective."

I laugh too. Then Saul is at our table. He kisses me. Then he kisses Evelyn. "You're late," she says.

Where was Saul last night? I wonder. Why isn't he following the schedule? I would like to ask him, to get things back on track. But time is short and there are many business matters to discuss.

Saul falls into a chair. "It's a wonder I'm still alive. I've been at the lumberyard all morning with Jen and the client. We were trying to get him to make up his mind about the paneling. There was nothing there he liked. Jen is going to have to do it all."

"Oh, Saul," I say, "we're so far behind. Jen has to finish up the Bedell job before she even touches this."

"I know, I know," Saul says. "We'll just have to juggle things."

"You have never learned to say no," Evelyn says. "You want everyone to like you." She pulls out the contract and we start to go over it. "We'll have to renegotiate."

"Can't we leave that part till later?" Saul hates to renegotiate.

"No, we can't. If he wants custom work, he should know up front what it's going to cost. Helen says he has money to burn. So what's the problem?"

Saul sighs. "It's been a hard morning." But under Evelyn's prodding, he makes out a new schedule and together they work out the figures on their calculators. We stare at the numbers. The new budget is almost twice what the old was. "I don't know," Saul says.

"I do," Evelyn says. "Either he agrees to pay or we tell him to forget all the extra details."

"He'll pay," I say. "He told me money was no object."

"They all say that until you bring them the bill," Saul says. He stares at the contract, nibbling on bits of food we have left on our plates. He marks one passage with his pen and then another. While he reads he eats the remnants of our meal. Without looking up, he gropes for the saucer with our fortune cookies and pulls it toward him. He breaks a cookie in half, glances at the fortune, chuckles, eats the cookie, and then breaks open the second one.

Evelyn and I exchange looks. "Hey," she yells, "you ate our fortune cookies." People at nearby tables turn and stare at us.

Saul, looking mystified, lifts his face. "I what?"

"You do that all the time. You gobble things up."

"I don't. That's absurd. Anyway, they were sitting here."

"I intended to eat mine."

"So did I," I say. "At least give me my fortune so I can see what it said."

"Your fortune?" Saul scans the table, rummages among the dirty dishes and crumbs. He goes through his pockets. "I don't know what happened to your fortune."

"What did it say?"

He looks perplexed. "Something about—oh, hell, I don't remember."

"Damn you, Saul, you're always doing things like this."

"Like what?"

"Grabbing things without asking, taking what isn't yours."

"I'll order more." He starts to beckon the waiter. I try to imagine what my fortune said: a message of love, praise for my strength, my stalwart character, a promise of something wonderful to come. "Forget it," I say. "I wanted that one. Another wouldn't count."

"Me too," Evelyn says.

"Oh, hell," Saul says.

3

Jen called earlier. "Where was he last night?" she said. She and Kelly had waited and waited, but Saul never appeared. A friend had asked them out to dinner. Someone they knew was giving a party.

While she was naming all the things they had needlessly given up, it gave me the chance to think of an excuse. "He got stuck with a client," I said.

"He should have called."

"He should have," I said.

What's going on? Saul takes his conjugal visits seriously. He is like a boy scout picking up litter or helping old ladies across the street in the belief, the hope, that good deeds are the way to build character. In Saul's case, fidelity to his conjugal schedule is his deed, for even when he is tired, preoccupied, or not in the mood he sticks to his routine. Each time he leaves the house for a visit with a wife, he says, "Duty calls," as if he had invented the phrase at that very moment.

I keep waiting for Saul to tell me where he has been spending his nights. Sooner or later he tells me everything. In the meantime, I make excuses to the other wives.

Now Connie is asking Saul why he didn't come over Thursday night. "I was so worried. I thought something awful had happened to you," she says. She is having dinner with Saul and me. I tend to be protective of Connie, to have her over on occasions separate from our group meals, for she is less close to the other wives than they are to each other.

From the kitchen area where he is fixing us a drink, Saul calls out, "I'll be there in a minute and explain the whole thing." He hands me a martini, Connie a glass of white wine. He himself is drinking a Perrier with lemon, an indication of the care he takes of his body. "When you have the claims upon your person that I do, you have to keep in shape," he often says. "My body is a responsibility, like the bodies of athletes or dancers."

"You never even called," Connie says. She is waiting for the explanation.

"I know, I know. It's awful. I've been bogged down with work. Absolutely snowed under. Ask Helen. We're behind in all our schedules. It's making me crazy. Every time the phone rings, it's an irate client."

"But you're always in that situation," Connie says.

"It's worse now," Saul says. He's lying. He's been away from home just about every night this last week.

I try not to look at Connie, for a nipple is visible through a tear in her T-shirt. Does she know, I wonder? Should I tell her? She buys all her outfits at Gabby's in SoHo, a boutique that specializes in conspicuous consumption. Garments are worn out before they are sold, seams opened, holes inserted. Haute cuisine food stains dot the front of shirts and sweaters. A truffle crumb adheres to Connie's T-shirt. At other times the oily residue from imported Scotch salmon or beads of caviar stain her garments.

The clothes at Gabby's are expensive. "But they're worth it," Connie says. "You can't get that throwaway look anywhere else in the city." She buys everything in duplicate.

Beryl's clothes are not unlike Connie's, except that she finds most of them on the street, hanging on fences or lying atop trash cans. "The best time to look for clothes is early Sunday morning," she says. "The streets are littered with discards, abandoned by Saturday-night revelers." She has invited the entire family to go out foraging with her. "Soon," we tell her.

Beryl brings her finds to me to wash and mend: a sweater with a slight bullet hole, a shirt stained with blood. I throw everything in the washing machine and set it on its longest cycle. It is hard to differentiate Beryl's clothes from Connie's expensive gear, except that Beryl's clothes are ultimately cleaner.

Connie disputes this. "They don't have the workmanship that Gabby's things have. Everything is made by hand in European workshops."

The martini loosens my tongue. "Your nipple is showing," I say.

Connie looks down at herself with pleasure. "They started doing holes before anyone else even thought of them. They manage to situate the opening at the exact right spot, even though no two women are built alike." She keeps glancing over at Saul to see if he has noticed her nipple staring at him like a third eye.

But Saul is standing at the stove stirring his specialty, a green sauce with seafood for the pasta he is about to plunge into the steaming cauldron. While he waits for the water to come to a full boil he says dreamily, "Can I get you more wine?"

"Is it Valery?" Connie whispers. "Is that where he's been spending his nights?"

"It's possible," I say, though I know it isn't Valery. In fact, it surprises me that Saul hasn't been spending more time with her. But she too called earlier.

"I'm sorry to bother you, but how does this thing work? I thought we each had an allotted night with him."

I made the same excuses I had given all the others, his heavy schedule, the impossible demands on his time, wondering as we talked why Valery had married Saul. The others married him because of some need, some weakness, some quirk, that only he might fix or remedy. But this one, Valery, young, lovely, and seemingly cheerful despite Saul's talk of gloom and self-doubt: why would she agree to such a small share of connubial bliss?

"Nothing like a little novelty to get a man all steamed up," Connie says. "I suppose we'll just have to wait it out until the shine wears off."

We are sitting at the table now; Saul carries in a huge platter of pasta. He tosses the pasta and heaps enormous mounds on our plates. Then he serves himself. He twirls a strand around his fork and then another and another, like a child toying with food it is reluctant to eat. "You'll never get any nourishment that way," I say.

"What?" Saul says.

His absence unsettles me. Where is he? I wonder. I long to put my hand on his, squeeze his flesh, feel his blood pulsing, return him to the moment, to us, to me.

He digs his fork into his food and takes a large mouthful. He looks at Connie, smiles, compliments her on her outfit, apparently not noticing her exposed nipple. "How's it going?" he says.

"A recent study on the bereaved found that eighty percent of widowers immediately sought another wife. And every single one of them was in the market for personal grooming aids." Connie is talking about her new job. She is working for a company that test-markets products of consolation. "Grief is a growth industry," she says. Since she lost her first husband, she has joined a grief group, taken courses at a university, learned a profession, and when that didn't work out she learned another profession.

At the grief group, she discovered in herself a capacity for mourning and remembering that was far above the average. "I was a charismatic presence," she recalls. The bereaved widows would sit around in a circle, recalling special qualities of their loved ones—a talent for organiza-

37

tion, saintliness, a lustful appetite, an appreciation of the finer things in life. In her capacity for remembering details of the past, Connie had no peers. She was able to dredge up many brilliant facts. For instance, long before the airlines were offering discount family tickets, Bert always invited her to go along on his business trips. He brought her coffee in bed, remembered her dress size, the brand names she favored, all the things that she herself could not keep track of. "I was his adored love object," she said. All these memories set her above the other mourners in her seminar. She became a leader of the bereaved and decided to make a career out of her loss.

She lost her husband on a tour. He went into a cavern to see the sights and never came out again.

Sometimes she imagines Bert coming among us unannounced. This possibility fills her with terror, for he was a very conventional man. "How conventional?" we say. After they got married, he immediately started making contingency plans should the unexpected come to pass. He told her how to probate and where he had hidden his will. "We must begin learning how to adjust to loss," he said. What neither of them could anticipate was the ambiguity of his death, for nobody knows what happened to him in the cave. Is he dead, or merely in hiding, or endlessly lost in some dark labyrinth? These are questions she puts to herself when she is feeling low and insecure. Then she imagines him someday flinging open a door, pointing a finger at her, and crying out, "What are you doing in all that muck?"

"But it isn't muck," we tell her.

After she discovered in herself a capacity for deep and sincere feeling, Connie decided to become a therapist. She took courses and engaged in group discussions with other fledgling therapists; after a while, she was assigned a patient to practice on. But suddenly in the midst of a confession, an illumination, a dream, Connie would leap up as though catapulted by some invisible mechanism and fiddle with a venetian blind. Sometimes she would grab a hair from a chair back or brush a crumb from her patient's vest, leaving him in a state of confusion and despair. "Your inability to sit still is a vocational flaw," her colleagues told her. They advised her to try something else.

Undismayed and still determined to make something of her life, Connie next found work at a travel agency, a job she felt herself qualified to do since she and Bert had taken annual trips to many distant places. She knew the pitfalls as well as the rewards of travel, was able to tell clients what kind of clothes to wear in the Southern Hemisphere and how to say "I need a doctor" in a dozen different languages. "But how could you organize tours when you could never organize your cupboards?" we said. "I was determined to overcome my vocational handicap," Connie said. Instead, it overcame her. Travelers destined for Rio ended up in Belize; some groups never left the airport.

Despite her failures, she is an optimist. Each time she begins a new job, she is convinced that this time she will make a go of it, this time she will overcome her problems. This is the situation she is in now, test-marketing products of consolation. She has given all of Saul's wives a grief quotient test that comes with the sales kit with which she was provided.

Now she reports our scores. "All your grief quotients were on the low side," she says. "Your sense of loss seems to be extremely shallow."

"Are you sure you added them up right?" I say.

"I'm sure." She looks at Saul. "I hope nothing ever happens to you," she says.

"So do I," he says.

She has tested us before for this project or that. Our opinions, often at variance with the general trend, have forced her to make up many of her findings. She usually ends up pretending she is a multitude of people.

"Connie makes up her findings," we tell Saul, but he refuses to believe this. He cannot bear to think that any wife of his would do a dishonest thing. He likes to pretend we are all perfect.

Saul changed Connie's life. "I was totally phobic about anything new until I met Saul," she says. She loves to describe the clothes she was wearing when she attended his seminar. "A navy blazer, a pleated plaid skirt, a shirt buttoned at the neck. Utterly preppie, utterly safe." We shake our heads. It is hard to superimpose that drab conventional creature on the Connie we know.

Saul was giving his annual talk, "Culture in Transition: Fear of the New." At one time he was a professor of aesthetics at an urban university. He quit his job in the early seventies to do something alternate, but once each year he returns to his old place of learning and delivers a lecture the way a bird might deliver an annual egg.

He has given the same basic talk many times. He knows when to pause, when to say something funny, when to engage the crowd in his thoughts (as though they were the crowd's thoughts too), when to be lofty and authoritative, an expert on all things new.

I know the lecture by heart, having sat through it many times. It goes like this:

"Every period in history is an age of transition, insofar as it is moving toward a new era, new ways of being, living, observing. Art has always reflected these changes, defined them, anticipated them, generally keeping pace with the slow and orderly procession of time. The art of one era impinged on the next. Abrupt cultural breaks were rare, iconoclastic clashes with the past sporadic. All this began to change early in this century, but even then nobody could foresee the accelerated tempo that would take place over the years.

"Now art time is counted off not in eras, not even in decades, but in years, seasons, sometimes in months. As time speeds up, our ability to look at art becomes more strained, blurred. We begin to suffer from a cultural vertigo, as though trying to view art from a fast-moving

40

train. And yet even this image doesn't do justice to the accelerated pace of aesthetic events.

"In this environment, art becomes anarchic and hermetic, accessible only to a small circle of artists and the people doing business with them. There is not enough time or stasis for anything like a consensus to develop, so that when ordinary people ask 'What is art?' the response can only be a cacophony of sound without sense or meaning.

"No wonder people feel insecure, defensive, hostile when they come face-to-face with art. If each visit to a gallery or a museum is accompanied by uncertainty and confusion, it becomes more like a visit to the dentist than a joyful, illuminating outing. What we experience is dread, a stripping away of our autonomy, our judgment, our sense of ourselves."

Now Saul shows a series of slides: a movers' pad covered with ketchup stains and blobs of food, a brown paper bag covered with graffiti, a Matisse, a Braque, a photograph filled with male genitals each positioned behind the one in front until they disappear into infinity, a Giotto, a crushed cat, a Picasso bull. . . .

When the lights go on, there is a long silence to allow people to absorb what they have seen. Then Saul says, "How do we differentiate art from the haphazard articles of daily life? Which of these slides showed a work of art? Some are easy to pick out. We know the Giotto, the Braque, the Matisse are art. If our own senses don't tell us, history will. But what about the others—the crushed cat, the paper bag, and so on?

"They are all art, if art is defined by how and where they are viewed. Each of those slides showed a work that hangs on a museum wall or has been shown in a gallery. Each of them represents the judgment of some dealer, some museum director, that the object is part of the contemporary aesthetic scene."

He holds up his pen. "Is this art?" His book bag. "Is

this art?" The centerfold of a magazine showing two males kissing. "Is this art?" He pauses. "It is if I say it's art."

Although this smacks of Philistinism, it never fails to get a laugh of relief, of complicity. How warming he is, how permissive! If people cannot appreciate art, there are reasons.

He winds up his lecture by summing up the cultural void we are positioned in, the lack of consensus, art's separation from a social or political function. "And yet in its separation from life, in its powerlessness, in its frivolous nature, its ugliness, its cruelty, current art does make a statement, a statement that reflects life. What it reflects is the drift in Western affairs, our sense of helplessness, the terrible feeling that we are on a space ship and nobody is in charge, that nothing can change, that we are speeding toward the edge of time. What it is saying is, There are no patriarchs, no band of men who know the truth, who can offer consolation, give out edicts that will tell the rest of us what to think and how to live.

"In this sense, contemporary art is all too relevant, for it depicts the void we are all living in. And yet there is something liberating about this idea. For if there are no experts, no wise men, we must each find the courage and the strength to look inward, heed our own opinions, listen to our inner voice; in effect, to be our own wise man."

Afterward Connie rushed up to the podium. "*You* are my wise man," she said. "My map, my dictionary of current opinion. You have changed my life."

That's the way Saul reported the encounter, and I have no reason to disbelieve him. He asked her to have a drink. She invited him to her place. He spent an hour or two telling her about himself: his early life, his business, his connections, his views of New York.

He told her everything except the important thing: that he had a number of wives in various sections of the city. Then they went to bed.

When Connie found out about the rest of us, she decided she wanted to be part of the extended family.

42

Knowing her now, I can well understand this. She has a passionate compulsion to change things, improve the quality of life, make us all better than we are.

She would like me to dress in a more assertive manner so people would begin to notice me. "We are what we wear," she says. She urges Evelyn to count calories. "I don't even have time to count my change," Evelyn says. She worries about Jen and Kelly being too emotionally dependent on each other, urges them to develop separate interests. "Their closeness restricts their growth," she says, adding, "take it from one who knows."

Connie was too dependent on her late husband. Since losing him she has had to learn things the hard way, through trial and error—how to change a tire, keep track of the bills, the charge accounts, the length of time you can keep food in the freezer. She has had to develop self-respect and the strength to listen to her inner promptings. She is trying to help Saul listen to his inner promptings too.

"Gabby's is having a sale," Connie says. Saul isn't listening. "Everything is twenty percent off. I got you something, Helen. I just couldn't resist." She hands me a package. Inside is a pair of pantaloons. "They had *you* written all over them," she says. She tells me to try them on. "They are replicas of the pantaloons worn by the first wave of feminists," Connie says.

Even so, I don't like the way they look on me. "Did the first wave of feminists really wear Day-Glo orange and yellow dots?" I say.

"That's just like you, Helen. You're too conservative. Honestly, they look fabulous on you." She turns to Saul. "Tell her how great she looks."

"What?" Saul says.

"Saul, where are you?" Connie says.

"I'm here." He glances at his watch. "I'm listening."

"The sale is still going on. They have some fabulous men's gear. We could all go over there Sunday afternoon after we've eaten."

"I have to see a client Sunday afternoon."

"You'll kill yourself if you don't slow down. What about Sunday night? I have tickets to the rodeo. It's part of my class assignment." Connie is taking a course on the culture of violence, primarily so she can discuss her studies with Saul, take him to lectures, impress him with her scholarship and her insights. "The critics loved it. They said the rodeo was a metaphor for contemporary life."

"In what way?" Saul says.

"The precariousness of each contest. It's like living at the edge."

"There are worse things than living at the edge," Saul says.

"Like what?"

"Not knowing you are living at the edge. The precariousness of modern life lies in its ambiguity. It's like the very beginning of a toothache. One keeps running the tongue over the tender area to convince oneself it is nothing, a mere irritation. It is the interval between hope and despair that is such a torment."

"How true," Connie says. She is eager to continue this discussion, for suffering is something she knows about. "Americans don't know how to suffer. They are ashamed to be sad. That's why it is necessary to provide public spectacles like the rodeo, a safe place to express our feelings. Our terror at the bucking bronco or the fierce bull allows us to scream and cry in a public place surrounded by other screaming people. Think how therapeutic it is to share in such an outpouring. It would do you a world of good, Saul. It would help you to lower your fences."

"I wish I could spare the time," Saul says. Connie looks disappointed.

"Why don't you ask Josh?" I say. "It sounds like something he would enjoy."

"He never wants to do anything with me."

"Beryl, then," I say.

"Beryl's busy," Saul says.

44

"Busy?" We both look at him.

"She's taking a course."

"In what?" I say.

"Inventory control."

"On Sunday night?"

"No, but she has to prepare for it then."

"I'm glad she's taking a course. That's good news," Connie says. "She owes it to herself to go back to school and get an education. If she waits too long, she'll get in a rut and never do anything to improve herself. I know. When I was married to Bert, self-improvement was the last thing I had on my mind."

Saul nods. He is afraid of Connie's persistence, her desire to improve us. "No wonder her husband disappeared," he has said on more than one occasion. Sometimes, I suspect, he regrets having married her. And yet they do have things in common, a love of clothes, a yearning for approval. They are both disorganized, but Saul does not necessarily see this as a bond. For although he forgives himself, saying, "That's the way I am," he is very censorious of Connie's chaos. "How can she live that way?" he says.

During the salad course, Connie looks at Saul. "Who gave you that haircut?" she says.

"Why?" Saul says.

"It doesn't suit you. There's something funny about it."

"How, funny?"

"I'm not sure." She studies his hair, frowns. "I think it's too symmetrical. It isn't you. It makes you look older. Don't you think so, Helen?"

At the word "older," Saul looks as if someone has punched him in the stomach. I refuse to get involved. "I am not a good judge," I say.

"How can you say that?" Connie says. "You of all people, with your eyes for spaces, your sense of the metric system. That's what I mean when I say you are too modest. Look at the left side. Don't you think it's too even? It makes him look like a banker or an insurance salesman. If it were just cut a little on the ragged side, the whole thing would give an impression of debonair youth." Connie leans over and pulls at his hair. "Right there," she says. Saul leaps up and dashes over to the mirror. While he stands there looking at his hair, he squeezes his eyes nearly shut in an effort to erase the wrinkles that are beginning to underline them. "You're right," he says. "I told him there was something funny about this cut."

"Come with me to Henri's. He's a magician with mousse," Connie says.

Before Saul can pursue this path, the phone rings. He rushes over to answer it, turns his back when he learns who is calling, and whispers, "Yes. . . . No. . . . Later, I promise. . . . Of course, of course." He tries to lower his voice even more. "I'll be there, I'll be there. . . . Yes, soon. Do your yoga, meditate. It'll help the time pass. . . . Yeah, sure, that'll be fine. See you soon."

I brush crumbs into my open palm, trying to avoid Connie's eyes.

"Another client," he says, after he hangs up. "Shall I make some coffee?" He dawdles in the kitchen, waiting for the kettle to boil.

I try to make small talk. "How are the dogs?" I say.

"Awful. Oh, Helen"—she raises her voice so Saul will be able to hear her too—"Aster hasn't eaten anything but fish sticks for days. And Belinda is totally apathetic. She won't move. I'm worried sick about them. They both seem to have lost all interest in life."

"What's wrong? Have you seen a vet?"

"I don't need a vet to tell me what's wrong. When I'm unhappy, they're unhappy. They keep searching the house for Saul."

We both look at him. He is pouring water into the coffee maker, his face so bleak and worried my heart falters. What's going on? Why should that telephone conversation have made him so miserable? I feel as if I am losing touch with him, that I am suddenly unable to understand the way his mind works, to follow his devious ways. Is he sick? Is he cracking under some strain? Perhaps this life is proving too much for him, as Evelyn keeps saying it will.

I watch him putting cups on a tray, pouring milk into a pitcher. "Does something hurt?" I say. Is it possible he has an ailment he is concealing from us, some wasting disease that is destroying his body? But that isn't like Saul. I have never known him to suffer anything in silence.

"Just tired," he says. "I've been working too hard. There are too many schedules. Too many people breathing down my neck." He summons a faint smile as he carries the coffee things over to us. He ruffles Connie's hair, tells her he will try her Henri and the mousse. His tone is flirting, his face fixed in a wide smile.

"That's wonderful," Connie says. "You won't regret it. He'll do fantastic things to it." Connie fishes her date book out of her bag. "When?" she says.

"Soon." Saul pours the coffee, sits down, and stirs.

Watching them, I think, It's a game, a fraudulent game, an imitation of affection, of desire. Is it always like that, the smiles, the jokes, the flirtatious manner? Is our whole life false, superficial? Does Saul feel anything for us other than a vague and shapeless lust?

The phone rings again. Saul rushes over to answer it. "Oh, my God," he says after a moment. "I'll be right over. Don't panic. Don't move. For God's sake don't try to free yourself." He hangs up and turns to us. "Beryl has glued herself to her lamp. I've got to go right over and try to unglue her." His face looks doomed; his voice has the portentousness of a Shakespearean actor announcing the death of the king.

"What are you talking about?" I say.

"She was trying to repair her lamp with some of that Krazy Glue. It sets in thirty seconds. She didn't move away fast enough."

"I told her not to fool around with that glue," I say. "I warned her." Saul is putting on his coat, wrapping his

47

scarf around his neck. "Do you need some help?" I say. "Do you want me to go with you?"

"Thanks, I'll manage. I've got to run." He opens the door, pauses as if to say something, changes his mind. "See you." Then he is out the door.

4

Are you sure he won't be back during the meeting?" Kelly says.

"He's gone to Connecticut to search out ruined artifacts," I say.

"He usually asks us to go with him," Jen says.

"He was going to ask you but I talked him out of it. I knew you wouldn't want to miss this meeting."

"Where's Beryl?" Evelyn says. "Is her hand still bothering her?"

"It's healing, but slowly," I say.

"But she *is* back on the job?"

"Yes," I say.

"She probably forgot."

"She's totally disorganized."

"She has no sense of responsibility."

"She thinks only of herself."

"It's a miracle she can hold a job."

A torrent of criticism pours out of everyone's mouth. Evelyn taps for order. "We're not here to discuss Beryl's character," she says. "We have more important things to talk about."

"I don't think we should wait for her," I say. My voice sounds peculiar, as if I'd started on a note too high. Sooner or later I will have to tell them that Beryl won't be coming to this meeting.

We are here to discuss Saul's errant behavior, his refusal to follow conjugal schedules, his lies, his disappearances, the foolish reasons he gives for his neglect.

He has stopped answering the phone. "Let it ring," he yells. The answering machine is no longer operational. He tried to put a message on it, both witty and enigmatic, that would soothe his irate wives and at the same time make sense to our clients. The witty remark sounded merely coy. He sang a song: "It's been good to know you." But when he played it back, he didn't like the song or his voice. I begged him to desist, simply to say, Leave your name and number and we'll get back to you. "It's not good enough," he replied.

Each time I answer the phone, a wife is on the other end. "Where is he?" they say. I am sick of making excuses.

Evelyn took matters in hand. She organized the meeting, asked me to help her gather everybody together. "We've got to get to the bottom of this," she said. "Perhaps if we piece together stray bits of information, we'll figure out what's going on, and why he is avoiding us, and where he is spending his time."

It is a Thursday evening. Kelly and Jen are in the kitchen space stirring a pot of chick-peas. Valery is washing lettuce. Evelyn is making an agenda. Connie has volunteered to take notes. Now we are all sitting around the long table eating while we discuss the situation.

"If you ask me, he's having one of those mid-life crises," Kelly says. "Succumbing to the general hysteria."

Kelly has pronounced the second *u* as if it were a double *o*. "Succooming?" we say.

Jen translates her remark for the rest of us. "Succumbing," she says. "She means he's having some kind of breakdown."

"I wouldn't go that far," Evelyn says. "A little strung out, perhaps, but that's his normal state."

"There are underlying causes," Connie says.

"There usually are," Evelyn says.

"In this course I'm taking on the culture of violence, we've been studying male hysteria," Connie says. "Since the dawn of history, men have been telling themselves that they're better than we are. You know why?"

"Why?" we say.

"To cheer themselves up. For actually they are evolutionary parasites, repositories for genetic waste. And they know it. Why do you think so many of them become female impersonators?"

"How do you know they do?"

"There is an increasing demand for gowns in the larger sizes." Now that regional cooking is in, haute cuisine stains no longer dot the front of Connie's clothes. The T-shirt she is wearing is flecked with corn bread crumbs, a tiny piece of blackened redfish. "Scientists are even beginning to suspect that sex is a kind of disease and that once a cure is found, men will become obsolete."

"The sooner the better," Kelly says.

"You can see, though, why they act out their gender anxieties in aggressive behavior or, like Saul, in sexual adventures."

"Poor Saul," someone says.

Valery looks confused. "You mean he's gay?" she whispers.

"I doubt it," I say.

Evelyn interrupts. "No theories." She tells Connie to strike her own remarks. "We are here to get a grip on things, to find out what he's up to and where he's been spending his nights." Suddenly they are all looking at me.

I shred my napkin, I drain my glass of wine. I have prepared various remarks, but now that the time draws near to say them, nervousness dries my throat. I choke, start to cough, reach for a glass of water.

"Are you all right?"

"I will be in a minute."

Valery is knitting each of us a sweater. Bobbins of every hue hang from her work. She takes up a sweater, holds it against a torso, and knits a row or two. Then she lays it aside and picks up another. Each sweater has a theme. On Evelyn's the scales of justice are emerging. Jen's has carpenter's tools scattered on a field of asters, Kelly's a picture of the Outback copied from a photograph of one of her paintings. On mine, a tiny figure is trying to shore up an enormous leaning tower. On Connie's a huge teardrop looms over huddled figures, ready to fall and possibly drown them. Many small objects—tweezers, pencils, a tube of Krazy Glue, superimposed on a giant calculator—are scattered over Beryl's sweater. Valery is knitting one for Saul too, but nobody has seen it or knows what theme she has chosen.

She is measuring Jen. "I think I've made it too large," she says.

"I like things big," Jen says. "Leave it the way it is." I am glad of the diversion, a few more minutes of grace before I have to tell them what I know.

"I love to knit where there are people and something going on," Valery says. That's how she met Saul. Like Connie, she attended his annual symposium. "I always try to go where there are cultural opportunities. I like to learn things while I knit." She has learned how to manage a trailer camp, prevent crime, use the legislative system for one's cause. "Of all the cultural events I've attended, Saul's was the best," she says. "He showed me a whole new way of looking at the world that is bound to have an effect on my life."

He is helping her to recognize that knitting is an art form, as creative an act as spray painting on burlap or piling broken crockery in mounds. She is trying to absorb this, to make it part of her belief system in an effort to free herself of her obsession with acting.

Hoping to be more effective in the world, she has recently joined a group called Knitters for Peace. "They

52

have an agenda—to interest large numbers of men in their craft. 'Knitting is basically an aggressive act,' they say; 'the thrust of the needle into a stitch and then the thrust of the needle into another stitch is brutal.' If they can teach warlike men to knit, perhaps they will lose all interest in war."

"It's worth a try," we say.

Valery's work is biographical. Her sweaters tell a story, delineate a life. "Saul and I have been talking about opening a store," she says. "He thinks my work is unique and that I should be able to charge large sums of money for knitting people's lives. We intend to call our store Biographies."

"He spreads himself too thin," Evelyn says. "That's just like Saul. He's always taking on more than he can manage. No wonder he's falling apart." She taps the table with her pen. "Let's try to have a little structure."

I am pouring coffee; Jen is cutting cake; Connie is rubbing conditioner into Kelly's elbows and explaining how a nightly application would eliminate rough skin. Valery, scraping dishes, says, "Someone told me she heard the President doing a commercial." Her voice sounds very bitter.

"What kind of commercial?"

"A dog-food commercial."

"Well, he's a very persuasive person."

"That's not the point," Valery says. "He has a job. Do you know how many unemployed actors there are?"

"Maybe the sponsor was a friend."

"What brand is it?" Connie says. "I won't buy it."

"Let's not go off on a tangent," Evelyn says. "We've got a lot of ground to cover." She reads from her notes. "The problem is this: our conjugal visits have stopped and nobody knows why. The explanations we are given are so spurious they insult our intelligence. We don't know where Saul is spending his nights or why he has chosen to upset the usual order of things. Our next step is to come up with some process."

"Let's tell him to straighten up or bugger off," Kelly says.

"We have plenty of things to do with our time," Jen says. She and Kelly do volunteer work at a battered women's shelter. They are putting up shelves; they are painting walls and ceilings. They are teaching some of the battered women how to saw and mix colors. "Our lives would be a lot simpler if we didn't have him hanging around."

"You better believe it," Kelly says. "We've been dying to join this study group that's tracing the matriarchy to its source. Only it meets on Sundays."

Everybody complains about our Sundays. "We can never make any other plans," they say. "Our social life is too confining." But nobody really wants to be anyplace else. On the rare occasions a wife has to miss a Sunday, the first thing she does is call to find out what took place. "Did I miss anything? Tell me what you talked about. What did you eat?"

Now, even though Jen and Kelly talk of distancing themselves from Saul, they both look forlorn. For the truth is they love to be with him. The three of them can spend hours discussing wood grains, paneling, hardware, paint; they swap gossip about the clients, go on shopping trips for supplies. They never tire of talking shop.

Talk is the sensual pleasure of our time, someone once said. I think they are right. I suspect, sometimes, that Saul would rather talk than make love, rather sit around hour after hour, telling us the story of his life, than to climb into bed and perform a sexual act.

We all love to talk. Sunday after Sunday, we sit around the table, long after the meal is over, discussing our lives. Saul dominates the conversation. Every Sunday he delineates the many pitfalls, twists, and turnings of his career. "How risky it was to leave the tenured academic world for construction," he says. "In the early seventies, renovation was not what it is now. People put up a bookshelf and considered it an extraordinary act. Nobody envisioned the current rage for gutting."

We have heard the account of Saul's struggles many times before, and it always has the pleasure of an old familiar song. At some point he turns to me and says, "Ask Helen. Remember those terrible days and weeks we would sit around waiting for the phone to ring?"

And I always say, "We didn't know when we were well off."

Now we are overcommitted. Irate clients threaten to sue unless we finish their renovations within the week. Suppliers promise deliveries that are never made. Inept bureaucrats lose our plans. Corrupt building inspectors discover violations. Each time Saul pays a bribe Evelyn grows furious. "I had to," Saul says. "It was the only way we could get the job done." "What's his name. We'll report him," Evelyn says. "Forget it," Saul says. "We'd have the whole damn department on our neck." "Someone has to take a stand," Evelyn says, and the two of them go on arguing.

At our Sunday gatherings, we discuss the state of the world, current events. Now that marriage is once more in, Saul feels smug. "I was one of the pioneers," he says. But this leads to a discussion of Josh and whether his refusal to do his assignments is somehow connected with Saul's craving for women.

Saul doubts it. The rest of us are not that certain. "You take wives the way some people buy clothes, in the belief that the acquired object will change your life, enhance your person. But once possessed, the garment or the wife loses its magic quality. And then you have to start shopping around again. This is a poor role model for any child."

"Not true," Saul says, but he wants the discussion to go on, for his ways fascinate him and he never tires of hearing himself analyzed or dissected. Only when we turn to other things—a movie, the latest disease, a recipe for crayfish—does his attention falter.

Our Sundays seem to last forever. There is so much ground to cover, so many subjects to be dealt with. Connie always brings reams of newspaper clippings, which she doles out to the appropriate person: an article on a new allergy treatment for Jen; for Valery, a story about the floor-length sweaters that are sweeping Paris; a new program in inventory control that is guaranteed to change Beryl's life.

We all vent our political anger at the current administration, the Star Wars program, environmental degradation. Then Beryl always infuriates everybody by claiming the bottle law is bad for business. This provokes arguments, an outpouring of moral indignation.

Sooner or later, the teasing starts. Jen usually initiates it. Last time we were all together, she said, "Where'd you get that jacket?"

"At Luciano's, where else?" Saul said. He paraded in front of us, waiting to be admired.

"It's gorgeous. . . . It suits you." Only Beryl and Connie had nice things to say.

"Luciano's?" Jen said. "I saw the exact same jacket at Canal Jeans for twenty-nine ninety-nine."

"Not this jacket," Saul argued. "This cost a small fortune. You couldn't get anything like it at Canal Jeans."

"Maybe," Jen said.

Then Evelyn spoke up. "I hate to tell you this, but in court when a client has done something really horrendous—killed and eaten his mother, or sold his infant daughter to a porn king—we dress him in a jacket like that so the judge will feel sorry for him."

We shrieked with laughter. Still Saul continued to extol the jacket's qualities. "It's part cashmere. Made in an Italian workshop. No matter where I've worn it, I have received only compliments. A leading city builder squeezed the fabric; a man on the street asked me where he could buy one."

He is so teasable, so earnest, so serious about himself. How can we do without our Sundays? What will happen if our family falls apart? Without Saul there would be no center.

Evelyn says, "Have we listed all the complaints?"

Valery raises her hand. "I don't know if this is a complaint or not. He offered to design a storage unit for my wool, but he never did anything about it."

"It's a complaint," Evelyn says. She tells Connie to write it down.

"On our last job, he forgot to tell me the client had decided on another color," Kelly says.

"He and I were supposed to have our hair cut at Henri's," Connie says. "Saul never even showed up. Some people have to wait months for an appointment. Henri said he'd squeeze us in. Now I'll never be able to go back."

"He lost Josh's paper on woodchucks," Evelyn says.

Suddenly there is a silence. All eyes are on me. "You haven't said a word," they say.

My heart is rattling. I am afraid to tell them what I know. But I can't continue to protect him, make up lies, pretend I have no knowledge of his whereabouts. My evasiveness fills me with disgust. And yet, my mind is in conflict. He has brought this on himself. His self-indulgence, his ability to justify his every whim, can only lead to disaster. Sooner or later they will have to know what is going on. Yet even while I argue with myself, my habit of protecting him almost overwhelms me.

I take a deep breath. "Saul's been spending all his nights with Beryl."

"Beryl?"

"Beryl?"

"You're kidding."

"Why?"

"He has developed a mad passion for her," I say. "I don't know why."

"All his nights?"

"It's crazy."

"Beryl?"

"Since when?"

"I think he's fallen in love with her," I say.

"But he loves us all."

57

"Not the way he loves her."

"But she's such a nothing person. It's disgusting."

"It's degrading."

"What is there to love? She's so totally self-absorbed."

"She takes herself so seriously."

"She's so immature."

"Since when did any of those things matter?" I say.

A dazed look crosses everybody's face, a look of confusion, doubt, denial. Despite all our teasings, it is difficult to believe Saul loves someone better than he loves us.

His greatest gift is making each of us feel we are the special one, the love of his life, the person he looks to for closeness, pleasure, understanding—the one person he cannot live without. For even in a roomful of wives, he has a way of seeking you out, of gazing at you as if he cannot look in any other place. Eyes meet in tender understanding, conveying a message, something only the two of you share. He does this with each of us, one at a time, and yet, even though I am aware of it, see it happening, I cannot help feeling he loves me the best, needs me the most.

"Say it again, Helen. Lay it all out."

"Saul has developed some kind of obsession with Beryl. I don't know what to call it: love, lust; you'll have to ask him to define it. But it doesn't really matter. What matters is, he's there all the time. Every night. He can't seem to stay away from her. I mean, I watch him pacing nervously around the loft. Or sitting at his desk trying to settle down to something. And suddenly he will jump up and leave the house. It's like a compulsion or something. Like he's under a spell."

There is a long silence. Then everyone starts to speak at once, a jumble of protest, denial, doubt.

"He's crazy. . . . I can't believe it. . . . Are you sure? . . . Beryl, oh, God, of all the wives. . . ."

"Anyone else, I could bear it."

"It's unbelievable."

"Insane."

"Why didn't you tell us sooner?" Evelyn says.

58

"I was hoping it would go away."

"How long have you known about it?"

"Tell us everything you know."

"It started about a month ago, just before she glued herself to the lamp. There were phone calls, unscheduled visits to her place. But the accident seemed to be the catalyst, the thing that really made a difference."

The night that Beryl glued herself to the lamp was the first time he spent an entire night at her hovel. I didn't think anything of it. Saul had rushed her to the hospital, stood by while they separated her from the lamp, comforted her, nursed her. What else could he do? But then there was the next night and the night after that and always the same excuse: "She's helpless. Her hand is in a sling. She can't do anything for herself with one hand."

"Why not bring her over here?" I said. "It'll be easier for you."

He looked stricken, confused. "No, she's better off at her place." That's when I began to wonder.

Saul loves his creature comforts: clean sheets, a bed that does not sag, coffee brought to him in the morning in a delicate china cup, all the services the rest of us provide, all the stupid, onerous, unnecessary things we do for him—enjoy doing, if the truth must be told. Always before, after an hour or two with Beryl, he would come crawling home, his back stiff from her lumpy mattress, hungering for his bed, a little nourishment. But that night and then the next night and the one after that, when he didn't come home, I began to worry, to wonder, ultimately to doubt his explanations.

My revelation has thrown the meeting into chaos. Curses, denials, and hindsights fill the air. "I knew something was funny when he was too busy to come for shortcake. . . . Bastard. . . . He left my library book on the train."

"He's a fucking psychopath," Kelly says, "that's what he is. I left Australia to get away from men. They're all cowboys there. I thought the men in America were more sensitive—more like us."

"The only totally sensitive man I ever knew was Bert," Connie says. "What a sweet nature he had. I'll never forget the time I left his laundry in the parking lot. 'It's okay,' he said. 'The economy needs a little shot in the arm.' Any other man—"

"Not now, Connie, please."

"I told that damn idiot this would happen if he persisted in taking another wife," Evelyn says. " 'Saul, you're spreading yourself too thin,' I said. 'You won't be able to handle the responsibility.' "

"Everything's always my fault," Valery says.

"I didn't say that," Evelyn says.

"People never say what they mean."

"Don't be paranoid," Connie says.

"We're not blaming you," Kelly says. "We're blaming the situation."

"I knew he was trouble the minute I met him," Valery says. "Something inside of me said, Stay clear of that man. But unfortunately, I've never learned to listen to my inner voice. I've never learned to trust myself." Her voice wavers. "He said he was going to help me—that together we would develop a belief system that would help me overcome my self-doubts. Now I see it's never going to happen."

Valery's hopelessness cheers Connie. "I have this book I want you to read. It's called *You Are Better than You Think*. It changed my life. It will change yours."

"He has no sense of proportion," Evelyn says. "He's totally incapable of seeing the consequences of his actions. Other people have to do his thinking for him."

"It could be worse," Jen says.

"How?"

"He could be chasing some stranger."

"It's a fact," Kelly says.

"That doesn't justify his irresponsibility," Evelyn says.

"I didn't say it did. But at least we know what we have

to deal with. And we can hope after all that it won't last, that he'll lose interest in Beryl."

"And what are we supposed to do in the meantime?" Evelyn says. "We can't wait for him to come to his senses. We've got to make it clear to him that he has to stop this nonsense. He has everything a man can desire: loving women, a thriving business, a nice place to live. Only a madman would jeopardize all of that."

"What if he won't listen?" Connie begins to weep. "I've had such a hard life. You don't know. You can't imagine what it's like to have a husband one moment, and then the next—nothing. If it happens twice, I'll die."

"It isn't going to happen because we won't let it," Evelyn says.

But Valery starts to cry too. "I was so lonely until I met Saul. The life of an actress is full of disappointments and broken promises. On top of that I am a geographical orphan. My entire family lives in the South."

"Josh must never know about this," Evelyn says. "It would disillusion him irrevocably."

"I doubt that anything could disillusion Josh," Kelly says. "He's very cynical about his father. 'Anyone else would be a misfit,' he says, 'growing up with a role model like that.' "

"He only says it for the effect," Evelyn says. "He doesn't mean it. You should see them doing calculus together." She bangs the table with her pen. "This meeting is getting out of hand. We're got to have some order," she says.

They all turn on Evelyn. "You're not in court," Kelly says.

"You're always on some kind of power trip," Jen says.

Evelyn flings down her pen. "Get someone else to run this meeting!" She runs into the bathroom and bangs the door shut.

"What's with her?" Jen says.

"What do you think?" I say. "She's in shock just like the rest of us." But it unnerves me to see Evelyn so upset.

61

She's the balanced one, the judicious one. It makes our plight real; our problems seem insurmountable.

"Tell us about it," Jen says. "How do you think I feel? When I think of the hours I have spent with that man choosing paneling, studying wood grains, I could just kill him. Remember the job on Wooster Street, the tilting floors? I didn't think we'd ever get the shelving and cabinets level. We struggled with it for days."

"What about the Dennison job," Kelly says, "when we had to match a violet to a violet in their painting? Saul and I spent a whole day mixing colors and then waiting for them to dry so we could compare our violet with theirs. We were so determined to get it right, we never even stopped to eat."

"But you loved getting it right," I say.

"It was hard work," Kelly says. "I wouldn't do it again. Not under the present circumstances."

Evelyn comes out of the bathroom. I hand her her pen. "We've got to separate them," she says.

"How?"

"Someone is going to have to talk to Beryl. She's the key. She's not a bad kid, a little flaky perhaps, disorganized, but she's not mean. We've got to make her see what a mistake she's making, how much she's hurting the family."

"You're right, Evelyn. It's a good idea. Maybe if we can convince her to go back to school, it'll distract her. She wouldn't have time for this nonsense."

"Why talk to her, though? Why not Saul?"

"Because she's more likely to do as we say."

"Exactly. Saul's an old hand at justifying his desires. He can develop a whole philosophical system around his appetites. We'd never get him to budge."

"Beryl's our only hope."

"If we can talk some sense into her."

"We've got to try."

"But who's going to do it? She would never listen to me," Connie says.

"Nor me," Jen says.

"And I'm too new here," Valery says.

They all look at me. "You talk to her," Evelyn says.

"Me?"

"Absolutely. You're the only one who has any hope of reaching her."

"Why me?" I say.

"You've been like a mother to her."

"People often resent their mothers."

"She won't resent you. How can she? You've always been so good to her. When she had the flu, you brought her to the loft and nursed her, fed her broth, dropped vitamin pills into her mouth. You probably saved her life. And that's not the only thing you've done for her. She has to be grateful. She'll listen. If anyone can make her understand, it's you."

"What can I tell her?"

"Tell her what an impossible person he is."

"Ask her if she's thought about what it would be like putting up with that man on a full-time basis."

"Remind her of his quirks."

"His egomania."

"His self-indulgence."

"The way he's always losing his keys."

"The parking tickets he's acquired just because he doesn't have the patience to find a legal parking place."

"The way he holds on to everything."

"His vanity."

"His hypochondria."

"You've got to try to convince her that she'd be better off the way things are."

"Make her see the disadvantages of a full-time husband."

"What a burden it would be."

"Will she listen? Whatever I say, will it make any difference?" I say.

"What else can we do?"

"Okay, I'll talk to her. All I can do is try."

5

Beryl is shuffling down the notions aisle of the five-and-ten. She is stomping one foot and then the other in time to the music on her Walkman. Her injured hand, swathed in bandages, swings back and forth like a pendulum.

Surely her hand has healed by now, I think. So why is she still wearing bandages? Doubtless for the dramatic effect. Unless, of course, there are complications, but if that were the case, we would have heard about them.

Beryl has a lot of red hair and a vague expression on her small, pinched face. She is wearing a skirt over another skirt and a man's huge shirt belted in with a metal chain, the kind used to hang ceiling lamps. Several scarves encircle her neck; earrings dangle from multiple holes in each ear. She looks like a person driven from her home by some catastrophe: a vicious city policy, perhaps, or some natural disaster that forced her to flee wearing everything she owned.

I call her name but the music blots out sound. "Beryl." I say it louder, but there is still no response. I tap her on the shoulder.

She turns around and looks at me, switches off her Walkman, removes her earphones. "Mozart's Quintet in G-minor," she says, although I clearly heard the Chopsticks playing "Gimme a Break."

"Hi, Helen, what's new?" We are in the greeting card section of the five-and-ten. Beryl turns away from me and begins to sort out cards.

Now that she is assistant manager, she is allowed to listen to music while she works. She tells me this while she removes a condolence card from the sweetheart section. She is in charge of inventory. A pocket calculator dangles from her belt.

The bandage covering her hand is filled with messages. *Pepi*, I read. *Ramon. Cora. To a swell girl. Beryl's a champ. Grow some skin soon.*

"How's it doing?" I say.

"They may have to do a skin graft," she says.

"I'm sorry to hear that," I say.

She is moving cards from one slot to another. "They never put them back where they find them. People are so irresponsible these days." She points to a sign saying 50% OFF. "We are clearing out our entire Friendship line," she says. "Now is the time to stock up."

"I'll think about it," I say. "How are things? We haven't seen you in a while."

"Ramon is giving me a hard time because I got promoted over him."

"I thought you two were friends."

"Not anymore," she says.

Beryl in the five-and-ten is queen. She has a handsome husband and a large family (us) who care about her welfare, drop in from time to time to see that she is all right. She spends much of her time in the basement with Ramon sorting out the merchandise—or did, until this falling out. Their closeness has always worried Saul. "What do they do down there?" he says.

Beryl likes us to come by. She greets us with an air of authority, is eager to put us on to good buys. "This

65

shipment of porcelain from the People's Republic of China is an incredible bargain," she says. "They are clearing cotton panties. . . . Our new insect repellent carries a money-back guarantee."

Now she is explaining the situation between her and Ramon. "He is convinced the promotion belonged to him but that due to Third World prejudice on the part of management he was passed over for someone with lesser abilities—namely, me. I try to tell him it isn't so. 'Ramon,' I've said time and again. 'It's not your nationality, it's your clothes. You don't look like management. You have to learn to dress for the fast track.' "

"And what does he say?"

She shrugs. "He thinks he's gorgeous."

"Beryl, we have to talk," I say.

"I thought we were talking."

"You know what I mean. Can you take a break and go and have a cup of coffee with me?"

"We're very shorthanded," she says. "Two of the girls are out sick."

"It's important."

"I don't like to take advantage of my new status."

"It'll only be a few minutes," I say.

"I'm supposed to be in the basement this very minute counting out a shipment of paper towels."

"I'll help you," I say.

"Only qualified personnel are permitted down there."

"Oh, Beryl, cut it out," I say.

The basement of the five-and-ten looks like an archaeological dig. Day-Glo hula hoops dangle from the ceiling. An early shipment of washboards rests against a wall. Paper dresses, yellowing and torn, hang from a rack. Dacron wigs, bell-bottom trousers, celluloid Kewpie dolls are piled one on top of another in chronological layers. The floor is littered with platform shoes.

I follow Beryl to a stack of cartons. She rips one open, curses. "They've made a mistake. They sent us buff. We

66

ordered pink. It's right here on the shipping label. Nobody is going to buy buff."

"Beryl, the other wives asked me to come and talk to you. We're worried about Saul."

"You're always worried about Saul."

"With good reason, don't you think?"

Beryl is ripping open one carton after another and stacking rolls of paper towels as if her life depended on it. "Will you stop that," I say, "and listen to what I have to tell you?"

"Don't treat me like a child," Beryl says. "I have two Third World men working under me."

"I'm here to talk to you as an equal. One responsible woman to another."

"He's too confined. That's the problem."

"What do you mean?"

"He's too locked into his life: the emotional demands, the schedules, having to be at a certain place at a certain time. It's killing him."

"Is it any worse than being in one place all the time?"

"You don't understand him, any of you. He's a very sensitive person. He needs someone who really cares, who—listens, who takes him seriously."

"Someone like you?"

"Oh, Helen, I don't want to hurt your feelings. You know how much I like you. You've been like a mother to me, only a whole lot better than my own mother, who thinks only of her body tone and diversifying her holdings. But I owe Saul something too. He saved my life. That day he found me crying in the doorway, I didn't want to live."

The day he found her crying in the doorway, she had had a fight with her boyfriend. A street musician, he had walked off with the day's take. Beryl was not a musician, but her boyfriend had taught her to make a noise on the recorder at a certain point in his song. Their fight had been over her performance. "It doesn't sound right," her boyfriend had said. "And after I had given him all my

67

marinated chick-peas, he didn't even leave me carfare." Those were her first words to Saul.

He found her weeping in a doorway; snow was turning to slush. Saul took her to her hovel, made her some oatmeal. They had a long talk. Then he climbed into bed with her, and shortly afterward she became another wife.

Her mother in the West liked the idea. IRREGULAR DOESN'T MATTER, she wired. MATURITY IS WHAT COUNTS. IT WILL BE GOOD FOR BERYL TO INTERFACE WITH CREATIVE SUCCESSFUL PEOPLE.

Although Beryl is always denying the effect her mother has had on her behavior, the marriage almost didn't take place when she discovered how much her mother wanted it. "She is under the impression I work in the five-and-dime to make her miserable. 'A low-paying, dead-end job . . . a waste of your talents . . . a refusal to try anything challenging.' " She quoted some of the things her mother was always saying to her. Then added, "Like all immature people, my mother thinks she is the center of the universe, that I plot my life to get back at her."

"Well, why *do* you work there?" we said.

"I happen to be the chief stock clerk, the only female in the entire store on that level." Ramon was her friend then, and they did everything together. Every morning, they toured each aisle, straightening merchandise, replenishing stock. "Ramon loves the cosmetics department," she told us. "The thought of all those lotions and powders adorning women makes him happy. Sometimes he opens a bottle and spreads some lotion on himself. Then he squeezes the cap tight and puts it back."

"Isn't that a little kinky?" we said.

"He's not hurting anybody," she said. "Unlike my mother, I am able to respect other people's choices." Ramon was teaching her Spanish. She had already learned to say, "*Mañana, hasta la vista, mira, buenas noches.*" She was teaching Ramon the periodic table of elements, for he was upwardly mobile and trying to impress ladies of a better type.

68

"It's a shame about you and Ramon not speaking," I say. "You were really close."

"I have other things on my mind," Beryl says.

"I can imagine," I say.

"Oh, Helen, it isn't something Saul and I planned," Beryl says. "It just happened."

"What happened? Would you mind telling me what's going on? Saul won't explain a thing. He pretends nothing has happened."

"Saul and I have fallen in love."

"What do you mean, fallen in love? Didn't you love each other when you got married?"

"Of course. But this is of a different magnitude. It was an accident, Helen. Neither of us planned it. We were suddenly drawn to each other in a new way, overwhelmed by intense feelings, a yearning to be together. Even so, it was the accident with the lamp that really solidified things. When he saw me standing there, trapped and helpless, his heart almost broke. 'You poor darling!' he cried. He started to run across the room to rescue me, but then a terrible thing happened. He slipped on my area rug and fell."

"He never told me that. Did he hurt himself?"

"It was quite a fall. I think he hit his head."

"He might have had a concussion. No wonder he's acting so crazy."

"If you mean loving me is crazy, we really have nothing more to say."

"Did he pass out? How bad was it?"

"I had to unplug the lamp before I could go to him, and it wouldn't come out of the socket. I've always had trouble with that particular plug. By the time I had freed myself, he was on his feet."

"How did he seem to you? Was his speech slurred? What about his vision? He probably shouldn't have moved."

"He was more concerned about me than he was about himself."

"That doesn't sound like Saul."

"He was afraid I might lose my hand. 'That glue is permanent.' He kept saying it all the way to the hospital. And then, when they peeled my skin from the lamp, I really thought he was going to pass out."

"You mean he was in the operating room with you?" Beryl nods. "Why'd you let him stay? You know how sensitive he is. He just about dies if he sees a speck of blood."

"He insisted on staying. By then—by then we knew something special had happened. 'I never want to leave you,' he said."

"What about the rest of us? What's going to happen to the family? Josh? Our Sundays?"

"Why does anything have to happen? Why can't we all be friends?"

"It just doesn't work that way. If Saul neglects his other wives, quits his conjugal visits, how do you think they'll feel? How would you feel if you were on the receiving end?"

"Honestly, Helen, we never meant this to happen. If we hadn't been in such an extreme situation, we probably would have been able to curb our feelings. But it was like the end of the world, me glued to the lamp, Saul down there on the floor. I suppose it had the effect on us that drowning does. Our lives flashed before us, and we both asked the same question: What does it all mean? And what it meant was—us." Although her voice is mournful, there is a certain bragging quality to her words.

"Give him back," I say.

"How can I do that? He's not a piece of merchandise to be handed over to others."

"Tell him that it isn't going to work, that you've changed your mind."

"I can't do that. I need him. Do you think I would be where I am today without his encouragement?" She points to the calculator dangling from her belt. "I'd still be on the street corner crying if he hadn't come along."

70

"Oh, come now," I say.

"Besides, even if I agreed to go back to the old arrangement, what makes you think Saul would want to? Do you realize how hard it is having seven wives?"

"Yes," I say.

"Saul feels he's being used—that everybody expects the impossible from him."

"He's always exaggerating his life."

"They all expect the moon. When Jen stopped biting her nails, she was in a tizzy because he didn't notice. And Evelyn treated him like a criminal because he didn't praise her for losing a few pounds. How can he keep track of every trivial change? He's not a priest, after all, just an ordinary mortal."

"You're quoting him," I say.

"He needs peace and quiet, a person who doesn't expect the impossible. He needs to be with someone who is self-sufficient and isn't in constant need of reassurance."

"You?"

"He needs to be able to hear himself think."

"Saul doesn't think. If he thought, we wouldn't be in this present situation."

"You don't appreciate him, any of you. You simply are not aware of his fine points, his sweetness. Just because he's an intuitive person, you think he's not an intellect. But that isn't why he quit the academic world. He couldn't stand the people, the long thoughtful silences, the constant editing of remarks."

"I know all that, Beryl. I was there when it happened."

"Even so, he feels that nobody gives him credit for how hard he works, how conscientious he is about meeting all his responsibilities. Everybody takes him for granted."

"Is that what he says?"

"He would like a little recognition; he would like to feel he's appreciated. It's not so much to ask. He's no different from anyone else."

"I'm glad to know that," I say. "Would you mind telling me what's going to happen now?"

"Well, as soon as my hand heals, I'm going to take a week's leave and we're going on a canoe trip along the Bleak River."

"You're kidding!"

"We have it all planned."

"But it's winter."

"That's the best time. It's more of a challenge in the winter."

"But Saul hates the cold. You know that as well as I do. His idea of a brave act at this time of year is to walk to the corner for his newspaper."

"It's just a phobia. People can overcome their fears if they really want to. And he wants to. He intends to be a different person from now on. No more shrinking from the elements. He wants to feel at one with nature, be someone who isn't afraid to take chances."

"He'll be absolutely miserable. He'll freeze to death."

"There are ways of keeping warm. It isn't difficult. Anyway, we've signed up for a survival seminar. They teach you everything about hardship trips, how to read maps and what to do if your canoe tips over in the icy water."

"Oh, God," I say. "He'll die. He's totally inept out-of-doors."

"Naturally if you keep saying that to a person, they start to believe it."

"He was that way when I met him. He didn't learn to walk until he was three."

"He'll be okay. It isn't hard to learn to paddle. We'll take along down sleeping bags guaranteed to keep you warm at five below, and at night we'll camp out by the banks of the river."

"Saul camping out by the banks of a river? Beryl, are you sure you have the right man?"

"He'll be okay. I was a camp counselor two summers in a row. I know how to take care of myself in the wilderness."

"Is that what you want me to tell the family? That

72

you're taking Saul on a canoe trip where he'll either drown or freeze to death?"

"Tell them what you want. Why are you picking on me?"

"Beryl, you'd better give this some thought. We could all be in real trouble if it continues."

"Continues? You can no more stop us than you can stop the sun from rising." She waves a roll of paper towel at me to underline her feelings, stacks one on top of another in an effort to control herself. "Listen, Helen, he needs a little breathing space. He needs to get away from his life. He feels as if he's living in a pressure cooker."

She is still trying to explain the situation when Ramon comes down the stairs. "We're out of number ten envelopes. Must be about twenty-five customers up there waiting to buy envelopes."

His voice is angry; Beryl's equally angry when she answers. "Twenty-five customers, I just bet. Anyway, they're over there. Help yourself."

Ramon glances where she points, but he does not move. "I don't see them," he says.

"Maybe you need glasses." She gives Ramon a hard look, begins to search herself.

"Some inventory control," he mutters. "This place is a mess. It's a miracle the store don't go bankrupt."

Beryl puts her headphones on and switches on her Walkman. She turns her back on Ramon and begins to rummage through various boxes.

It is obvious our discussion is over. I stand up. "I'm going, Beryl," I say.

"Okay." I start for the stairs. "Thanks for coming, anyway," she says. "I appreciate what you said."

I try to harden my heart, to blame her for the trouble. She has no sense of responsibility, no genuine feeling for the rest of us. But Saul is the one, the culprit, the person who is spoiling our lives. And yet, instead of feeling angry at him, I feel only bemused.

I climb the stairs in a daze. Saul on a canoe trip,

sleeping by the banks of a river in the dead of winter. How is such a thing possible? Do I know so little about my husband that his pleasures are a secret and a surprise? Has Beryl made it all up, created a dream world inhabited by the two of them, a world of icy water and cold?

I'd like to believe that it is her idea and not his. He is always placating his wives, saying yes when he means no. It is possible that he agreed to go canoeing with Beryl in the belief that it would never come to pass.

I can even visualize the scene—taking place on the way to the hospital—a weeping Beryl, a frightened Saul, a jolting taxi, and both of them clutching for dear life at the lamp adhering to her. I can imagine Saul saying some comforting nonsense: "When this is over, we'll take a trip, just the two of us, to some far-off place where neither of us has ever been." And from that this terrible journey evolved.

That's the way it must have been, I tell myself, as I leave the cavernous five-and-ten: an accidental commitment made in a moment of stress. But suppose it wasn't that way? Suppose it was something else, a serious and enduring tie that won't go away no matter how the rest of us argue and protest?

6

The phone rings constantly. Each caller is a worried wife. "We've got to get him to a therapist," Connie says. She knows just the right person, one who specializes in restlessness. Jen is next. "Kelly can't keep anything in her stomach," she says. Then Valery calls suggesting we try to interest Saul in a course in needlepoint. It has helped many high-strung executives learn how to center themselves. Also it would give Saul a creative outlet. Next Kelly calls to badmouth Evelyn. "Her approach to life is too damn intellectual. That's why Saul feels so inadequate." Evelyn calls to say she has a plan. "We'll lure Beryl into signing up for a course in merchandising. Then she won't have time for Saul."

Each time a wife calls, I get up to answer the phone. "Yes, okay, we'll talk later. I'm busy right now," I say, for I am with Saul in the workroom going over a plan. We are designing a space for a couple who do catering. In less than a thousand square feet they want us to design a working kitchen, a place to sleep, another to entertain clients.

It is getting late. Nothing suits Saul. I have drawn up

one plan and then another. Now I am trying a third. "We will start with an open floor plan. Instead of partitions, six columns will divide the space into its components. All their storage needs will be concealed within the columns." I make a rough sketch of what I have in mind, a Doric column sliced down the middle, its insides revealed. Within this area, which would be concealed, I draw shelving, hooks to hang things from, bins. "The columns will open at the press of a button. Each one will have a revolving mechanism that moves the interior space around. Within one column, they can store clothes and linens. Another would hold kitchenware. And so on."

The more I expand on this idea, the more I like it, for its application seems to go far beyond this particular job. "There's a vast urban population out there with unmet storage needs," I say. "We could manufacture prefabricated columns, easily assembled, and market them nationwide."

I look at Saul and wait for some response, hoping he will share my excitement at the commercial possibilities of these columns. He stares at my rough sketch and rummages around on the desk for a T square that is not there. He gets up and sorts through a pile of rubble nearby and, still unable to locate his T square, returns to the desk. The workroom is always a mess. Things merge with other things and disappear. Saul is incapable of throwing anything out. He studies the drawing, shakes his head. "It's too gimmicky," he says.

"What do you mean, too gimmicky?"

"Too many columns breaking up that small space. It would feel like you were living in a forest."

"It is a bold, simple concept."

"Simple?" Saul stares at me. "It's anything but simple."

I study the sketch. Is he right? Am I losing my outlook? Is worry obscuring my sense of style? Why should it be me? Nothing pleases Saul today. If I had designed the Sistine chapel, he'd have found fauit. "It is not gimmicky," I say. "Those columns would serve a dual purpose.

76

In a thousand square feet, we have to make use of all our structural components."

"But not at the expense of austerity. Without that we are nothing. Any two-bit designer could work out a design like that." His criticism infuriates me. I feel as if he is dismantling me, removing my essence.

"Two-bit designer." I throw my drawing pen at him. "Everybody is saying bad things about you."

Saul rubs his eye, presses his hanky to it. "Jesus, Helen, you almost took my eye out." He stands up, looking injured and haughty.

"You were supposed to help get Aster to the vet. The dog could have died if Connie had waited for you."

"You could have blinded me."

"Valery is totally confused. She doesn't know what being married to you entails."

Saul is standing before a mirror, examining his injured eye. "It hurts," he says.

"I'm sorry," I say. "I didn't mean to hurt you."

"This isn't like you," he says.

He is using this as a diversion, turning the tables, trying to make me out the assailant, him my innocent victim. "Sit down," I say, "and tell me what's going on."

"What do you mean?" He gives me a puzzled look.

"You know damn well what I mean. Are you going on a canoe trip or aren't you?"

"Who told you?"

"Who do you think?"

Saul stares down at my rejected design, makes a notation in the margin.

"I saw Beryl yesterday."

"How is she?" he says.

"We talked about the canoe trip, and other things too."

Saul puts down his pen and looks at me. "Is that what's bothering you?" he says.

"It's not just me, Saul, we're all in this. The other wives asked me to go see her."

77

"It's no big deal, Helen. Don't look so distraught. It isn't the end of the world if I paddle down the Bleak River for a couple of days."

"But why would you even want to go, the way you hate cold weather? You'll be miserable. I just don't know what to make of all this."

"They've developed cold-weather equipment that makes it easy to be out in the cold. They have this personal environment equipment now, these insulated suits. They invented them for the Alpine troops. They're guaranteed to ward off cold as low as ten degrees below zero. It's never going to get that cold."

"That's beside the point. It's crazy going off like this with all the work piled up. Where's your sense of responsibility?"

"A few days isn't going to make all that difference. You and Jen and Kelly can cope while I'm gone. Evelyn is drawing up contracts, and—"

"Beryl says you and she have fallen in love."

"Is that what she said?"

"Madly, hopelessly, insanely in love."

Saul blushes. "She said that?"

"What about the rest of us?" I say.

"You know the way Beryl talks. She overstates. That entire generation dramatizes their lives."

"Then you're not in love? Is that what you're saying?"

"Not exactly."

"Not exactly what?"

"It's just a momentary infatuation."

"But Beryl isn't even your type." In his essay on the defeminization of women, he deplores boniness. "You like wives with a little flesh on them."

"Several of my wives are bony," he says.

Who does he mean? I wonder.

"So you're determined to go off on this crazy trip where you'll either drown or catch pneumonia or both."

"I would just like to have a little monogamy for a while. Is that so hard to understand? Think of this as a

78

vacation, me from you and you from me. Everybody needs a change. You can enjoy yourself while I'm gone. Think of the fun, the freedom—"

"Whose fun, whose freedom?"

"Wouldn't it be nice not to have to worry about calendars? Wouldn't you like to be able to say to yourself, His whereabouts are not my responsibility? I should think you'd want a change, a vacation from schedules. You can go out, see a few movies, have dinner with Evelyn or whoever else you'd like to see. You never have any time to yourself. The burden is always on you. Everybody expects too much from you."

"You mean you're going off to give me a rest, sacrificing yourself for my welfare. Your generosity overwhelms me."

"I'm trying to be straight with you, and you're being sarcastic."

"How else should I be?"

"Why can't you think of it this way? When I get back, everything will be new again. It'll be like beginning all over."

He puts an arm around me and rubs my shoulder. Does he mean it? I put my arms around him and press him against me. My heart beats rapidly. A powerful longing seizes me. Oh, Saul, hold me, love me. I lift my face. Saul squeezes my chin. "You're still the best-looking woman of your age group I've ever seen."

"Go to hell." I wrench myself away from him. "I don't believe a word you've said."

"Then what's the point in talking? I don't know what's got into you, Helen. You're getting hard. You never used to be this way."

"Let's just finish the job." I will not look at him. I will not try to discuss personal matters with him. Not anymore. If this is the way he wants it, okay. I used to be his friend as well as his lover. But that time is long gone. He doesn't deserve friendship or understanding. He is on his own now. I have no intention of protecting him from the others. From this day forward, we are business partners—nothing more.

We sit down opposite each other and stare at the blueprint. The phone rings and I start to get up. "Don't answer it," Saul says. "Let them leave a message on the machine. Otherwise we'll never finish."

My thoughts are bitter. I see him wrapped in insulated sheeting, huddled in the prow of the canoe, his lips blue, his body shaking, while Beryl paddles erratically down the river. His face is yellow as well as blue, for he is seasick from the turbulent water. Or perhaps, at this time of year, there will be large chunks of ice bobbing around, their edges sharp. One of them will pierce the hull of the canoe, which must surely be made out of something soft and therefore easily penetrated. Then they will sink and our troubles will be over.

I stare at the blueprint, trying to expunge such thoughts from my mind, for in truth I feel as if I am orchestrating their deaths. But I can't focus on the work. What was I trying to do? We sit across from each other like strangers; worse than strangers, like ancient enemies, determined to destroy each other come what may.

Such thoughts. They make me guilty and afraid. Why am I reacting so powerfully to this betrayal? It isn't the first time he has rejected me for someone else, and I am sure it won't be the last. Is it Beryl, her youth, her lack of accomplishments in the world that make his passion for her seem so unfair and cheapen what the rest of us are and feel for him? I try to focus on the work, the problem in front of us.

We continue our discussion, our voices cold and businesslike, our comments perfunctory. "Change this wall. Add a partition there. Shelving here." As we talk, I sketch out the most conventional of designs. I am through caring about the quality of our work. If this is what he wants, this is what he'll get.

Saul nods. He agrees to all my suggestions as if originality and brilliance had never been part of our vision.

80

"Okay," he says. "Now the only problem left is where they hang all their kitchen things. They have a million utensils and pans they need to get their hands on at a moment's notice."

I try to think of a solution. Work is a relief, a truce, a shield between me and my bitterness. "I have an idea," I say. "Suppose we staple a fishnet to the ceiling, across the entire length of the kitchen. We could hang hooks from it and. . . ."

Saul stares at me; my voice wavers.

"What's the matter?" I say.

"You're not serious."

"Why do you say that?"

"Because it's cute. You've never designed anything cute before."

"It's not cute," I say. "It's practical. We could place the hooks in rows, achieve a certain symmetry. And if we chose a color for the fishnet that matched the ceiling, it would blend in and disappear."

"I can't imagine anything more cluttered and busy."

I lay down my pen. "You figure it out," I say. "I don't care whether the job gets done or not. What difference does it make? You are ruining our lives."

"How am I ruining your life? Just because I'm leaving the city for a couple of days? It isn't like you, Helen, to exaggerate things this way. I wish you would stop crowding me."

"You did it to yourself. Nobody forced you to marry so many women."

"That's not the point. I've never regretted my marriages. But now I need a little space, a little quiet time. Why is that so hard to understand?"

"You always have an answer. You think you are better than other people."

"Not better, merely more imaginative, more adventurous. I'm not afraid of living at the edge." But he does consider himself better. I have heard him on the subject of living dangerously. Saul sees himself as a saint, his lust a calling, a form of spiritual dedication, himself a priest, part Catholic, part pagan. Each time he gives himself to a wife, his body is an offering, a form of sacrifice, a penance for the sins of the world.

"No, you think you are better. You always manage to conceal from yourself what your selfishness is doing to others. You manage to convert whatever you crave into a moral imperative."

"It really hurts me when you call me selfish. How can you say that about me? Selfish is the last word I'd use to describe myself. If you see me that way, you don't understand what I'm about."

"Prove you're not selfish, then. Don't go on this trip."

"I promised Beryl."

"Tell her it's a mistake. Or that you can't get away. It's crazy, Saul."

"I'm not a slave. I give of myself every minute of the day. Someone's always there wanting something from me. I have a right to a little vacation. It isn't fair to make me out such a monster."

"I'm not trying to make you out a monster. I just don't want you to go."

"I'm going."

"We have all this work—"

"We always have work."

"Damn you. What's the matter with you?" I start to yell. "Why can't you act like a decent person for once in your life?"

At that moment, Josh walks into the studio. "The door was open," he says.

Saul looks stricken. "You should have knocked," he says. Above everything, he wants his son to think well of him, to look up to him, to walk around thinking, I want to be just like my father when I grow up. He hates for Josh to see him in any negative situation, weak or angry or not in charge of his life. "Why is security so lax?" he mutters.

"I'm not in charge of security," I say.

"The door should be locked at all times."

"Then lock it," I say.

"Anyone could walk in. A burglar. A psychopathic killer."

"Even a philanderer," I say.

Saul glances at Josh, obviously uneasy. "How come you're not in school?"

"We had a half holiday," he says. Josh is setting up his video equipment. He is doing a visual history of the family. He points his camera at a huge blueprint pinned to a wall.

"It seems to me there are more school holidays than there are schooldays," Saul says, trying to sound humorous. He gives me a sweet, complicit smile, but I refuse to return it.

"Too bad you ever left your teaching post," I say. "That was one long holiday. A safe, enclosed world where anyone could cope."

This is more than Saul can bear. His academic career was filled with disappointments, a sense of inadequacy. He hates to be reminded of it. He tried to write a paper on the aesthetics of women, the differing modes of beauty from one era to another, to develop a thesis of cultural sexuality, the transformation of the senses through aesthetic events. "At one time, women were beautiful," he wrote. "Their features even, their bodies soft to the touch, yielding. Now their rude and brutal manner, their unkempt hair exemplifies. . . ."

This is as far as he got. He would sit in front of his notebook and nibble at his pen, add a word, then another word, then cross out the first word or the second word or both and stare into the middle distance as if he might read a message of inspiration there. Then he would close his spiral notebook and thrust it into a drawer. "If only I had an entire irresponsible day," he would say.

Mentioning the academic world infuriates him. "Without me there'd be no business," he yells, "and then where would you be?"

If I weren't so angry I might admit the truth of this. Saul has the ability to take my concepts and translate them into living spaces: a place to eat, a place to work, a place to make love. He brings logic, a rational approach, to the environments I conceive—a sense of proportion, illusions of depth, of infinite expanses.

But I am unwilling to admit this now. "I could manage," I say. "There are plenty of people who know my work and appreciate it."

"You couldn't even install a partition without me."

Josh is focusing his camera. He sets it down gently on the floor. "There is justice in both your arguments," he says.

"What half holiday is it?" Saul says.

"It's the principal's birthday," Josh says.

"Jesus," Saul says.

Josh smiles sweetly at his father. "Don't be so grouchy," he says. He is taking a course in childrening, an adjunct of parent effectiveness training. But unlike parenting, childrening does not teach you to be a more effective child. It is a course in tactics: when to avoid conflict, when not; how to understand the hidden agendas of your parents, when to meet their eyes. Josh is studying manipulation; he is practicing diplomacy. Now he is testing his tactics on Saul and me.

"Just because you have troubles does not mean life is over," he says.

"That's not what's bothering me," Saul says.

"Silence is the worst enemy of a harmonious family life."

"There is too much talk in this family," Saul says.

"But what kind of talk? Is it clear and straightforward or is it double-talk, concealing what people really think and feel? It makes a difference," Josh says.

"We're working," Saul says. "We're very busy."

"That's what I mean. You're trying to change the subject to avoid painful discussions."

"We have a deadline, a client who's breathing down our neck."

"Just because I'm a minor doesn't mean I don't have

84

thoughts worth listening to. Try to get a grip on yourself; try to get a perspective. I've learned to overcome my sorrows by saying to myself, 'Tomorrow is another day.' "

"What sorrows?" Saul says.

"That's the way with most people. They think they're the only one with problems. I shot ten minutes of my mother marking up a brief. It was the most utterly truthful footage I had ever taken—and then, when I ran it, I discovered the lens of my camera had an eyelash on it."

"Are you hungry?" I say.

"A little bit."

"There's some nice bananas in the kitchen. Go help yourself," I say.

Josh goes through the workroom into our apartment. I turn to Saul. "He's right, you know."

"What are you talking about? He was spouting clichés."

"He was right about speaking the truth, facing our dilemmas."

Saul nods. "I suppose so." He stares at the blueprint in front of him, then at me. "Remember when I put my back out? It was so bad I couldn't move. My sacroiliac was a total wreck. Anyway, as a result, all conjugal visits came to a halt. Well, this is like that too, only on a spiritual plane. If you can think of it that way, if all of you try saying to yourselves, 'Saul has a spiritual bad back,' it won't seem like I'm rejecting you and it will give me a chance to mend."

"Mend? Are you sick? Is Beryl some kind of medicine?"

"A tonic, yes. Something that will renew my hold on things, so that I'll be more generous, more involved with the rest of you. Doesn't that make sense?"

"No," I say. "You could justify murder, if you had to."

"What murder? Whose murder?" Josh comes back clutching a glass of milk with a plateful of cookies on it and a banana he is munching on.

"We are talking metaphorically," Saul says. "And you shouldn't talk with your mouth full."

"I hear you're going on a canoe trip. Can I go with you? I would like to take some footage of the banks of the Bleak River at this time of year. I've never taken footage of a river in winter. Plus I could help with the portage. If you put your back out it would finish you. Plus I know a lot about camping. I could be a real help to you on this trip."

"Thanks, but it isn't possible," Saul says.

"Why not?"

"You can't afford to miss school."

"Beryl said she'd help me with my math if you let me go. We could do it at night while the food was cooking."

"Beryl never said such a thing."

"Ask her."

"She never invited you along."

"Ask her, why don't you? She's my best friend. We do everything together. Of course she wants me to go."

"You don't do everything together. It's a bad habit to get into, exaggerating what people say to you," Saul says. He looks hurt and confused and frightened.

"She and I have been talking for months about canoeing down the Bleak River."

"This is a different plan. It's just Beryl and your daddy. And besides, I'm sure Evelyn would not want you to go during the school term."

"Evelyn wouldn't give a damn. She's really upset at what's going on. Everybody is. The whole family is about to collapse. I used to think that with all your wives I'd at least have a stable life—not normal, maybe, but dependable—and that there wouldn't be bad feelings the way there are in a lot of families. But now you're ruining everything. Why can't you leave Beryl alone? Why do you have to spoil things?"

Saul and I look at each other, shocked by his son's words. "I'm not ruining things. You have to try to trust me a little," Saul says. "This is just a little trip. I don't know why everyone's making a mountain out of a molehill. Trust me, Josh. I'm not abandoning my family."

I echo Saul's words, suddenly united by a need to keep Josh at bay, outside the community of adult ways and secrets and compromises. "Trust him," I say. "Everything is going to be okay."

7

"I t's me," Valery says.

"What makes you say that?" Connie says.

"Everything was fine until he married me." Saul was right about Valery. She is essentially a gloomy person, filled with a sense of error and blame, one more refugee who sought safety in our midst. We are all running away from something: Connie from her frozen sorrow, Jen from her childhood, Kelly from the hostile Outback. But perhaps Valery's sense of inadequacy and failure is of a different magnitude, for she keeps trying to gather in all the blame. "He was disappointed in me. And that disappointment drove him into Beryl's arms."

It is evening. We are gathered together in the workroom to discuss Saul's defection. We are here rather than in the living space because Jen has work to do. She is gluing molding to the door of a cabinet long overdue. A muscular accident has caused her to fall behind in her work.

"It can't be that bad," we tell Valery.

"You don't understand. There is no me," she says. "I am like a straw woman waiting for a human soul to come and inhabit her. If I didn't pattern myself after others, I would barely exist. I bet you'll never guess who I'd like to be."

"Who?" we say.

"Julie Christie," she says, blushing.

"But what has that to do with Saul's defection?" Jen says.

"Everything. He thought I was going to be an interesting companion, full of ideas that would be of help and inspiration. He thought we'd have fun together."

"Fun? Saul doesn't believe in fun," Evelyn says.

Jen drops a clamp and rummages through piles of debris at her feet to retrieve it. She keeps tossing things aside. "I can't believe it," she says.

We should be used to it by now, Saul's chaos, his inability to throw anything out, not even a bent nail, not even a rusty screw. But we keep complaining about the mess to each other and, when Saul is around, to him. "I may need it," he says.

His mother, a maniac for order, threw out all his childhood possessions—the comic books, the magic candy dispenser, the wind-up robot, the General MacArthur doll—the year he graduated from college. The loss of his beloved toys was sharpened when his cousin (the one who won the yo-yo championship) made a fortune selling his collection of classic comics. The only way we can ever throw anything out is to sneak a piece of debris downstairs when he is away on business.

While Jen tightens her clamp, Valery continues to accuse herself. "He expected better things from me: a new interest in life, a more informed companion. When he discovered my inability to share his aesthetic concerns, he turned to Beryl for solace."

"You couldn't be more mistaken," Evelyn says. "Beryl is the last one he'd look to for intellectual companionship. And anyway, as you ought to know by now, the only thoughts that interest him are his own." She drains her glass of wine and pours another, passes the bottle around so we can all refill our glasses. We are drinking wine to comfort ourselves and nibbling on strips of green and red peppers for our health.

"Well, if it wasn't my intellectual inadequacies it was something else," Valery says. "Wherever I go, affliction follows."

Valery is knitting while she talks. She is working on our sweaters. But none of them satisfies her. She keeps spotting flaws, ripping back a row and then another row. "That hammer doesn't look right," she says. "You could never tell it from an awl. There's something wrong with the shape of this sleeve." At this rate she will never finish.

"Valery, please." We beg her to desist. "We don't mind a flaw or two. Perfection is an illusion. Just finish the sweaters."

Valery is insulted. "You don't respect my work," she says.

"We do, we do."

She holds up a sweater. "Is that a neck opening or a disaster? Can't you see that it's totally asymmetrical?"

"Asymmetrical is in," Connie says. "Everyone is wearing off-center gear."

Valery shakes her head. "It's no good." She pulls the stitches from her needle and starts to rip.

"Oh, Valery," we groan.

"I have to get it right. I can't sleep at night as it is. I keep having this nightmare. Everything I make starts to unravel." In this dream an angry mob, brandishing sleeves, neckbands, cuffs, chases Valery down the street. "It's horrible," she says. "I'm afraid to go to sleep."

"Poor Valery," we say.

"Poor all of us."

Saul and Beryl have been gone five days, and they haven't even sent us a card. "For all we know they may be dead."

"Or dying of pneumonia in some foul hospital."

"And none of us there to comfort him and bid a sad farewell."

90

"Even if he were dying, I don't think I have it in me to comfort him at this moment," Evelyn says. "What I really want is to teach him a lesson that he will not soon forget."

"Me too. . . . Me too." We all agree. Our hearts burn with anger, a hunger for revenge, a craving to be exonerated from all blame, all sense of inadequacy. Yet even with the wine, the solidarity of the others, I feel bereft, as if I too were lacking in some quality Saul hungered for.

We were incompatible, he and I. And the wonder is it took this long to surface. Our personalities, our outlook, our habits make us unfit to be together. Our inner clocks are out of sync. I am orderly. I love schedules, live by routines, eat at regular intervals, go to bed at the same time each night. Saul is just the opposite. His work habits are slovenly and irregular. He procrastinates, is late for appointments. He eats all day long.

I am circumspect, reserved. He dramatizes his life. "They are crucifying me," he tells the seltzer man, the dentist, our wine dealer, the paper man, his wives. His childhood is a sequence of disasters and sorrows, dreadful deeds inflicted on him that grow more monstrous each passing year. "One Passover, she"—his mother—"threw my tropical fish into the gefilte fish," he says.

"Tropical fish are not edible," I say.

"She did not know that at the time," he says.

Beryl is just like him, persecuted by her mother, irregular in her habits. She too eats all day long. No wonder they went off together. Yet when I try to imagine life without Saul, all I can think of is silence, and the order I crave seems like a death. Without Saul, I feel empty. Sudden tears fill my eyes.

I avert my face, but Jen notices. "Oh, Helen," she says. "It's worse for you than anyone." She throws her arms around me. "Don't cry. I can't bear it when you cry. Not you. It feels like the end of the world when I see tears in your eyes."

"It's like a death in the family," Connie says.

"It's like the President shedding tears during a speech," Evelyn says.

"Or the Pope weeping while he blesses the multitude," Kelly says.

"I'm sorry," I say. "I'll be okay in a minute." But my tears are catching. Eyes fill. Self-pity and uncertainty are in everyone's heart.

"I had no childhood," Jen says. "I don't deserve this."

"I had a childhood but it was terrible," Kelly says.

"Even when I was a small child I had to watch my weight," Evelyn says.

"My mother was a gender foe," Jen says. "My entire childhood was spent in litigation. While other children were enjoying themselves, doing whatever children do, I was testifying before some judge about the lack of female role models in our history book."

"In the Outback people used to stand around and watch me paint," Kelly says. " 'Call that a tree?' they would say. 'What's that supposed to be, a bridge?' Then they would nudge each other and laugh."

"I didn't know what life was all about until I lost Bert," Connie says. She pulls out a picture of her late husband, passes it around. We have seen this picture many times before. "Isn't he a lovely man?" she says. In the picture, he is stepping over the threshold of the cave. The entrance is low. The brochures and travel books described the cave as one of the wonders of the region. But they exaggerated its qualities. It was little more than a crevice in the side of the mountain. Connie didn't want to crawl inside. "You go," she said.

"Those were the last words I ever said to him. As he entered the cave, I snapped that picture." It is a view of his stooping back.

"I've never had a life," Valery says, "not even a sad one."

"Everybody has had a life," Jen says.

"Saul is the first person who ever took an interest in me. It's my own fault, of course; my obsession with acting has isolated me from humanity," Valery says. "You don't know how many hours I spend staring at myself in a mirror, teaching myself to convey disappointment or anguish. I made up this scenario to help me do my emotional exercises. It goes like this: I work in an office and this man follows me to the water fountain. When I bend over to get a drink, he sexually harasses me, thereby giving me the opportunity to express a variety of emotions—thirst, fear, outrage, and so on." She begins to make faces to show us her emotional range.

"Very good, Valery," we say.

"How can you say that?" Valery says. "My facial expressions are totally unconvincing."

Kelly opens another bottle of wine and passes it around. "We've got to figure things out," she says. "What are we going to do?"

"I'm not giving Beryl any more of my clothes," Connie says. "From now on everything goes to the Salvation Army." She has changed all her sleaze outfits for metal. Everything she wears glitters and shines.

"Why did you switch?" we say.

"Because people kept brushing off my crumbs," she says. "It got to be too much trouble to keep running back to Gabby's for a resoiling."

"We ought to keep one thing in focus. Beryl isn't the perpetrator," Evelyn says. "Saul's our problem. He's simply defaulted on all his responsibilities."

"I don't know why we're all so shocked. We should have expected something like this," Jen says. "Has he ever thought of anyone but himself? Last time we loaned him our Volvo, he left it in a no-parking zone and they towed it away."

"And who do you think had to go and reclaim it?" Kelly says.

"He left my Calvin Klein umbrella at the hardware store," Connie says.

"Every time we're supposed to meet with a client, he's late," Evelyn says. "He has no regard for my time."

"He doesn't respect us," Jen says.

"I knitted him a scarf. It's the only thing I've made that turned out right," Valery says. "The first time he wore it, he left it somewhere."

"I'd like to punch him in the face," Jen says. She is still working on her cabinet door, drilling a hole where a knob will go. "Make him wish he'd never left home."

"Maybe being in a canoe with Beryl for five days will be punishment enough," Evelyn says.

"He'll learn a lot about floor mops and camphor balls," Kelly says.

"She can give him a rundown on Ramon's personality problems."

"They can compete to see which of them had the worse mother."

"He may even learn to love Mallomars."

"It ain't funny," Evelyn says. "He's done us all an injury, running off this way. If we let him get away with it this time, he'll go off any time he chooses. We've got to teach him a lesson."

"Let's throw away all his health books," Kelly says.

"Be serious," Evelyn says.

"I *am* serious. He's preoccupied with his body. Convinced that his heart isn't going to last unless he learns all the ways it might malfunction. Without his health books, he'd be dead. Nothing in his body would work right."

"You know what would really send him around the bend?" Jen begins to giggle. "If we tidied up this place and threw everything out."

"He still broods over the G.I. Joe doll that was stolen from him when he was nine," I say.

"Let's do it," Jen says. She jumps to her feet and rummages in a corner for a carton, which she carries to the center of the room. She picks up some wood scraps and throws them in, a drill that is no longer operational, bent nails scattered all over the floor, a wrench, a pickax, three broken hammers. The rest of us watch her, laughing uncertainly. Then Evelyn stands up and hurls her empty

94

wineglass into the carton. It is like a signal, like the command in a military movie to fire torpedoes or drop the bombs. Suddenly everyone jumps up and starts running around the room, seizing bits of leftover material from this job or that—pieces of plasterboard and molding, chipped cornices, surplus knobs. We toss everything into the carton.

As soon as it is filled we search out another. But now we ignore the debris and begin to seize Saul's possessions. We toss in tools, architectural journals, books on art, on European churches, on effective fathering. We gather up his body-building equipment, his diagrams on effective loving, his diagrams of the human interior, his models of early skyscrapers, his crystals, his marbles, his nutritional supplements. We fill one carton and then another, and the pile grows higher. We toss in his albums of spaces we have created, his prize for a gazebo we built on top of an industrial building, his paint samples, his wood samples, his early building codes.

"This is your life, Saul," Jen yells. She lets out a war whoop and starts to dance around the pile, Indian fashion.

"Be careful of your shoulder, luv," Kelly shouts. But in a minute, she is dancing too.

The rest of us join hands and encircle the debris, chanting curses, shouting insults. "Prick, fraud, cheat," we scream. "Hypochondriac. Egomaniac. Glutton. Liar." I picture our words drifting down onto the pile of debris, settling there like garbage—cleansing us of our anger, bitterness, jealousy, despair.

We break apart, our dances growing more elaborate and passionate. Connie does a new-wave slither; Kelly, the kangaroo. Then Valery begins a dramatic depiction of our dilemma. She weaves in and out of the circle, a tragic look on her face while her body moves in intricate suggestions of despair.

We stand around her, clapping our hands. Her movements accelerate. She twirls and somersaults, jumps and twists, forcing her body into impossible postures as though trying to convey our selflessness in the cause of Saul. But instead of feeling sad, I want to laugh. I try to stifle it, but all around me I hear giggles, bursts of muffled laughter as Valery sinks to the ground and slithers abjectly along the floor in hopelessness and submission.

Now we are laughing loudly and applauding too. Why should sorrow be so hilarious? I wonder. "Valery," we say, "you are a comic genius."

"I didn't mean to be," she says.

Flushed and breathless, she gets to her feet and, grabbing her knitting bag, she pulls out a sweater. It is the one she has been making for Saul that nobody has seen. We gather around to look at it. The sweater is beautiful. On the front is a city skyline, buildings of varying heights and styles, trees, cars, tiny figures walking along the street, the kind of urban scene that Saul loves. She turns the sweater over and we gasp. On the back, a nude man— Saul—stands in a rural setting. Vines and leaves are threaded through his hair like Botticelli's *Spring*.

"Oh, Valery, it's beautiful," we say. "The most wonderful sweater we've ever seen." But even as we admire it, she pulls it from the needles and starts to rip it out.

"No, don't," we cry. "It's too beautiful to destroy. Stop. Don't. Give it to someone else." We reach toward her but Valery shrugs away from us and continues to pull out the sweater.

"Valery, it isn't right. . . . You mustn't destroy your own handiwork. . . . It's art. It's like a wall hanging. . . . Like an early tapestry. Don't!"

But Valery ignores us and continues to rip. Suddenly Kelly lunges at her and tries to wrench the sweater out of her hands.

While they are tussling, the doorbell rings. We look at each other in wonder and consternation. Could it be the delinquents returned from their canoe trip, without any prior warning, not even a phone call, a postcard? We look around the room at the empty wine bottles, our flushed faces, our hair in disarray, the cartons in the center of the

96

room containing all Saul's possessions. And feeling like culprits, like children caught in some unseemly act, we stand immobilized, staring at one another.

The bell rings again. Evelyn goes over to answer it. A muffled voice says over the intercom, "Let me in."

"It couldn't be Saul," I say. "He has a key."

"Who is it?" Evelyn yells again.

"Me."

She shrugs, presses the complicated entry system, and we wait to see who will appear.

It is Beryl who opens the door. Dressed from head to foot in foul-weather gear, she enters the room. Only her eyes show, glittery, wild, not in the least like their usual dreamy selves.

My heart jumps with fear. "Where's Saul?" Everybody is in a panic. "Why are you alone?" we cry. "Did something happen to Saul?" He drowned, I think. She's come to tell us that he's dead.

"Where is he?" Evelyn whispers.

Beryl tears off her poncho, sits down heavily on the couch. "Oh, God," she says. "What a mess, what a time." She looks exhausted.

"Is Saul—is he . . . ?"

"Saul's in jail. They took him away in shackles."

"Took him away? Where? What are you talking about? Where is he? What happened?"

"It's the parking tickets. They've finally caught up with him," Evelyn says. "I knew this would happen. I warned him not to let it go on. 'Throw yourself on the mercy of the court,' I kept saying."

"It's a lot worse than tickets," Beryl says. "They've arrested him for bigamy."

"Bigamy!"

"But he's not a bigamist. He's a polygamist," Valery says. "Why would they make such a mistake?"

"It's the same thing under the law," Evelyn says. "But how did all this happen? Who arrested him? Where is he?"

"Someone must have turned him in. Oh, it was horrible. There we were paddling peacefully down the Bleak River, and suddenly there was a roadblock and men staring down at us from a bridge."

"What do you mean, a roadblock? How can you roadblock a river?"

"Stop interrupting. Let Beryl tell us what happened."

"They had this chain across the river. About twenty feet from the bridge. I had to back-paddle to keep from running into it. And there they were, about a dozen men with guns drawn. Would you believe it? A dozen men pointing their guns at us. Standing above us on the bridge and yelling at us to drop our weapons."

"What weapons?"

"Were they crazy?"

"Who did they think you were?"

"Armed bigamists," Beryl says.

"Armed bigamists?"

"There's no such category under the law," Evelyn says.

"It was a mistake. They must have been after somebody else."

"I don't think so. They were after us—Saul. Someone must have called the police and told them he was on the river. And armed. They acted like he was a dangerous criminal. One false move, and I swear they would have shot him. Shot both of us, for that matter, since I was right there with him."

"Poor Saul."

"My God."

"How could such a thing happen?"

"It'll kill him."

"He's so delicate."

"He'll never be the same."

Valery, sniffing, picks up his sweater and begins to pick up stitches. "He'll need this," she says.

"I knew this would happen," Evelyn says. "Every time he took another wife, I told him he was jeopardizing himself."

"How could you know this would happen? That they'd pick him up for armed bigamy?"

"Not the exact charge, but I knew he was in danger."

"Someone must have turned him in," Beryl says.

"What are you saying?"

"Who would do such a thing?"

"Who knew where he was?"

"You all knew we were going canoeing on the river."

"We didn't know where you were. We haven't heard from you in days. How could any of us have turned him in?"

"Nobody else knew," Beryl says.

"How can you be sure?"

"Saul said so. He didn't mention this trip to another living soul."

"He always says that. He probably told everyone on the block where he was off to."

"I refuse to believe it."

"None of us would do such a thing."

"It's so vicious."

"So vindictive."

"So self-destructive."

But even as we disclaim the evil act, we look around the room at each other, searching for some sign, some hint of betrayal.

"How could anyone do such a thing?" I say.

"That's exactly what Saul said as they dragged him away in chains."

PART II

8

"My life is unraveling," Saul says. "What am I going to do?" He looks very tired. "Should I discontinue my conjugal visits, lie low for a while?"

"Oh, no," everybody says. There are sighs and protests.

"If you discontinue your conjugal visits, it will look like an admission of guilt," Connie says.

"On the other hand, if he continues them, they are likely to cite him for contempt," Evelyn says.

"Who's to know?" Connie says.

"The whole world," Evelyn says. "We're living in a fishbowl."

We are gathered together in the loft for a strategy meeting. Saul is out on bail. With the exception of Josh, who is on his way over, and Jen and Kelly, who are at a fund-raising meeting for the women's shelter and will join us later, the entire family is here.

Connie, taking advantage of the crisis, has brought her dogs, Belinda and Aster, to the meeting. They are nibbling palm fronds, knocking over lamps, eating out of the garbage pail. They punctuate each destructive act with a howl. We glare at Connie, raise our voices about their tumult.

"The way I see it, the best strategy would be to try to live the way we've always lived," I say. "Keep up a front, act as if nothing has changed. We can't succumb to the —" Aster bounds up to me, a chicken carcass in his mouth. "Oh, God," I say.

"Bad dog," Connie says. She jumps up and tries to grab the carcass from Aster's mouth. A chase ensues. "I just couldn't leave them at home all by themselves. Their anxiety level has peaked."

"All our anxiety levels have peaked," I say.

"I've tried everything to calm them down—long walks, soothing music. I've even been adding brewer's yeast to their dog food. It's supposed to be a nutritional tranquilizer, to encourage a more positive mental attitude. But nothing seems to lower their anxiety level."

"The problem is a lack of discipline," Evelyn says. "They've never been taught how to behave."

"They're very sensitive to stress," Connie says. "They act out whenever I'm upset." She snatches the chicken carcass from Aster's mouth and carries it into the kitchen. The dog howls; the rest of us exchange looks.

"How can we have a serious discussion with all that noise?" Evelyn says.

"Please, Connie, either lock them up or take them home," I say.

Connie looks to Saul for support. "I can't take them home."

"They'd be better off in a quiet place," Saul says.

"If I take them home, they'll howl all afternoon," Connie says. "Then the neighbors will call the police."

"How about the workroom, then?" Saul says.

"They'll feel abandoned in the workroom."

"Not if they hear us talking in the next room."

"We'll have to talk loud," Connie says. "Come here, sweethearts." She lunges at the dogs. "Come here, babies.

The family needs a quiet time, and we all have to make sacrifices in this emergency." The dogs bound off, Connie after them.

While she chases them around the loft, the rest of us try to continue our discussion. "You're right, Saul," Evelyn says. "The most prudent thing might be to hole up here for a while."

"But I was just getting the hang of it," Valery says. "I've never been a wife before."

"This is not the time to think of our own selfish needs," Beryl says. "Our entire way of life is at stake. We must put that before anything else."

Evelyn and I look at each other in disbelief. She says, "Too bad you didn't feel that way sooner. Before all this happened."

Beryl bows her head and closes her eyes. "I wish we'd never gone canoeing. I'll regret it for as long as I live."

Evelyn returns us to the strategy discussion. "We must figure out a modus vivendi. The worst thing we can do is flounder, let events dictate our choices."

"Events have already narrowed our choices," I say. "The publicity has turned our lives upside down."

"Helen's right. Our normal lives are a thing of the past," Saul says.

"It's like living in an occupied country," Valery says. "The media have marched in and taken over."

"I'll tell you one thing," Evelyn says. "I'm not going to let them dictate to me." She grabs a sheath of legal documents from her briefcase and begins to put them in alphabetical order, as if to prove to us that she is in control of her life.

All week long, the newspapers have been full of the case. The first story was a factual account of the arrest: HUSBAND OF SEVEN ARRESTED BY UPSTATE POLICE. But since then, the stories have grown increasingly sensational. Shrill headlines scream at us. POLYGAMOUS RITES IN LOWER MAN-HATTAN. NEIGHBORS IN TERROR OF SEX CULT. A CRIME

105

Every time we read an account of ourselves, we are in a state of shock. "Is that us?" we say.

"How can they write such lies?"

"They make us sound like a bunch of sex maniacs."

"Like some lower form of life."

"They are robbing us of our identity."

"The really important stories they ignore," Saul says, "the public corruption, the private greed, the plunder of our resources. How they love to waste space on scandal."

"They are insatiable," Connie says. She has finally captured her dogs and shut them up in the workroom. "Here's one you haven't even seen yet." She rummages in her voluminous purse, pulls out a clipping, and reads: " 'A neighbor's account of the SoHo harem. For a while I thought it was an illegal discount place selling stolen designer goods. There had to be some explanation for all those women coming and going. But the truth is far worse.' " At the sound of Connie's voice, the dogs howl and hurl themselves against the door.

"To think a neighbor would say such a thing," Valery says.

"Wait, there's more." Connie plucks another clipping from her purse. "Listen to this. 'Mrs. X, one of the women involved in the polygamous scandal, had this to say about their mate. "It's like a pressure cooker at the loft. Sex is always on his mind. It hovers in our midst like the Host at a religious ritual. There's no escaping it. You can't get up and stretch without him staring at you; every time you walk across the room, he is studying your contours. You'd think, with all his women, he'd be calmer, cooler, more in control of himself, wouldn't you? But it doesn't seem to work that way. In the final analysis, he is like a Woody Allen character, only bigger." ' "

Saul makes a disgusted sound. "Host at a religious ritual. That's absurd. Who said that?"

Connie shrugs. "It doesn't say."

106

"It's disgusting."

"It's not even true."

"Not me. . . . Not me. . . . I wouldn't dream of saying such a thing."

"It wrote itself," Evelyn says.

"We are in a state of siege," Saul says.

"He's not exaggerating," I say. "I can hardly bring myself to listen to our answering machine anymore." The media leave endless messages demanding interviews—with Saul, if possible, but if not, a wife will do, particularly if she is both shapely and photogenic. Perverts call, offering information: a new posture, an unusual attitude. Some leave numbers pleading to be included in our sex games. A person from the Religious Right prays that our sexual parts will wither, shrivel, and putrefy. A woman calls wanting to be Saul's eighth wife. "I make a wonderful lasagna," the woman says.

"That's all I need, another wife," Saul says, but for the first time since his arrest, a wan smile crosses his face.

"Our lives are like an early myth," Valery says. She was in a play once with parallel events, a happy family brought down by malignant, jealous gods. She is explaining the plot when Josh arrives, loaded down with equipment. In addition to his cameras he is carrying a slide projector so Beryl can show us the pictures she took on the canoe trip.

"Did you put the milk away?" Evelyn says.

"Did you remember to bring the book on pantomime you borrowed?" Valery says.

"Did you finish your assignment on the dinosaurs?" Saul says.

"Ignore me," Josh says. "Pretend I'm not here." He carries his equipment over to a corner. Beryl joins him. Together they move a table to an appropriate spot, set the slide projector on top of it, and darken the room.

Josh focuses the projector onto a white wall, and the first of Beryl's pictures appears. In it, Saul, slightly out of focus, is huddled in the prow of the canoe looking cold, miserable, and frightened. "This is where the river forks,"

Beryl says. Josh clicks to another slide. "This is where we found the embers of a fire." *Click.* "This is where we found an abandoned mill." *Click.* "This is where the doe and her baby were feeding."

She keeps up a running commentary, although each picture looks exactly like the one before, showing a cold, frightened Saul huddled in the canoe. "This is where they arrested us." In this picture, a dozen enormous men pointing guns, their badges pinned to their hunting gear, hover over a tiny Saul cowering at the bottom of the canoe.

"Oh, my God, how awful," we say. This picture makes their ordeal real, provoking fresh outcries of indignation and sympathy.

"Awful isn't the word for it," Saul says. "I thought we were goners. I thought they were going to kill us." Josh turns off the slide projector and heads for the light switch. "Show that last picture again," Saul says. "I want everyone to get a good look at those men."

The picture of the arrest leaps upon the wall.

"Look at their faces. They could be a textbook illustration of abnormal behavior. And that was exactly the way they acted, like crazy men. Standing over us with their weapons and yelling at us to drop our guns. There was no reasoning with them. I kept saying, 'I don't have a gun.' It was like yelling at the wind."

He has described this part to us before—the sudden encounter with the law, the standoff, the guns. But much of it is still not clear: how and why and who engineered the arrest. Each time we try to clarify the sequence of events, he grows vague and evasive.

He signals to Josh that the viewing is over. Josh turns on the lights. We look at each other with dazed faces, still trying to understand what happened. We ask questions. "Who did they think you were? How did they know where to find you? What was the charge? Why were they waiting by the river?" But neither Saul nor Beryl answers any of our questions. Instead, he continues to describe the horrors of their encounter with the law, she to tell us how confused and frightened they were.

"They wouldn't explain anything," Beryl says. " 'What is the charge?' I kept yelling. And all they did was yell back at us to drop our guns."

"They made us stand up in that tippy canoe with our hands in the air," Saul says. "Had we fallen into the river, we would have died within seconds from exposure. It must have been about ten below zero."

"I thought my hands were going to drop off from the cold," Beryl says. "They kept us there for a good ten or fifteen minutes, maybe more. And yelling at us the whole time to drop our weapons."

"By then I was wishing they would shoot. I've never been so cold," Saul says. "I could barely lower my arms when they finally took us into custody."

"The weather made them mean," Beryl says.

"It didn't help matters," Saul says. "All the way to the station house, they kept saying what a day to have to come out in, and if they got sick they would hold us personally responsible."

"They also held us responsible for interrupting their poker game," Beryl says.

"I finally said to them, 'We didn't ask to be arrested,' " Saul says.

"Were you both arrested?" Josh says.

"Well, they never actually charged me with anything, but that didn't prevent them from treating me like a criminal," Beryl says.

"How come they didn't confiscate your film?" Evelyn says.

"I had the camera hidden in the folds of my foul-weather gear," Beryl says.

"Lucky for her they didn't find it, or God knows what they would have done," Saul says. "They were monsters. When I said we hadn't asked to be arrested, they called me a wise guy and said they had special ways of dealing with wise guys. They asked me if I'd like to know what those ways were. I said not really, but they told me anyway. It involved cattle prods and other instruments of torture."

"They're Nazis," Evelyn says. "It's as if due process never existed."

"Due process!" Saul says. "What those jokers know about due process, or any other aspect of the law, you could put in an eyedropper and still have room for the medication. They must spend most of their time sitting around the station house playing poker. It was obvious from the shape they were in. They were flabby and over-weight, and their potbellies hung over their belts."

"But I still don't understand why they arrested you in the first place," Valery says. "It doesn't make sense."

"They were after a bootlegger, some guy who ran illegal drinking parties. They thought I was their man."

"They had been ordered to watch the river and wait for him to show," Beryl says. "Instead, we came along and the rest is history."

"Okay, but then why did they charge you with big-amy? If they were looking for some bootlegger, why didn't they just let you go once they realized you weren't their man?"

Beryl and Saul exchange looks. "It was a mistake . . . a trap." They both fall silent.

"Look, fellas, this isn't fun and games," Evelyn says. "If we're going to fight this arrest, we've got to know exactly what happened. How did they come to charge you with bigamy?"

"I told them," Saul says.

"You what?" Evelyn says.

"This bootlegger, whoever he was, was wanted for attempted murder. That's why the sheriff and his men were so rough with us. They kept questioning me about various assaults and robberies. They couldn't believe we were on the river just to go canoeing. Not in that weather. It seemed to me a straightforward explanation would get them off our backs. So I told them. First I said my wife and I had gone on a canoe trip to get away from it all.

110

Then when that didn't satisfy them, I said we'd taken this trip to get away from my other wives."

"Oh, God." Evelyn groans.

"I know, I know. But I'm so used to them, my marital arrangements no longer seem strange to me."

The room falls silent. "Then what happened?"

"They laughed," Saul says. "They didn't believe me."

"They acted like it was the funniest thing they'd ever heard," Beryl says.

"They thought I was a joke," Saul says. "It made me a little crazy. I started naming names."

There is a stunned silence. Then we all look at Beryl. "But you blamed us. Last Sunday when you got back, you said one of us had turned him in."

"I know. That's before I sorted it all out. I thought one of you had tipped them off and that's why they'd stopped us."

"So the reality was a case of mistaken identity," I say. "It was just some stupid mishap."

Beryl nods. "It was a mistake."

"It's so awful I could die," Connie says. "Our lovely life trampled in the dust, all our happy occasions mere memories."

"It's a little premature to talk that way," Evelyn says. "They don't have a case. We'll countersue for false arrest."

"They do have a case," Saul says. "I told them everything."

"Everything?"

"I was so angry at those idiots, I hardly knew what I was saying. I named each wife. I gave the dates of every marriage."

"Did they read you your rights?" Evelyn says. "The charges won't stick unless they followed due process."

"They read me my rights. At least they started to read me my rights. The sheriff had a card on his desk: the rights of the accused. But he was barely literate. He read in this halting voice; he mispronounced words; he started over. Anyway, by then I'd told them everything and I couldn't stand listening to him, so when he started over for the third time, I said I knew my rights."

"You told him you knew your rights," Evelyn says. "No lay person knows his rights. If you knew your rights, you never would have incriminated yourself."

"They shouldn't have laughed at me," Saul says. There is a long, gloomy silence.

"What are we going to do?" I say.

"It's hopeless," Saul says.

"It isn't hopeless. Don't say that," Evelyn says. "Don't even think it. They have no case. They questioned you without a lawyer present. They used undue force. We have the photograph to prove that. We'll ask the court to drop all charges. We'll demand a thorough investigation of arrest procedures in Bleaksville County."

"It's their word against mine. They'll deny everything."

"Beryl was with you. She can testify on your behalf."

"Evelyn, they have the goods on me. I told them everything. And now every newspaper in the country has the story."

"You're not in jail yet," Evelyn says.

Saul sighs. Beryl sighs. "It was unreal," they both say. "We felt so isolated there, so far from civilization. There were WANTED posters all over the walls. Reading them made us feel as if we were in a kind of criminal limbo."

"One of the wanted men had drowned his buddy in a vat of bootleg moonshine," Beryl says. "Probably the bootlegger they were after when they arrested us. This other guy ran his pickup truck into a busload of Korean businessmen because a Korean grocer had sold him a rotten pear. The entire wall was like that. Full of mindless violence. In fact"—she cannot suppress a grin—"one of the posters had come loose. While they were fingerprinting Saul, I took it off the wall."

Although nearly a week has passed since the arrest, Beryl continues to wear her foul-weather gear. She reaches in the voluminous garment and pulls out a rolled poster. "I thought Josh would like to have it," she says.

Beryl unrolls the poster and holds it up for us. Josh runs over and points his camera at it. A man and a woman stand side by side, arms around each other, a demented smile on both their faces. They are wearing identical T-shirts with bad words written all over them. Many of the bad words are misspelled.

We are all indignant at the theft. "Suppose they'd caught you? Aren't we in enough trouble?"

"Nobody was watching."

Evelyn and I exchange meaningful looks; this act of larceny reinforces our suspicions that Beryl filches things from the five-and-ten. I study Saul's reaction to this theft. He says nothing, stares down at the floor. He has seated himself as far from Beryl as he can, and whenever she speaks he tenses, as though warding off blows.

Evelyn steers us back to our discussion. "Beryl, I'd like to have the negative of the picture of the arrest so I can have some glossies made from it. We'll introduce it as evidence of undue force. We'll circulate the picture to the media if necessary. We'll make them wish they'd never set eyes on you. We'll teach those jokers in Bleaksville a civics lesson they'll long remember."

"I've never even heard of Bleaksville," Valery says. She is knitting Saul still another sweater, copying a pattern from some ancient runic embroidery which is supposed to have magic qualities. "It will protect him from his enemies," she says.

"Bleaksville is the discard capital of the world," Beryl says. "There's a sign above the entrance to the town hall that says HOME OF UNDESIRED THINGS. YOUR GARBAGE IS OUR LIVELIHOOD. The entire town lives off garbage. Everybody makes things from other things that have been thrown away."

She shows us a pencil holder made from a beer can that she bought while she was waiting for the bus back to the city. Nobody likes the pencil holder. "It's tacky," we say.

Saul is also wearing a Bleaksville artifact—a digital watch made to run on an old computer chip. "They were selling them at the station house," he says. "In addition to doing the usual things—time/date functions, the ten-melody alarm, cycles of the moon—the watch will hold a conversation with its wearer." Saul presses a button. "Yes, no, maybe," it says. "Well, I never. Tell me more."

"How primitive. . . . How boring," we say.

"I don't know how you could bring yourself to buy anything there. They don't deserve our patronage." Evelyn, still fuming at the lawlessness of the Bleaksville lawmen, continues to plan reprisals. "We'll file a suit. . . . we'll instruct them in the law. . . ."

Her spirit of combative righteousness is catching. We all cheer up and dismiss the trial as some minor inconvenience, soon to be behind us. "When this is over," Connie says, "we should try to do more constructive things together—take a course in wine-tasting, learn a language." Beryl knows where you can buy Spanish tapes for half the retail price.

"It's never going to be over," Saul says. His gloom is total. He sinks into his chair as if his bones have melted and he has lost his ability to hold himself erect. His posture suggests a return to an earlier evolutionary stage before bones were thought of and everything that lived sagged.

"Oh, Saul," we say. "You must not lose hope."

"Hope? What's that? I feel like someone who's been shipwrecked. I feel like someone condemned to spend the rest of his life in solitary. Do you know what it feels like when you lose trust in others?" He looks at each of us, his eyes reproachful. "It feels like death."

"What are you talking about?" we cry. "We're all in this together."

"Are we? I don't know who I can count on anymore."

"You can count on us. We're your friends," we say.

"Then we'll have to redefine the meaning of the word."

114

I thought friends were people you could depend on. People who would respect your possessions and not pile them all in cartons with the intention of disposing of them as soon as your back is turned."

"Who told you?" Our shock is total.

"When I think of all the years it has taken me to acquire a credible library of architectural details. And the money and time I put into my collection of precision tools."

"We never . . . we didn't . . . we were just tidying up a little."

"How come Jerry the super is now wearing one of my jackets?"

"What jacket?"

"My beige buckskin with the fringe."

"Oh, that. You haven't worn that jacket in years. You gave it to him yourself."

"Never. Not that man. I don't like him. I don't like the way he looks at me."

"He looks at everyone that way."

"And all the other things you were planning to get rid of? What about them? It makes a person wonder if real friendship between men and women is possible."

"Don't say that. We never intended you any harm. It was a joke. We were just fooling around. You can't really believe we would throw anything of yours away."

Who told him? I wonder. I look around the room studying each wife for indications of guilt, complicity: shifty eyes, a twitchy mouth, nervous hands.

As soon as Beryl appeared with news of the arrest, we unloaded the cartons. "Saul must never know," we told each other. We put everything back—everything but a few unusable items: a hammer without a haft, a wrench that no longer gripped, an obsolete copy of the city building codes, a set of telephone directories going back to the early sixties, expired pills, the buckskin jacket.

Did Valery tell him? Perhaps she has not yet developed a sense of solidarity with the rest of us. Connie? She is

115

always trying to curry favor. Beryl? It is hard to predict what Beryl might do. Evelyn? Did she blurt out the truth in a fit of tough-minded truth-saying?

"What did I do to make you all so vindictive? They say women take advantage of a man who is too nice, too self-sacrificing. I never believed that until now. I was too stupid, too naïve. I refused to believe that altruism no longer existed."

"It depends on how you define altruism," Evelyn says. "That vacation was not exactly an act of self-sacrifice."

"A few days on an icy river—a vacation? I would hardly call it that. It was more like a retreat, a quiet time, a chance to meditate. I wouldn't know what a vacation was. I haven't had one in years."

"Who has?" I say.

"I wish we could. I wish someday the whole family could take a vacation together," Connie says.

"It's too complicated," I say. "Our schedules don't mesh. And can you imagine everyone in the family agreeing on a destination?"

Saul gives Evelyn a saintly smile. "If I've hurt anyone, it is not what I intended to do. I have always been a willing hostage to domestic tranquillity. If there are things I've overlooked, people I've neglected, I'm sorry. Yet any further discussion seems academic, since the life we are dissecting will soon be but a memory."

We all fall silent, incapable now of speaking a single word of hope. Is it really going to end? How will we live? The doorbell rings. "It must be Jen and Kelly," I say. Nobody moves. It rings again. Finally Josh goes to answer it. But even he has been infected by our hopelessness. He walks slowly across the room as though some terrible affliction has aged him prematurely.

Jen and Kelly bound into the room. "Hi!" they say. The rest of us say a listless hello. "What's the matter? It's like a funeral in here," they say.

"How else should it be?" we say.

116

"Obviously, you haven't seen the latest papers. The Mayor made a statement that is just unbelievable."

Jen opens the newspaper she is carrying. "Listen to this," she says. She reads: " 'In this great city of ours, we encourage a variety of lifestyles. As long as people pay the sales tax and are not scofflaws, who counts the number of wives? Where else but in the Big Apple can such tolerance go hand in hand with cultural enrichment, great hotels, and restaurants of every conceivable ethnic group?' "

"The Mayor said that?"

"I don't believe it."

"It's fantastic. It puts everything in a different light."

"People listen to the Mayor."

"He's got a lot of influence in the city."

"I never expected him to be in our corner," Saul says. "Read it again, Jen."

She reads it again.

"This might even make the media a little more responsible," Saul says. He looks a shade less assaulted by life.

"Maybe he remembers meeting you that time he dedicated our gazebo," I say.

"I doubt it," Saul says. "It's probably political, some opportunistic reason for the statement."

"His motives don't matter," Evelyn says. "He's thrown a little perspective on the case. Maybe people will be a little more tolerant after this. That's what matters."

"I'm hungry," Beryl says.

"I wouldn't mind a little nourishment myself," Evelyn says.

"There's nothing in the refrigerator," I say.

"Let's send out," Connie says.

A long discussion follows on what to order. Everybody wants a different thing. Saul wants stuffed cabbage the way his mother might have made it if she'd been a different kind of mother and cooked anything but convenience foods. His Jewish mother is an invented character, made up of longings gleaned from books and other forms of

117

popular culture. His real mother ran a business, had little time for maternal concerns. Saul and his sister were given a dollar a day and sent out to forage for food. While he's reinventing his past, he decides he wants some blintzes too.

Kelly and Jen want spinach pies and a Greek salad with feta cheese; Connie wants Cajun; Evelyn and I, Chinese. While I phone in the orders, Beryl and Josh rush down to the bakery. They return a short time later with a Sacher torte, cream puffs, and a Key lime pie. Valery is the only one without a specific preference. "I'll eat whatever's left," she says.

The food arrives and we sit around the long table, the dishes spread in front of us. Our ordeal has made us hungry. We serve ourselves from our chosen dishes, cram our mouths with food. When we've finished what is on our plates, we look around the table, studying other people's choices. Everybody wants what someone else has ordered. Forks are thrust at distant dishes, across the table, down its length, poked onto plates, and retrieved speared with tender, dripping morsels.

From the corner where his equipment is positioned, Josh eats huddled over his camera, taking footage of the meal. He aims his camera at his father trying to stuff a whole blintz in his mouth, at Jen with strands of spinach descending from her teeth like fangs, at Connie licking whipped cream from her lips, at Evelyn leaning far across the table in an effort to capture a piece of pie.

His mother looks at him and glares. "You are not helping matters," she says.

"Art must be ruthless," Josh says. He is trying to compensate for the footage he missed, the dramatic entrance of Beryl the previous Sunday with news of Saul's arrest. "I missed the chance of a lifetime," he says. "The raw emotions, the element of surprise, the sense of doom."

This only sets his father off again with thoughts of his impending trial and imprisonment. "They will sodomize me," he says.

118

"Oh, no," we say, but this grim possibility unnerves us and we eat everything in sight, every crumb, every dab of sour cream, every speck of chocolate from the Sacher torte, every grain of rice.

The room slowly empties. Connie, accompanied by her howling dogs, leaves first. Then Evelyn and Josh. Each person carries down a bag of trash from the meal: disposable plates, plastic utensils, aluminum foil containers.

Alone with me, Saul drops all his disguises: the sweet saint, the brave martyr, the innocent victim. He moves around the loft picking things up: scattered newspapers, cushions, chewed-up bits of food abandoned by Connie's dogs. He scrutinizes the palm tree fronds for dog bites; I sweep the floor, feeling the need to move around after the long afternoon.

I am glad everybody has gone. There are moments, and this is one of them, when I long to go back to a simpler time, ordinary days, normal meals, uncomplicated routines. Saul and me. So different from our current life with its endless complications—each meal a smorgasbord, every decision a debate.

"I could use some air," I say. "How about a walk?"

"Good idea," Saul says. We put our coats on and start to leave the loft. But feeling suddenly shy, Saul wraps a muffler around his neck and thrusts a hat onto his head to hide his face, hoping no one will know who he is.

On the street everybody recognizes him. Some shake hands, others look the other way. A street person at the corner asks for change. As Saul digs in his pocket, the street person stares at him. Saul thrusts a dollar at him. The street person thrusts it back. "I may be down, but I'm not out," he says.

"Let's go home," Saul says.

We pick up the morning papers and return to the loft. Each one of them contains a story attacking the Mayor for his support of Saul. "Condoning polygamy is against the law," a noted attorney says. The church asks the Mayor if he has turned his back on morality, a rabbi reminds him

119

of the Judeo-Christian edict on adultery, a feminist spokesperson wonders whether the Mayor would be as supportive of a woman if she had married seven men. Out-of-town visitors say they are fearful of a city in which the Mayor encourages immorality and therefore they are curtailing their stay. Irate hotel owners accuse the Mayor of insensitivity to the needs of the business community. Real estate interests threaten to withdraw their support.

The Mayor retracts his earlier statement and puts out a new statement. "I was misquoted," he says. "Let them send the bastard to jail and throw away the key."

9

Saul and I are still in the workroom when Connie arrives. "You're early," I say.

"I need your help," she says. She is trying to get a job in the consumer affairs office and wants us to look over her application letter before she sends it out.

"Can you wait a few minutes?" I say. "We're almost done."

We are sitting at our workroom desk struggling with the design elements of a space we have contracted to construct: a gallery for a photographer who specializes in dead things—a tree defoliated by bagworms, dessicated cornfields, African cows lying legs up in the red dust. Although we have built our reputation on austerity, we have not yet been able to come up with a design that satisfies the client. "It is not bleak enough," he says.

It is evening. We have spent most of the afternoon trying to get it right. We have eliminated all extraneous details, each door deprived of its knob, every window its sill. After a hasty meal, we have returned to the workroom in an effort to finish the floor plan. I feel our commitments pressing in on us. We are behind on all our schedules. I study the layout. "It is too empty," I say. "Austerity is a relative condition. It is more than an empty space."

Saul stares at the blueprint. "We need something to give the emptiness a focus," he says. He is striving for an Olympian detachment. He is trying to view his life as if it were someone else's. To achieve this, he has sectioned off his personality, adopted roles: the wise, affectionate patriarch, the shrewd businessman. At present, as we sit across from each other, he is the efficient contractor, the man who gets things done.

But now that Connie is here, his posture collapses. He looks up from the blueprint and gives her a sad, stoical smile. He says a listless hello. In keeping with this tragic stance, he lets his ruler fall to the desk and turns off his calculator. If only Connie had arrived a little later. She is a bad influence on Saul, encouraging self-pity and torpor.

Our business has suffered since his arrest. One client canceled, another tried to renegotiate his contract. A third, wanting to cash in on our publicity, has been after *People* magazine to shoot us working on his space. Even those who haven't tried to take advantage of our plight are worried about our completing their work on time. With good reason.

"You're right," I say. "It does need a focus." I try to recapture Saul's attention. "What if we placed a cube slightly off center? Right here." I sketch in what I have in mind. "That will give the eye something to rest on." He stares at my addition without really seeing it. Connie is a magnet pulling him away from the work. He looks up at her. "Did you bring newspapers?" he says.

"They're inside."

"The newspapers can wait," I say.

But Saul is already on his feet. "It's been a long day," he says.

He follows Connie out of the workroom. He's not the only one with problems. The lack of order in our lives has affected my work too. My mind is cluttered with irrelevant details; Connie's vocational difficulties, the disorder in our living space, the ringing phone. Jen has developed a new complaint, an allergic reaction to almost everything she eats. With the breakdown of our conjugal arrangements, people wander in and out as they please. Nearly every night, one wife or two or three drops by on one pretext or another. Sometimes they appear when we're eating and then they eat too. I never know how much food to prepare.

Every day there are new leaks to the media, anonymous statements attributed to some wife. They make everybody edgy. People say things they do not mean, question one another's integrity, make accusations that lead to denials, tears, scenes.

The chaos in our lives has spilled over to Josh. Because of our notoriety, everybody feels compelled to spoil him. They buy him expensive video equipment, hi-tech state-of-the-art editing devices, complicated sound mixers. People lend him money, forget to check on his school assignments, ignore his nutritional needs. He seems to eat nothing now but giant slices of pizza. Even Evelyn, who considers herself a disciplinarian, lets him do as he pleases.

I force myself to remain at the desk. I erase the cube, sketch in a column instead, and then another column, join them with a partition. I study these additions. Do they objectify the bleakness or do they violate the space? Drained by the emotional intensity of our lives, I am unable to decide. I close my notebook, put away my drawing tools. I could bear anything if there were some order in my life.

I join Connie and Saul in our living space. They are standing over a stack of newspapers. Saul is turning the pages of a paper, searching out stories that will reinforce his sense of persecution. When he finds a story he likes, he reads it aloud to us. A building and loan president was exonerated from any wrongdoing after lending himself one hundred and thirty million dollars. A county welfare supervisor sold surplus cheese, intended for the indigent, to a gourmet take-out store. A welfare cheat was jailed after buying beer with his food stamps.

He reads these stories in a triumphant voice, for they foster his sense of his own virtue. He has developed an obsessive need to amass evidence of the imminent collapse of the Western world. Connie feeds his obsession. She spends much of her time buying out-of-town papers, for although the crimes in other places are fewer, they are frequently more flagrant. I offer Connie a cup of tea, a drink. "What time does the show go on?" she says.

"Ten thirty," I say.

Saul suddenly stops turning pages and stares at a story. "Oh, Christ," he says, "Another leak. POLYGAMIST'S WIFE TELLS ALL IN EXCLUSIVE INTERVIEW." He shakes his head and sighs. "When will it ever end?"

"What does it say?"

"The usual slop." He reads in a falsetto voice: " 'Of course there are problems in our kind of matrimony. How could there not be? One of the dangers we live with is catching one another's quirks. For instance, a wife who shall be nameless is slightly paranoid. She distrusts everybody and everything. Once I saw her counting out pills. "What are you doing?" I said. "Does this look like a hundred to you?" she said. Well, she really started something. Before you knew it, everybody was counting everything—vitamin pills, tranquilizers, aspirin. It wasn't so much distrust as a need to show we were alert consumers.' "

Saul flings down the paper. "Who is putting out these stories?"

"I've heard worse," I say.

"It makes us sound like flakes," he says.

"The world is a harsh judge," Connie says. While Saul continues to scrutinize the newspapers, she shows me her letter of application. She is eager to get the job at the consumer affairs agency. "I understand products," she says. But because she has had so many job interviews that led nowhere, she is nervous. She has applied for work at various places—as a shopper's helper in a large depart-

124

ment store, in the botanical gardens tending plants, as an earn-while-you-learn telemarketer.

Now she is taking a course in job methodology to develop an effective career strategy. She is learning how to prepare a résumé, write a letter. "The main thing is to impress them with your ability to get things done," she says. She reads us what she has written. "I am an individual of rare talents, a self-starter, a person who other people like. I play to win. My eyes are on the main chance; I have the courage of my convictions. I am not afraid to fail." She looks at us. "What do you think?"

Saul looks up from his paper. "Whom," he says. "A person *whom* other people like." Connie makes the correction.

"You think it might be a shade too aggressive for the department of consumer affairs?" I say.

"Too aggressive? Oh, no, Helen. A person has to learn to value herself, to be able to communicate a belief in her abilities. If you don't sell yourself, who will?"

She gives Saul a yearning look, as though seeking corroboration. He is still leafing through the newspapers for stories that will reinforce his dark view of things. He comes upon one and cries out with joy. "Listen to this," he says. " 'EVANGELIST ACCUSED OF SEXUAL MISCONDUCT AND GREED DENIES ANY WRONGDOING. "THE DEVIL DID IT," HE SAID.' "

"They always blame someone else," Connie says. She is crossing out *fail* on her job application and replacing it with *try*. She writes another sentence. "How does this sound? 'I have the courage to manipulate my fellow workers in order to get things done.' "

"Perhaps 'motivate' is a better word," I say.

While we are working on her application, Jen and Kelly arrive. They are both giggling. "Who did you buy silk undies for, Saul?" Jen says. They too are loaded down with newspapers, which they drop upon the other papers scattered over the long table.

"What are you talking about?" Saul says.

Jen pulls a paper from the top of the pile, points to a story she has encircled in red. "Listen to this," she says. "It's in a column called Lifestyles of the Kitsch and Infamous." She reads: " 'He tended to prefer a decadent lifestyle, thought nothing of spending thousands of dollars on silk lingerie for his wives, expensive chocolates and wines, tailor-made suits. He could not pass a haberdashery without going in and buying himself some smart accessory. At the same time he would lecture us on our too materialistic natures. He must own a hundred belts, socks of every hue, dozens of pairs of shoes. Yet when one asks him, "Why do you need a hundred belts?" he looks amazed.' "

"Who could have said such a thing?" Saul says. He reaches for the story and reads it to himself.

"What time does the show go on?" Jen says. Her arms are covered with welts. Each time the doctor pinpoints what she is allergic to, some new substance sets up another reaction. Connie is convinced her allergies are symptomatic of a carnal ambivalence.

"Ten thirty," I say.

"I wish there wasn't going to be any show," Saul says. "This family doesn't need any more publicity. These leaks are killing us. And it's all such lies, such gross exaggerations."

As usual, everybody denies being interviewed. "I wouldn't give them the time of day. . . . I have always been extremely circumspect. . . . The airing of confidential matters is anathema to my nature."

"But these stories don't just materialize out of thin air," Saul says.

Kelly begins to giggle again. "Saul, just tell me one thing—who'd you buy silk lingerie for?"

Jen giggles too. "It wasn't me."

"It was Beryl, what do you want to bet?" Kelly says.

"Beryl wears only cotton," Connie says. "She told me that in strictest confidence."

"Was it you?" Jen ask Connie.

126

"Me?" Connie says mournfully. "No."

"I bet it was Helen. Saul has always had a soft spot for Helen," Jen says.

"You know what kind of gifts I get?" I say. "Cookbooks, graph paper, T squares. Practical things."

"So who was it? C'mon be a sport. Tell us." The two of them are laughing so hard they can barely talk.

"Nobody," Saul says. He is not amused.

"Confession is good for the soul. Just say a name."

"If confession is good for the soul, I'd like to know which one of you told the media I was vain and selfish," Saul says.

"Where did that come from?" Jen says.

"In one of the anonymous interviews," he says. He rummages through the mass of papers littering the long table. "Here it is. 'He has convinced himself that were he not so bogged down by domestic demands, he would long since have become rich and famous. He tells everybody how brilliant he is, that the only thing he lacks that the rich and famous possess is selfishness and vanity. "My wives have always come first," he says. He's kidding himself. He may not be rich and famous, but he is a vain and selfish man.'"

"You selfish? That's insane," Connie says.

"Maybe a little vain," Jen says.

"Vain? That's the last word I'd ever apply to myself," Saul says.

"Anyway, silk is disgusting," Kelly says. "It means the death of millions of silkworms just to weave one silken crotch."

Kelly is explaining the silk-making process when Beryl arrives. "What time does the show go on?" she says. "I can only get channel seven on my set." She is loaded down with presents, articles she found on the street—a chipped picture frame for Kelly, a container of flea eradicator for Connie's dogs, a limp Chinese evergreen for me, a copy of the *Buffalo Inquirer* for Saul. He immediately opens the paper and begins turning its pages.

"Did Saul ever give you silk underwear?" Jen says.

"Me? Never! He knows better than that. Silk was what I wore before the enlightenment. My mother always said that only the Mexicans wore any other kind. When I left home, I gave all my silk things to the Latino housekeeper."

"Poor Bert used to buy me things of that nature," Connie says. "He had this catalog hidden in his desk. Whenever there was an occasion to celebrate—my birthday, a lowering of the interest rates—he would order me a silken something from Private Nights. Now, of course, I realize that his carnal appetites were walls."

"Valery's more the silk-underwear type," Beryl says.

Saul looks up from his newspaper. "If I hear the word 'silk' one more time, I'm going to kill myself," he says. "Has everyone in the family gone crazy? We're in a crisis situation. There is nothing funny about those leaks."

"Why are you all looking at me?" Connie says. Her voice quavers, her eyes fill with tears. We all deny looking at her. She doesn't believe us. "I never told them anything."

Evelyn arrives during this discussion, carrying a metal case containing some of Josh's video equipment. Hearing the word "leaks," she says, "They are definitely weakening our case."

"Well, I never leaked," Connie says. She is leaking now, the tears running down her face. We murmur words of reassurance, of belief in her integrity.

"I made a statement," Kelly says. "But it was merely to publicize the plight of the kangaroos. All I said was that if they kept on slaughtering them the way they're doing, there'll soon be no kangaroos left."

Josh comes in, carrying another metal case, a giant pizza slice between his teeth. He puts his equipment down and slumps to the floor, munching on the pizza with somber concentration.

"What's with you?" his father says.

"I am very depressed," Josh says. He forgot to press an important button on his video when he was taping the family, and when he ran the film, nothing appeared on the screen. "First *Challenger*, now this," he says. "I have lost all faith in technology."

His papa interrupts his grumbling to tell Josh a story. "When I was a boy, my cousin the yo-yo champ was the first person in our family ever to ride in a plane. As a result of winning the yo-yo championship, they took him on a flight to Pittsburgh. In those days planes were tiny; the trip was bumpy and it took many hours to get there. When they landed his face was green. He told everyone that planes were a thing of the past."

Josh likes this story, but he doesn't understand its significance.

"Sometimes things get better," Saul says. "Planes go faster than they did then. They are currently developing a driverless truck that will go from coast to coast in less than thirty hours. Take courage from these stories." Josh says he will try.

"I wish they would develop some mechanism for closing off leaks," Evelyn says. Connie's eyes fill again.

"What we need is a press secretary like the President's," Saul says. "Somebody who knows how to deny or retract."

"Hey, everybody, it's time for the show," Josh says. He turns on the television set. Valery is being interviewed on a talk show. We tried to dissuade her from appearing. "It will not help the case," we said. She promised not to say anything of a personal nature. "I will talk only about acting."

The picture appears on the screen. Valery is sitting in a shiny chair knitting, next to her a tiny man, legs crossed. He stares at Valery's needles while she talks.

". . . not flying saucers exactly, but something similar," Valery is saying. "Beings we can neither comprehend nor see. Try to imagine the relationship between pigeons and people. The pigeons perceive us as a hand tossing out bread, a body passing among them and moving them aside. But never a whole person, never an entity. Well, think of larger beings moving among us, as we move among the pigeons. We sense them in clouds passing in front of the sun, a breeze ruffling our hair. But since they are of a different magnitude, we can neither see nor feel them."

"Let me get this clear. What you are saying is that these things, these beings, are to blame for your—for your husband's present trouble?" the interviewer says.

"Exactly. Everything was fine until he married me. They are basically a fun-loving, happy-go-lucky bunch. As soon as I came into the picture, it all changed. It is ever thus. I have never had a relationship that did not end disastrously. A man I was involved with borrowed library books on my card, and when we broke up he took the books with him. Guess who paid the fines. There is something about me that invites disaster."

Valery knits rapidly as she talks. The interviewer, watching her busy hands, looks bemused. "But why you?" he says.

"Why me? Because I've always refused to compromise. Integrity maddens these beings. They want to punish people who won't sell out."

"Oh, God," I say, "everyone will think we're total flakes."

Saul grows defensive. "She seemed perfectly normal when I married her," he says.

"Everybody is into the supernatural these days," Connie says. "How else can you explain current events?"

Josh is shooting the family watching the television screen. His father is trying not to notice him. But each time he moves in with his camera, Saul sits up straight and sucks in his stomach.

"I wish you wouldn't do that," Josh says.

"Do what?"

"I am trying for truthfulness. Stop sucking in your paunch." Saul denies having a paunch.

"Okay, but let's get back to this extended family," the

130

interviewer is saying. "This polygamy. How do you explain your part in that? Weren't you jealous of the other wives?"

"Of course I was jealous of the other wives. I have a jealous nature. As a child, they had to separate me from other children. I took their toys. I hit them if they appeared to be having fun. I could not bear to see anyone having a good time."

"I kicked a boy once because his father won a Toyota," the interviewer says. "But let's stick to now. What we'd like to know are the details of group marriage. You are, after all, in the forefront, the avant-garde of a new lifestyle."

"I was just beginning to get the hang of it when the trouble came. Mostly it had to do with food, who brought what to our Sunday dinners. It was a very complex situation. There were endless phone calls, sometimes five or six between one Sunday and the next. They'd tell you to bring a salad, and then, an hour later, they'd call and say No, don't bring a salad, someone else is bringing a salad; bring cheese. Then an hour later, there would be another phone call, and this time they would tell you to bring a loaf of bread. But not just any bread. One of the wives has a wheat allergy, so you have to get a bread with seven grains, which is not easy to find."

"Yes, but"—the interviewer is getting restless; he shifts in his interviewer chair, puts his left leg over his right, and then reverses them—"there must have been more to it than that."

"Yes indeed," Valery says. "Everybody in the family was a health freak. They were always reading the ingredients listed on labels. Someone would say, 'Lactalbumin, riboflavin, diglycerides,' and everyone would groan. Sometimes we felt so nauseous, we couldn't eat."

The interviewer makes sympathetic sounds. Then he says, "But what we really hoped you'd talk about was the personal, the intimate. The—er—arrangements."

"What arrangements?"

"Well, surely you must realize that everybody in America is dying to know: did you or didn't you?"

131

"Did we or didn't we what?"

"Engage in polygamy. I mean, how does a marriage like this work?"

Valery stops knitting and stares at the interviewer. A long silence, perhaps eight seconds, transpires. "I thought you were interested in me," she says. She knits a stitch.

Sitting in front of the TV, we all applaud. "Good girl, Valery. . . . She put that joker in his place. . . . The nerve of that man, thinking he could worm information of an intimate nature from her."

"I told you she was okay," Saul says.

"She has developed a lot of insight since she became part of this family," Connie says.

A commercial flashes across the screen, and we turn away from it. "Well," we all say, "it was not as bad as I feared."

"But did you notice how heavy she looked?" Evelyn says.

"The screen adds pounds to a person's body."

"I'm going on a diet," Evelyn says. "Starting this minute."

"It's that suit," Connie says. "Valery doesn't know how to dress. I begged her to go shopping with me. Red is not your color, I told her. Wear gray. Or jade green. Colors that convey sobriety, solid family values." She herself has shed her metal clothing and is wearing indigo. "Metal implies that you are not a serious person," she said. She gave all her metal castoffs to Beryl.

The commercial is over. Valery and the interviewer are back on the screen. He is saying, "Tell us about yourself. What are you really like? What makes a beautiful young woman like you take up with a—well, with a roué?"

"Saul is not a roué and I am not beautiful," Valery says. "Without all this makeup they plastered on me before the show, you would be able to see what I really look like. My nose is too long, for one thing. It gives me a look of austere severity that puts people off. It is the Meryl Streep look, only more so."

132

"Oh, Valery," we moan, "why can't you learn to accept a compliment?"

The interviewer interrupts this monologue of self-disparagement. "I understand you wanted to be an actress."

"Wanted to be? I *am* an actress. My entire life has been devoted to developing my craft, fine-tuning my ability to convey emotions." She lifts a hand and twists a wrist. "What does that convey to you?"

The interviewer looks bemused. "Belligerence? A warning?"

"Watch carefully." Valery does it again.

The interviewer leans forward and squints his eyes. "I don't know," he says.

"Contempt," Valery says. "It is supposed to convey contempt. It is discouraging when people don't understand its meaning. I spend hours every day doing these conveying exercises. I intend to be in total control of my body. Every muscle, every nerve." Her hands fly as she talks, the click of her needles an accompaniment to the conversation.

The interviewer watches her knit as though hypnotized. "Is that part of your exercises?" he says.

"I design knitted things. That's how I make my living." Valery holds up the sweater she is working on. A château with many chimneys is emerging. "I am knitting this sweater for a client with high government connections. This building that you see, this château, is actually a safe house. I am not at liberty to say where it is located. I had to get top government clearance before I could start knitting this project."

"Engaged as you are in this most irregular marriage, I should think you would be a security risk."

"Saul is not a Russian."

The studio audience applauds. Josh trains his camera on his father looking pleased.

"How she rambles," I say.

"As long as she is discreet, it doesn't matter," Evelyn

says. "If we are going to base the defense on the First Amendment, it is essential that we appear wholesome. Otherwise arguing that Saul's marriages are simply an extension of free speech will not hold water."

But now the tenor of the interview suddenly changes. The interviewer's benign look disappears. His face grows fierce, his voice harsh and insistent. "How does this marriage work? What did you do?" he says. "You owe the American public an explanation."

"I don't know what you mean." Valery's voice falters.

"Yes, you do," he growls. "What did you do and when did you do it?"

"Do what?" she whispers.

He continues to probe. Valery stares down at the knitting in her lap. "Answer the question," he snaps. Valery's hands grow limp. Her knitting slides to the floor. "America has a right to know," the interviewer thunders. "What did you do?"

After a moment she says, "What did we do?" Her voice is hushed and quavery.

"What did you do?" There is a long silence. "America is waiting."

"Well," Valery whispers, "it was just a game. He loved to engage in fantasy. Undressing me, things like that. Then he would have me stand legs apart, working a yo-yo. Then he would lunge at me, grab the yo-yo, and—"

Saul turns off the set. He covers his face. After a moment he looks at us, first one and then another. "It never happened," he says.

"Of course not," we say.

Josh, resting his head in his hands, groans. "I can't believe you turned off the set," he says. "After all the footage I've lost."

"She has a very tenuous hold on reality," Saul says.

"I've been trying to help her," Connie says. "I gave her this book to read, *The Underground Self*, so she could get in touch with her carnal self. Before I read it, I didn't know what my body was trying to tell me."

134

Josh has his camera trained on Connie. "Can I borrow it after Valery?" he says. "I too would like to get in touch with my carnal self."

"You don't have a carnal self yet," Saul says. "Why are you always trying to rush things?"

"Just let me turn on the television and I'll slow down," Josh says. Saul says no. Evelyn says no. By the time Saul gives in, the program is over. Josh looks disconsolate.

"I think we all need a little refreshment," I say. "How about some cocoa?"

While I start cocoa in the kitchen area, Saul goes back to his pile of newspapers. He reads us an account of a postal clerk who threw his town's Christmas mail into a creek, of a banker who spent the pensions of widows and orphans on his matchbox collection.

Connie, sitting at his feet, is helping him. Each time she comes upon a story of sufficient turpitude, she hands it up to Saul. The pile in front of him grows higher and higher.

"Oh, my God, here's another leak," Connie says. She reads us the story. " 'Yes, we did all our socializing at Sunday brunch. But quite frankly those meals scared me. Certain wives weren't clean. They had a very primitive notion of hygiene. One of them particularly—I won't mention names, but she'll know who I mean—you were afraid to open her refrigerator. There were things in the recesses of that box that were no longer identifiable. They'd been there so long, they were pulsating and groaning like simple forms of life. I was sure we were all going to get ptomaine poisoning.' "

She lets the paper drop to the floor and sits there, head bowed. When she finally lifts her face, her eyes are tragic. "It's me they're talking about, isn't it?" she says.

"Of course not. They made it up. Half the stories they write about us are fiction."

"I used to be like that, but no more," Connie says. "It's so unfair."

I carry in the cocoa and pass it around. "Anyway, they

135

probably were referring to me," Beryl says. "Something once turned green in my refrigerator." She is wearing one of Connie's discards, a metal tunic, and playing with a dog leash that serves as its belt. The dog leash is part of a new pet line featured in the five-and-ten. "The name of the line is Pampered P-yuppies," she tells us.

Beryl sips at her cocoa and eats a Mallomar. She eats another and another and another. The rest of us munch on rye thins and apple quarters.

Beryl's Mallomars begin to make everybody uneasy. We watch her eat them in fidgety silence. Saul finally says, "Maybe someone else would like a Mallomar. You were always good at sharing."

"I can't spare them," Beryl says.

"But there must be hundreds of them in that giant box."

"That may be, but I am eating for two these days."

"You are what?"

In a voice husky with drama, she says, "I am going to have your baby."

She pulls the metal tunic tight around the middle so we can see her little round belly. Josh brings the video camera almost to her stomach. "Don't move," he says.

10

The three of us—Jen, Saul, and I—are in a taxi on our way to Fred's lumberyard. Saul is sorting through the morning's mail. He deals it out, some for him, some for me, a huge volume of letters. I tear open a lavender envelope; inside is an obscene poem. I open another letter, an invitation to participate in a seminar on sensuality for the sexual underachiever. That's me, I think.

Each mail brings Saul additional offers of marriage. A sensational redhead longs to build a cocoon around him. A fitness expert with a terrific sense of humor would like to help him with his muscle tone. *You're cute*, she writes.

Saul grins at these letters. "How many is that?" he says.

"I've lost count," I say.

"Hundreds?" Saul says.

"Close to a dozen," I say.

Men write him too, offering love, a new interest in life. "What can you have in common with all those women?" they ask.

"Now I know what it feels like to be a sex object," Saul says. But he's always been a sex object, I think.

Saul seems a little more cheerful today. Since Beryl announced her pregnancy, his moods have shifted between hope and black despair. In his good moments, the idea of a baby in the abstract pleases him, the idea of renewal, of getting things right. "This time I will know what to do," he says. He will be wise, he will be patient, a loving guide and mentor. Poor Josh was practice.

But when he thinks about Beryl mothering a child—his child—his mood changes and he is filled with doubt. "She is in love with novelty," he says. At the five-and-ten her allegiance shifts from one new item to another—first the perfect garlic press, then a brilliant self-stick hook. He wonders if such a person could sustain love for a child.

"A baby isn't a garlic press," I say.

"She wants this baby," Jen says.

"She wants this baby now, but what about later? She loses interest in things."

In him? I wonder. It's possible. We haven't seen Beryl since the night she announced her pregnancy. Each time we call, she says she is coming by. "When?" we say. "Soon."

Saul wonders if Ramon has anything to do with her absence. "They've always been so close," he says. "They're not even speaking," we tell him. "There are other ways of communicating," he says.

Now he opens another letter. "Oh, my God, here's one from my cousin the yo-yo champ, berating me for blackening the family name." *I always knew you were a depraved person*, the yo-yo champ writes. He is now heavily into naturopathy. *Had you been eating right, sexual deviation would have been kept to a minimum.* Enclosed with the letter is a list of acceptable foods.

Saul shoves the letter into his pack. "Another crazy heard from," he says.

Our notoriety has made us the target of many demented people. One advises us to send a prayergram to God, another to eat only foods beginning with the letter *b*.

This will rid you of all your poisons, the letter writer says. A vitamin distributor urges Saul to try his upwardly mobile virility supplements; he promises a lifetime supply for the whole family if Saul will only endorse them. An entrepreneur wants us to join his road show, which presently consists of three Latin beauties astride an exotic mammal. He would like to have the entire family onstage telling jokes about our lives. *Can any of you sing?* he asks.

"And they call *us* oddballs," Saul says.

He opens the last of his mail, then picks up the newspaper at his feet. He turns the pages slowly, pausing when a story catches his fancy. After a few minutes, he looks up. "This will interest you," he says. "A missile museum in Arizona has attracted thousands to its subterranean display. It is the only place in the entire country where you can tour an intercontinental missile."

"I have always wanted to tour a missile," Jen says.

Saul continues. "Several guests have signed *Mikhail Gorbachev* in the guest register, a sign that many tourists share a sense of humor."

"It becomes more enticing every moment," I say.

While Saul reads his paper, Jen and I stare out the window at the passing scene. I count the stretch limos clogging the streets, try to identify the dead animals adorning women's bodies. On nearly every block, a luxury highrise is emerging from a construction site like some noxious weed. Amid these signs of plenty, people huddle against buildings surrounded by plastic bags filled with filth. A family is cooking yams over a hibachi in the doorway of an empty store, while nearby two elderly people in pink Afro wigs are setting out old shoes and torn sweaters and other merchandise on a dirty blanket. From under a tree, a ragged man collects deposit cans, which he drops into a plastic garbage bag. A barefoot drunk has plucked crocuses from a bed growing under another tree, which he is trying to sell to passersby.

"The two cities seem to coexist without really impinging," I say.

"I know," Jen says. "It's as though the rich and the poor were invisible to each other."

"Or different species, each with its own territory," I say.

Still absorbed in his newspaper, Saul misses all this. Suddenly he curses. "Another anonymous interview." He reads rapidly. Then looks up at us. "Did you know I was a gynethologist?" he says.

"A what?"

"A gynecologist?"

"No, a gynethologist. Listen to this:

" 'In a conversation with one of the alleged polygamist's wives, she told us her husband was the quintessential gynethologist. "I mean," she said, "he watches women the way ornithologists watch birds. He likes to study women in their various manifestations—old women, new women, women in the process of emerging from their chrysalis. Change is what interests him, the movement from one stage of life to another. He particularly likes to watch women shedding their bad traits and developing good traits. 'I love to see them improving themselves,' he says." She explained that this was the reason the alleged polygamist has so many wives. "He needs to have numerous women around him, since no one person could embody all the aspects he is interested in. 'It would be like attempting to study a disease by observing a single germ,' he says." ' "

"Did you actually say that?" I say.

"Of course not. I've never thought of my wives as a disease. The whole article is a fabrication."

"I wonder which wife they were interviewing," Jen says.

We speculate on the source. "It doesn't sound like any of us," I finally admit.

"I think they must take raw facts and make up a story out of it," Saul says.

"Well, it could be worse," I say.

140

"Yes, it could be worse. They could have compared me to Jack the Ripper."

"Put down the paper so we can talk about the job. We have to figure out what we're looking for at the lumberyard," I say.

"I'm almost done," Saul says. He turns to the science section and glances through it. A column at the bottom catches his eye. He reads a story, his face intent. After a moment he shakes his head. "It says here that children are becoming more primitive."

"In what way?"

"In their intellectual development. They're regressing." He reads from the paper: " 'Contemporary children are leading such passive lives, their brains are no longer developing normal intellectual patterns. Pathologists have discovered, when early death intervenes, smooth places in the brains of children where once there were folds. "This may portend a return to an earlier evolutionary state," a leading doctor speculated.' "

Saul shows us two diagrams accompanying the story. In the first, the brain looks like a normal brain with all kinds of complicated indentations; in the second, the brain is only faintly marbled with thin lines. "It all comes from a lack of stimulation," he says. He stares out the window. "If this continues, they'll end up like vegetables."

"How they love to exaggerate their findings. Josh is a modern child. I'll bet his brain has millions of indentations."

But mention of Josh is a mistake. He is so busy being befriended by the parents of his schoolmates, we hardly ever see him. The fathers take him to sporting events, the mothers on walking tours of the city. "I should have spent more time with Josh," Saul says. He reproaches himself for neglecting his son. He ponders the things he might have taught Josh, questions his own virility. "If only I'd learned to pitch a curve," he says.

Jen and I look at each other in despair, searching frantically for ways to ward off this onslaught of doubt, for once he gets started on this track, we know what to expect. "He's at an age now where he needs outside contacts. It isn't good for him to hang around all the time," we say.

But it is too late. Now virility is on Saul's mind, the fear of being taken for a sex object should he end up in prison. "If seven wives have not established your manhood, what will?" we say.

"They'll think I've been overcompensating," he says. He ponders a more manly stance, rough ways; practices snarling, cursing. He curls his hands into fists and studies them, wondering if he ought to take a crash course in boxing or one of the martial arts—something, anything, that would shield him from the erotic desires of men.

"Anyway, as far as Beryl's baby is concerned you're just borrowing trouble," Jen says. "Who's to say what the world will be like by the time the baby is a teenager? For all we know, it might be a wonderful place to live in, full of stimulation and cultural delights."

"All the signs point the other way."

"Okay, but regardless of the state of the world, Beryl will be a fine mother."

"Absolutely. She's very serious about her pregnancy," Jen says. "She's joined a prenatal exercise group, and she's studying early nurturing. The trouble with you, Saul, is you don't really give her credit for the things she can do. After all, she orchestrated your entire canoe trip. That's hardly the work of an underachiever."

Saul makes a bitter sound in his throat. "You should have been there," he says. "She said she knew how to paddle, but she couldn't keep the damn thing on course. We almost drowned."

"You're kidding!" we gasp.

"We kept running into the bank; hitting submerged objects; sometimes we'd go around in circles. I began to wonder if she'd ever even been in a canoe before."

"Well, she's doing very well with her Spanish."

142

"And we'll all give Beryl a hand; whatever she needs, we'll get for her. Now please, let's get down to business."

We are on our way to Fred's lumberyard to look for materials. We are planning to start the construction of a dozen columns for the gallery we are building. These columns are central to the overall concept of the gallery, fusing the viewing spaces and at the same time separating them. Placed at irregular intervals throughout the space, their hollow insides will be carved neo-totem poles turned outside in. Post-historic monsters will twine up the implosion, as if the weight of events had crushed the outer forms of culture and turned all art in on itself. A mechanism will open and then close the columns throughout the viewing day, not all at once but in some sequential order. Kelly is making a series of sketches of these post-historic monsters, basing them on rare Australian fauna.

The client liked this proposal. He liked the hermetic quality of the columns, reiterating the emotional statement of his photographs: the dead cows, the defoliated trees. "I like the moral authority it confers over the space," he said.

Despite our troubles, I have managed somehow to get on with our work. This gallery for photographs I consider one of my best concepts, its proportions elegant, its spatial elements both perplexing and bold, concealing the practical flexibility that lends itself to display. For instance, the movable partitions, interspersed among the columns, will be at odd angles to one another, creating an element of surprise that will both alienate and delight, thereby intensifying the emotional relationship between viewer and photographs.

Jen thinks the imploded totem columns are brilliant. "It forces the viewer to turn to the photographs to get her bearings. It should be a very intense experience."

"That's what I'm striving for—symbiosis," I say.

Both Jen and I are dressed up. Ordinarily, she wears blue jeans and T-shirts to work, a jumpsuit when she is dressing for a social occasion. Even in her work clothes, Jen always looks nice. She brings the same aesthetic attention to her clothes that she does to her work—an interesting belt, an unusual scarf, some detail that makes everything she wears look elegant, a touch surprising. But not today. Today she is in a solemn creation that Connie picked out, a tentlike dress that engulfs her as if she had become entangled in a huge black umbrella.

Do I look as bad as she does? I wonder. I am wearing a suit that I loathe, for its severity makes me feel estranged from myself. Connie's Henri has constructed my hair in strands that form a pyramid. I keep wondering how long it will take to grow out. The entire family went there for a hair styling, even Josh, whose hair now stands away from his head in spikes as if he had recently been electrocuted. Saul's hair frames his head in perfect curls, like the early Shirley Temple, and Jen's wispy hair is in little cocktail-sausage ringlets.

Henri was trying to help. He was striving for a wholesome, all-American, extended-family look. But somehow he ended up robbing us of our individuality and turning us all into generalizations.

Desperation drove us there. Everybody in the family is trying to look nice, for each time we go out, photographers lurk, waiting to record the moment.

Our story grows and multiplies as if our lives were reflected in a thousand mirrors. They have photographed me in the produce store squeezing a grapefruit, Kelly smelling a cantaloupe, Evelyn in court pointing a finger at a judge, Jen and Kelly dancing together at a benefit for the women's shelter. They have trapped Connie in a tanning center, scantily dressed, eyes blacked out, lying prone under a blue light, like some victim of a hi-tech torture system, soon to be exported to our Third World allies.

From nearby roofs, they have trained a camera on our workroom and run pictures of us in glossy magazines showing us arguing, our faces wild and angry, or searching frantically through mounds of rubbish for some lost object. In one photograph, Saul is trying to push a cruller into his mouth while he talks on the phone; in another, Beryl is extricating a shirt from a garbage pail.

Our lives are not our own. Saul has finally had to abandon all conjugal visits. For a brief time, he tried to resume his schedule, if only to prove to himself that he was capable of surmounting all difficulties. Late at night or very early in the morning, he would leave the house disguised as someone else and scurry through the empty streets like a displaced mouse. Now the huge calendar that once dominated our lives is empty. It no longer brings an orderly sequence of days; its unmarked spaces only intensify our sense of chaos, our loss of control. It is weeks since Saul visited a wife.

Ordinarily, he enjoys our trips to the lumberyard. But not today. He is self-conscious about appearing there in his new guise—notorious polygamist—and worried about how they will receive him. "What will they say?" he keeps muttering. "How will they act?"

"We give them plenty of business," I say. "That's all they care about."

"They've always liked you at the lumberyard," Jen says.

"They didn't know," he says.

"At least nobody is following us today," I say.

Sauls looks out the rear window. "How do you know? There's a whole line of cars behind us. Every one of them could be filled with nosy reporters ready to pounce on us as soon as we leave this cab."

"Let's not get paranoid," Jen says. "That's normal city traffic." She is studying the blueprint. "Ten columns of varying circumference and height. But you haven't indicated their measurements. I'm not sure I understand exactly what you have in mind."

"I'll know better once we choose the fabrication," I say. "I need to get a sense of its solidity before we get locked into dimensions. Once I see a construction, we'll have a clearer idea of their relationship, not only to each other but to the space as a whole."

145

"Hmm." Jen looks puzzled. "What do you think, Saul?"

Saul has taken up the newspaper and is studying the death notices. He looks at Jen blankly. "What do I think about what?"

"The columns."

"They're okay," he says.

Jen and I exchange looks. She continues to study the blueprint. "So," she says, "the way I read this is you are striving for a sense of permanence even though the dividers are movable. Yes?"

"Yes. Solidity and subterfuge," I say.

"It won't be easy," Jen says. "Not if we are to avoid having it look like a compromise, a kind of middle ground between vision and need. I always find that tacky."

"Me too," I say. "It's exactly what I want to avoid." In our analysis of a job, Jen and I are nearly always on the same wavelength. I nudge Saul. "What do you think?"

What Saul thinks is important, for he knows the way a job should be, what makes a space both workable and satisfying. He is always quick to spot flaws, point out potential construction problems. He brings this sense of certainty with him in his dealings with the clients. He knows when to cajole, when to compromise, when to stand firm. He is our interpreter, our bridge.

Jen and I lack this ability. She's too uncompromising, I'm too locked into my concepts. Evelyn thinks of herself as a diplomat, but her forceful, aggressive style puts people off.

I nudge Saul again. "Is it going to work?" I say. He stares at the blueprint. "Have you any thoughts on what we should use to fabricate these columns?"

"We'll think of something," he says.

"Saul, pay attention," I say. "We need to get started today. We're way behind. If we don't meet the schedule, he won't be able to have his showing in the fall."

"It wouldn't be such a loss," Saul says. "His work lacks

authenticity. As far as I'm concerned, all that gloom is a pose."

"It isn't a pose, it's very moving. A vision of heroic despair. That's the way the critics put it, and I happen to agree."

"The critics say that about everybody," Sauls says. "It's become a cliché—heroic despair, wrestling with nothingness, staring unblinkingly into the void. But what does he know about despair? What do any of them know?"

"Not just despair, heroic despair," I say. "Refusing to submit, to give in, that's what it's about."

"It's all a pose. His vision is pasteurized to make sure he doesn't offend the sensibilities of the collectors."

"*Newsweek* said his work was prescient, the wave of the future."

Saul and I are glaring at each other, our voices raised. I can feel the anger rising and swelling in my throat as though all my fears, all the frustrations of the last months, were pouring out.

"That's easy to say, since everybody alive will be dead sooner or later," Saul says. "But that's not really what the future is all about. What those two-bit critics don't realize is that people get off on pain and despair. And then they get bored with it and ultimately coarsened and hardened. Until they can no longer respond to real suffering."

He means me. How unfair, how totally wrong. "That's not true. Just because I loathe sentimentality, just because I hate exaggeration, doesn't mean I am coarsened," I say. Now I feel like hitting him. I feel like tearing up the blueprint and throwing the pieces in his face.

"Is it unreasonable to worry?" Saul says. He looks at Jen. "Am I being oversensitive about what lies ahead? Is it egotistical to worry about going to jail?"

"The gays are forming a support group," Jen says.

"A support group for what?" Saul says.

"For you. They want to protect your rights."

"What rights?"

147

"Your civil liberties. They see a parallel between your legal troubles and the persecution of same-sex lovers."

"I have no rights," Saul says, looking lost and frightened.

The anger leaks out of me. "It's going to be okay," I say. "More and more people are on your side." I squeeze his hand.

He takes my hand between his. "Sure," he says.

As we pull up to the lumberyard, the cabdriver says, "I'm just from Jordan. I like the way you speak."

"It's just ordinary American eloquence, the New York sound," Saul says.

At the doorway to the lumberyard, Saul hesitates. It is his first visit since the arrest. He scrutinizes his costume, tugs at his sweater, tucks in his shirt. Each time we visit the lumberyard, Saul dresses for the occasion, casting off his elegant tweeds for worn blue jeans, a wrinkled work shirt, a sweater riddled with holes. As Jen and I nudge him through the doorway, he tries to muss his hair.

The lumberyard, a cavernous room, is long and narrow. Along the perimeter, materials are stacked: boards, cornices, plywood doors, carvings, fiberboard, ceiling tiles. The center is a cluttered corridor of workbenches and tables holding saws and other machinery. Ordinarily the noise of all this machinery is deafening. But today the place is deserted and all is quiet. "It must be lunch hour," I say, as we head for the glass-enclosed office at the back.

The entire crew has squeezed into the office. Above the desk, a giant television set sits on a shelf. The men are watching a soap opera.

Fred, the owner, is sitting at his desk, his grown son Billy next to him. We stand in the doorway waiting to be acknowledged. The men turn briefly to look at us. Then they turn back to the set. Then they do a double take. Heads swivel in our direction, eyes stare at us.

"Hi," we say.

"Hi," they say. They turn away from us slowly and

148

look once more at the screen, as though torn between that spectacle and us.

The are watching an episode of *Cast the First Stone*. A man sits in a chair talking to another man standing over him. "I never meant any harm," the seated man says. "I'm going to call the police," the standing man says. "No, don't, please." The first man falls on his knees and presses his hands together in a gesture of supplication. "I'd rather kill myself first, Uncle." "That's not a bad solution." The uncle reaches in a pocket and pulls out a gun. "Here." He hands it to his nephew and stalks out of the room. Still on his knees, the nephew strokes the gun, studies it, and then slowly raises it to his forehead. A close-up reveals a tear in his eye.

The screen darkens and then a commercial flashes on. The men turn away from the set. "He's innocent. . . . That rotten bastard of an uncle. . . . Making him think he killed the gardener while under the influence. . . . Oh, God, I hope he doesn't pull the trigger." They file slowly out of the room, a dazed expression on all their faces.

Fred turns off the set, looking stunned. "He wasn't even there when the gardener was run down," he says.

"I knew something bad would happen as soon as his uncle returned from the Hebrides," Billy says. He stands up and greets us. "How do," he says.

"How do," we say.

Fred stands up too. "You've got to admit he's taking it like a man," he says.

"While there's life, there's hope," Billy says.

"It's always darkest before the dawn," Fred says. Their words are measured, their tones portentous, as if the soap opera had leaked character traits all over them.

They shake each of us by the hand; Fred squeezes Saul's shoulder. "You're looking well," he says.

"Couldn't be better," Saul says. "I'm sure it will all turn out for the best," he says, commenting on the program.

Saul admires the soaps. "They're folk art, like subway

149

posters or directional signs," he says. Occasionally, in order to establish a bond with the lumberyard crew, he watches an episode or two. He longs to be one of the boys. The male environment of the lumberyard makes him expand. He feels defined, his role in life clarified, the distance he has traveled since his academic days marked off in miles. "I am truly alternate, " he says after each visit.

Jen loves the lumberyard too, the raw materials of her craft. She loves to handle things, to run her hands over the stacks of lumber, the piles of paneling, from which she can visualize a regal wall system, a handsome cabinet emerging. She and Saul can spend hours searching for the right grain.

"What can I do for you today?" Fred says.

"We got a real sweetheart we're workin' on," Saul says. His voice grows coarse, he abandons final letters, his grammar becomes slovenly. He rubs his day-old beard. "I mean this one's a bitch."

"Nothing's easy," Fred says.

"Ain't that the truth," Saul says.

"Nobody's perfect," Fred says.

Saul smiles. "All we can do is try," he says.

"And how's the missus?" Always before when he came to the lumberyard, I was Saul's wife, Jen his chief carpenter. Now Fred's eyes swivel to me and then to Jen.

"Can't complain," I say.

"Never better," Jen says.

Saul relaxes. He gets out his pocket calculator. We unroll our blueprint, spread it out, and show Fred and Billy the columns. I explain what I have in mind. Saul analyzes their structural components. "We're going to need something special to build these babies," he says.

"Follow me." Billy shuffles along the perimeter of the enormous room, where all the materials are stacked. The men are working now, sawing, measuring, planing. I can feel their eyes on us as we follow Billy.

He leads us to a stack of fabricated columns fashioned from fiberglass. We study their contours and then move on to some of molded polyurethane. We rummage, weigh, handle, hold things up to the light, stand them in lines. As we study the fabrication, I am aware of people watching us, whispered comments, smirks. I can tell by Saul's posture that he hears them too.

"What do you think?" Jen says.

"We need something denser, something with more substance," I say.

Fred joins us in our search. "Have you thought of a wood-pulp core?" he says. "Everybody's using it. I can hardly keep it in stock."

"It has to be hollow." I explain about the imploded neo-totem poles, and we study the blueprint together. "The columns have to be mobile but they also have to look permanent, as though they are part of the basic structure."

"I have an idea," Fred says. He drags us down the length of the room, shows us some wire sheeting. He snips off a length and rolls it into a cylinder, holds it upright so we can stand back and study it.

"I don't know," I say. "The question is, will this be strong enough? It has to support the imploded carvings in addition to an outer skin."

Jen looks doubtful too. "It looks awfully fragile to me."

"Fragile? This stuff has the durability of steel," Fred says.

"But it doesn't *look* solid. These columns have to look as though they've been there forever."

"It might work," Saul says. "Suppose we used a heavy industrial canvas on the outside, stiffened with glue. We could make them look like ancient columns, dug up in some ruin."

"That's a possibility," I say.

We lose track of time. It is nearly three before we find materials we are willing to experiment with. In Fred's office, Saul taps at his calculator, Fred at his.

Suddenly there is a murmur behind us, the sound of many voices getting louder. Two of the men are pushing a

151

trolley across the floor, the entire lumberyard crew following. On the trolley is a cake, a bottle of wine, plastic cups. They push the trolley into the office. Across the cake in red icing is written, *Cast the First Stone.*

"Where did this come from?" Saul says. He is trembling with a deep-felt emotion.

"We sent out," Fred says. "We wanted you to know who your friends are."

Someone cuts the cake and hands Saul a piece. Someone else pours wine. The men toast Saul. "More is better. . . . Keep it up. . . . Stay in there. . . . You must be doing something right."

One by one, they stand beside Saul while someone takes their picture. "Let no man cast the first stone," Billy says. Everybody drinks to that. Like the nephew in the soap opera, a tear shimmers in Saul's eye.

11

Tour buses, lined up at the curb, spew noxious fumes at all the passersby. A sign in the window says THE BERYL DOLL IS NOW IN STOCK. The entire window is filled with Beryl dolls; they spill out of large laundry baskets as if some pregnant machine had gone berserk.

The five-and-ten is full of tourists, senior citizens on a cultural visit to the city. They are clustered around a counter. Above the counter a sign dangles from a fluorescent light fixture. GET AN AUTOGRAPHED BERYL DOLL HERE. MEET THE ORIGINAL, the sign says.

I push my way up to the counter looking for Beryl, but she is nowhere in sight. The flustered clerk is telling the tourists that she will soon be there. "When?" they keep saying. Each senior citizen clutches an armful of Beryl dolls. The tour-bus leader is trying to herd them back to the bus: "We got a schedule to maintain." But even though the tags on their Beryl dolls have already been autographed, the tourists are reluctant to leave. "We are waiting to meet the original," they say. Everybody is very angry.

I look around the store trying to spot Beryl. Just like her to keep everybody waiting. The five-and-ten has been added to a tour that also includes a Broadway musical, a shopping excursion in a Third World neighborhood, and a five-course gourmet meal.

As the angry tourists are herded from the store, another tour group erupts from a bus into the store; they converge on the counter and start to grab up Beryl dolls. Ramon, staggering under an enormous carton, approaches the counter, yelling, "Watch yer back, watch yer back." He upends the carton, and dozens of Beryl dolls spill out.

The milling tourists push and shove to get at the new supply of dolls as though they were better than the ones already lying on the counter. I manage to extricate myself from the crush. "Where's Beryl?" I say. Ramon rolls his eyes toward the entrance to the basement.

Downstairs, Beryl is sitting on an upended crate, legs apart, a pile of Beryl dolls at her feet. She picks up a doll, signs a tag attached to it, and tosses it into a carton. She is wearing headphones, and while she signs, her lips mouth the words of the song she is listening to, her head sways in time to the music.

I am almost upon her before she notices me. "Hi," I say.

She removes her headphones and says hello.

"There are hordes of tourists upstairs waiting to see you."

"Oh, God." Beryl moans.

"You're a celebrity."

"I don't want to see them."

"Why not?"

"They make me feel like some kind of freak."

"They're getting angrier by the minute."

"Shit. I hate that part of it. You wouldn't believe the things they do."

"The senior citizens?" I say.

"They are not normal." She lowers her voice as though

154

reluctant to hear her own words. "They think nothing of putting their hands all over me. They snip off pieces of my hair. They pinch me. Some of them even want to smell me. It's really disgusting. You know how they act? As if I were a life-sized Beryl doll—as if I were a thing."

"You're not the only one. A magazine offered us big bucks if we would sit for a family portrait in the nude," I say.

"Plus they all want to tell me their life story—the fortunes that eluded them, the men that got away, their surgical procedures, how much harder life was then than now. One ancient woman wanted me to arrange a meeting between her and Saul. 'I'd like to meet that lover boy,' she said."

"At least he hasn't lost his touch. He'll be happy to know that."

"The men are even worse. One old man wanted me to autograph his underpants. Another stuck his tongue in my mouth."

"Well, if you're not going to put in an appearance, they should at least take down the sign."

"That was management's idea, not mine. Let them wait. I have all these tags to sign."

"How's it going?" I say

"Fantastic. The important thing now is to get the Beryl doll into stores before some other company tries to bring out a copy. What they do is change a detail or two so you can't sue. They'll make another color hair. They'll call the doll Berry, something so close the innocent consumer will not be aware that it isn't the genuine article, the real Beryl. How do you like the doll?"

"I haven't had a chance to look at it yet." I pick one up and study it. The Beryl doll is pregnant. Her maternity outfit is made out of sheeting. The fabric, in stars and stripes, lends a patriotic motif to the outfit. The face of the doll is a photograph of Beryl superimposed on a soft plastic head. Mounds of red Dacron hair encircle the face.

Beryl, too, is now noticeably pregnant. Over a Hawai-

155

ian print sarong, she is wearing a blue pillowcase with slits
cut out for her head and arms. She picks up a doll, signs
the tag, and tosses it into the carton. Then she picks up
another. "Actually it doesn't look much like me," she says.

"It's not a bad resemblance," I say. "How are you
feeling?"

"Not too great." She pats her chest. "I've been suffering from heartburn," she says.

"Are you okay? Saul's worried about you. He wonders
if you're getting the right food."

"Who put that idea into his head? Connie?"

"Why Connie?" I say.

"Who else is always telling everybody how to live?"

"She means well," I say.

"I wouldn't mind so much if she were capable of
running her own life. I at least have a job."

"Connie has a job," I say.

"Doing what?"

"She's working as a Vanguard Vicki."

"A what?"

"She drives a Decormobile to people's homes and
advises them on their decorating needs."

"I still don't understand. What's a Decormobile?"

"Just what it sounds like, a little decorating store on
wheels."

"Since when does Connie know anything about decorating?"

"You know Connie. She loves to learn. She took a
training course in colors and patterns. It's all very struc-
tured. She carries a looseleaf notebook full of charts and
concepts and guidelines. Then before she works out a
decorating scheme for the clients, she analyzes their personalities and lifestyles."

Beryl shakes her head. "It's the perfect job for her."

"She's dying to bring her color chips over to your
place and work out a color scheme. They have a whole
special section on decorating the nursery. This outfit did
an in-depth study on color. According to Connie, certain

colors stimulate a child's development while other colors stifle it."

Beryl picks up a doll, signs its tag, and tosses it into the carton. Then she picks up another. I lean over the carton and start to stack the dolls inside. Finally she says, "Is there any truth in that?"

"You'll have to ask Connie."

"I can just imagine what would happen if I let her loose in my place. She would want to beautify everything in sight. That's absolutely the last thing I want for my child—a beautiful nursery," she says. "I want this baby to be exposed to the world the way it is. I've been studying the subject of child care. The worst impediment to a person's development is sugarcoating. Telling a baby something won't hurt when it will."

"Is it always clear what's going to hurt?"

"It's not all that difficult to understand a baby's feelings. All you have to do is ask yourself, How would I feel in this situation if I were a tiny, helpless baby? and it will guide you to do the right thing."

"We never see you anymore."

"I've been putting in a lot of overtime," Beryl says. "It's work, test-marketing the Beryl doll."

"I bet it is. But if upstairs is any indication, it's going to be a winner."

"I hope so. Things look pretty good. The manufacturer is waiting to get some initial sales figures before he decides on heavy-duty production. It's selling like hotcakes here in the store. I don't see how it can miss. It's the first pregnant doll to come on the market. It's at the cutting edge of doll technology."

"That's great, Beryl. I hope you make a lot of money," I say.

"The tourists keep pouring in. Yesterday there was a whole busload of Germans. And keep in mind it's not just the doll. There are all the spin-offs—a Beryl T-shirt; a line of Beryl greeting cards, each one containing a witty remark; possibly a Beryl maternity line, though that's still up in the air."

"Are you going to talk to Evelyn about all your business deals?"

"I can handle it."

"You need a lawyer. Let her go over your contracts. Evelyn knows how to look at those things."

"So do I. I wasn't born yesterday. And besides, I have a partner. Between us, we're not going to let anybody get away with anything."

"Who's your partner?"

"Ramon."

"I thought you and Ramon weren't speaking."

"We made up," Beryl says. "He said I'd suffered enough."

"What's his role in this?"

"Ramon's my adviser. He's been taking courses in the business field; he's a very ambitious person. He hopes to buy into a cosmetic franchise eventually so he can advise people on their beauty needs. He is very interested in these matters. Meanwhile he's been talking to a record company about doing my song. They are definitely interested."

"Your song? What song? I didn't know you were into music."

"You didn't know I was into music? I used to live with a musician. I was part of his live performance in front of Lincoln Center."

"I'd forgotten," I say. "What's the song?"

"It's the Saul and Beryl story. Would you like to hear what I've done so far?"

"Yes," I say, but I really mean no.

Beryl puts down the Beryl doll she is holding and takes a deep breath. She closes her eyes, and after a long pause she starts to sing. "Oh, they took my man away and I will have to pay. Oh, they threw him in a cell and sent him straight to hell. My outlaw lover, come back to me soon."

She opens her eyes and waits for my response. "It's nice," I say.

"You don't sound very enthusiastic."

"I was thinking of Saul. How do you think he'll feel if this song comes out?"

"It can only help his cause."

"I hope so. He needs all the help he can get."

"It gets even better. The second verse is about how the world misunderstands a person like Saul. It compares him to all the misunderstood martyrs." I wait to hear it, but it isn't ready. "It's coming," she says. "I think about it all the time."

The ceiling rattles while we talk. "What's going on up there?" I say.

"Ignore it," Beryl says. "It's all those tourists."

"I still think you ought to talk to Evelyn before you sign anything," I say.

"You sound just like my mother. She thinks I'm totally incompetent."

"Are we incompetent? The construction company? We wouldn't dream of starting a job before Evelyn has gone over everything."

She picks up a doll and scrawls her signature on its tag. "I'll think about it," she says.

"Do you want to stay at the loft for a while after the baby's born?"

"I don't think so. I'm thinking of buying my own space once the Beryl doll takes off."

"Okay. Whatever happens, I wish you luck. The main thing is to keep in touch. You are part of the family. And people miss you."

"They do?"

"Of course they do. Everybody keeps asking, Where's Beryl?"

"I thought they blamed me for Saul's predicament. I blame myself. Oh, Helen, I feel so rotten. Such a total failure. If only we hadn't gone on that canoe trip."

"You didn't exactly kidnap him."

159

"But it was my idea. Saul never would have gone if I hadn't sort of challenged him. I think I made him feel that the only way he could prove his manhood was by going on this trip."

How typical, I think. "It wasn't your fault, Beryl. He should never have told them about his wives. Nobody in the family blames you."

"Are you sure?"

"If that's why you've been staying away, forget it."

"I wish I could forget it."

"What about baby clothes?" I say. "What do you need?"

"Nothing. I found everything I need on the street. A whole bunch of baby clothes were hanging from a railing."

I can't bear this.

"Don't look at me that way, Helen. It was in a very good neighborhood."

"Valery is knitting the baby a sweater." Beryl sighs.

"It's a beautiful sweater," I say.

"I wish I could make you understand why I hate gifts. My mother tried to regulate my life that way, always giving me things. She would bring home a cashmere sweater to get me to go to body rhythm class. And then when I'd tell her no, I didn't want the sweater, she'd tell me how much I loved cashmere. Or she'd try to get me to lunch with her and her astrologer so they could conduct an analysis of me. 'We're having shad roe,' she'd say. 'You love shad roe.' "

"I'll tell Valery you don't want the sweater."

"She was always telling me what I liked as if I didn't really exist as a separate being."

"Valery has enough trouble owning herself."

"I don't want to hurt her feelings."

The ceiling continues to rattle. "It sounds like a herd of wild animals have been let loose in the store."

"It's been like that all week," Beryl says.

"Saul's worried about you. He's very low."

"Are they really going to bring him to trial?"

"I'm afraid so. Evelyn and I went with him to Bleaksville for the pretrial hearing. The D.A. can hardly wait.
He has political ambitions and Saul's case is a platform, a
stage on which he can show the world how brilliant he is
and how much he deplores sin."

"Has Saul found a lawyer yet?"

"Not yet. Evelyn keeps arranging for him to meet
lawyers, but so far he doesn't like any of them. Either
they're too opinionated, or their idea of a defense doesn't
jibe with his. For a while, he toyed with the idea of
defending himself. And he started working on an exoneration document in his own defense. What he did was
collect newspapers stories showing all the evil in the world.
'I want to be tried in context,' he said. Fortunately we
managed to talk him out of it. The lawyers think his only
hope is to plead temporary insanity. Each one has a
psychiatrist who will attest to his derangement."

"That's so typical of Saul. Wanting to conduct his own
defense."

"Evelyn has threatened to quit trying to find him a
lawyer. If he doesn't decide on one soon, she says she will
just bow out."

"Actually, it wouldn't be all that hard to prove he was
deranged," Beryl says. "I've been reading a book on the
psychology of men, and I'm beginning to understand what
Saul's all about. It's his weak inner structure that's causing
all the trouble, plus his lack of a solid belief system. That's
why he needs so many wives. Without them, he'd probably
collapse."

"What's the name of the book?"

"*Disconnected Men.* Men who are unable to synthesize,
to incorporate all their parts into a total human being.
They all crave things in an effort to make themselves
whole. With some, it's cars or large sums of money. With
Saul, it's his collection of women."

"I suspect he's lost his taste for numbers. He has too
many things on his mind. Especially you."

"I'm okay. Tell him not to worry about me. Promoting

the Beryl doll is a full-time occupation. This is my chance to make something of myself, to prove to certain parties that I am not an incompetent child. I really enjoy wheeling and dealing. I've discovered I have a real talent for business matters."

"That's great," I say. Is she seeing a doctor? I wonder; is she eating anything but cookies and cupcakes? I won't allow myself to ask. I stand up. "I hope you make a fortune."

"So do I," she says. She scoops up a handful of dolls. "I'd like everybody in the family to have one." She drops them in a bag. "Josh too. I especially want him to have one for its educational benefits."

She starts to hand me the bagful of dolls. The noise from above seems to be intensifying. We hear thumps, running footsteps, voices shouting. "Beryl, something's going on up there," I say.

"They're trying to push their way up to the counter. You have no idea how they act." As I reach for the bagful of dolls, she says, "Wait, you haven't seen the best part." She lifts the skirt on a Beryl doll and presses its stomach. A tiny baby shoots out. It is a miniature of the Beryl doll, same face, same Dacron hair. She picks the baby up and pushes it back inside through an aperture between the legs which clicks shut when the baby is in place. "It's state of the art," she says.

I pick up the bagful of dolls and head for the stairs. A wild, disheveled Ramon suddenly clatters down them, almost knocking me over. "They are rioting upstairs," he gasps. His shirt is torn, his face is scratched.

"The senior citizens?" we both say.

"Some fanatics from the Religious Right. They burst into the store and started confiscating Beryl dolls. They intend to take them to a presidential commission on pornography as evidence."

"Evidence of what?"

"A conspiracy against the government, communist infiltrators, how the hell do I know?"

"The nerve of those people," Beryl says. She stands up, eyes blazing, and heads for the stairs.

"They'll kill you if you go up there," Ramon says. He picks up a Beryl doll and dabs at the scratches on his face, now oozing blood. "They are tearing them out of the hands of the senior citizens. They are making accusations, telling everyone the doll encourages welfare mothers, that it is a plot of the Russians to undermine the American family."

"I'm not going to take this," Beryl says.

"You can't go up there."

"Nobody's going to push me around anymore."

Ramon blocks her way. "You haven't heard the worst. They have taken wire from Hardware and they are stringing up Beryl dolls all over the store. Management is very angry."

12

"Keep it up,'" Saul says. "What does that say to you?"

I look up from my book. "What are you talking about?" I say.

"'Keep it up. . . . Stay in there.' How could I have missed it? How could I have been so stupid?"

"Missed what?"

"The double meanings. The lewd intent. All the time the men at Fred's lumberyard were saying those things, I thought they were wishing me well. I was too dumb to see what they were driving at. What a fool they must think me."

"You're crazy," I say.

"Everything they said—all those toasts—they all have a sexual connotation. What do you think of when somebody says 'Keep it up'?"

"Juggling."

"No, seriously."

"Oh, Saul, cut it out. Why do you do this to yourself?"

"And what comes to mind when a person tells you to stay in there? How they must have laughed when we left."

"It was a show of kindness, a simple act of friendship. Why can't you let it go at that?"

"It wouldn't have been so bad if I'd shown them I was aware of what they were saying. If I'd kidded with them. If I'd maybe winked or smiled. It was my stupidity, my naïveté, that gets me. Do you realize I was close to tears when they cut the cake?"

"Saul, for the last time, all they were doing was being friendly. Those men don't deal in irony. Why do you have to eviscerate yourself? Keep it up and you'll float away. Now leave me alone. I'm reading."

"How do you know they were being friendly?"

"I know. Now let me read."

We are in bed. I am reading the journals of an architect, Lady Jane X, who designed doghouses for the nobility in the time of King James I.

> Were I a man, my buildings would have been of a proper scale, gracious, noble, fit to house the greatest of men. But being a mere woman, scarce the ghost of any man, I must content myself with small offices lest I be ensnared in the envy and malice lying in the hearts of men. Someday, not in my lifetime, but perchance in the lifetime of my daughters, this will change. I pray devoutly for that time.

Her structures were so complicated, the dogs would get lost in them and small maidservants would have to crawl inside to rescue them. "Woulds't I were a hound and could dwell therein," a small maidservant said after emerging from one of these doghouses with a lost dog.

How I long to see one of these structures, one of these noble late-Gothic buildings in miniature. But not a single one has survived.

Saul is still deconstructing his life. "If they weren't laughing at me what?"

165

"Shut up," I tell him, staring at the printed page. Lady Jane writes:

I work upon a house that grows very high. It has many storeys, set one upon another. And a pulley, similar to the machinery used in the hanging of men, shall hoist people from one storey to the one above it.

I turn to Saul with great excitement. "She invented the skyscraper. She invented an elevator. She was another da Vinci. Or would have been, were she a man."

"You're getting awfully hard," Saul says. I deny this. "You used to be a much more thoughtful person. More generous. Kinder."

"No, I wasn't," I say. I turn back to my book.

This is a dark day indeed. I am undone. Unbeknownst to me, there came in the night a band of dwarfs which stole the house of the dogs of the Duke of Essex thinking themselves to dwell therein. This came to the king's ear, who outlaw'd my works. The king said, "Her work foments treason and other vicious acts. Henceforward she is to attend to her family and her household." His edict came by royal messenger this day. Oh, woe is me!

My poor Jane. "Imagine being prevented from doing your work!" I say.

"I used to think I could depend upon you above all others," Saul says. "That you would never turn your back on me. But I suppose I was expecting too much."

I force myself to put down the book. "What do you want?"

"Nothing."

"Saul!"

"It's my greatest flaw. Believing people are nicer than

166

they really are. There's no reason you should concern yourself with me. You've done your bit. I can understand your wanting to live for yourself. People get tired of other people's troubles."

How I miss those conjugal visits, I think. Quiet evenings when I could read in bed. "Your greatest flaw is not your mistaken judgments of people. It is your obsession with yourself."

"You think so?" Saul relaxes now. We can settle down to a good talk about him, discuss his obsessions: at this particular moment, the incident in Fred's lumberyard; at other times Josh, a design problem, an aesthetic riddle that defies solution. Each of his wives, at one time or another, has been an obsession, an object of lust and fantasy and insatiable craving, provoking an endless discussion between the two of us. Until the fixation dribbled away in words and lost its power.

I give my book one last ardent look as we begin to discuss Saul's character. "You are like some simpler form of life," I say.

"What do you mean?" Saul says.

"I mean you are unable to hold more than one thought at a time, because you hold it so fiercely it crowds out everything else, all the simple pleasures—a sunny day, the smell of clean sheets, fresh bread."

As the dissection of his character continues, Saul looks happy. I suppose there are worse ways of pleasing a man.

Our discussion overstimulates us; it is late and we cannot sleep. We make cocoa and carry it back to bed, and, wearied at last of the subject, or perhaps momentarily sated, Saul flicks on the television set.

An image leaps upon the screen. Cowboys on horseback are chasing other cowboys on horseback. He switches channels. A car is chasing another car. He switches again. A boat is chasing another boat. He switches again. A fleet of planes is chasing another fleet of planes. "Try cable," I say.

A man is licking the chest of another man while a

167

group of men surround them, applauding. "Jesus," Saul says, "a licking contest. Just what we need." He tries another channel. Now we are in a studio. Three people are talking, two women and a black person in an ornate evening gown. "It's Jen and Kelly!" I say. "Did you know they were going to be on television?"

"They never said a word," Saul says.

We stare at the screen. The black person is saying, "Welcome to Private Vue, the program that tells the truth. This is Dennis your host, crowned Miss Transvestite of 1985, in case you've forgotten. The gown I am wearing tonight is courtesy of Larger Than Life party dresses. A thousand sequins dot the front, forming a gorgeous hydrangea. No counting tonight. Trust me, they're there."

While he describes his outfit, we stare at Jen and Kelly. The camera angle elongates Kelly, exaggerating her thin frame so that she looks like a famine victim. She is wearing painter's overalls streaked with paint, a large tear at one knee. Is that deliberate? I wonder. Jen is wearing her black umbrella dress and has done something weird to her hair. All the sausage curls are standing away from her head as though they have been stiffened with florist wire.

Now Dennis is introducing them. "Princess Jen and Princess Kelly. Royal polygamists who are here tonight to share their lives with us. Let's hear a welcome for these two beauties." There is a roar of applause and the camera pans in on the audience, which seems to consist of a row of Japanese tourists holding cameras to their eyes.

"I need a drink," Saul says.

"So do I." He gets out of bed and goes over to the bar. While he is gone Dennis asks Jen and Kelly how they came to get involved with a husband. "You girls don't seem like the type."

Kelly: "I'm not here to discuss my life. I'm here to tell the public about the plight of the kangaroos." She holds up a picture. It shows dead kangaroos piled one on top of the other. "Kangaroos are not pests. They are part of the Australian ecology. If someone tells you they are being eliminated because of damage to the environment, it's a lie. The real reason is greed. They sell the pouches to a bag manufacturer, who adds a strap and sells them for big bucks."

Dennis: "And you, Princess Jen, do you have a cause?"

Jen: "Not anymore. I spent my childhood in litigation. My mother was a gender foe. We sued the school board, the Boy Scouts, the American Legion. She was trying to change the world, to remove the weight of gender from my life and from the lives of others."

Dennis (giggling): "Is that why she called you Jen?"

Jen: "It's short for Jennifer." She falls silent and stares thoughtfully at the camera. "Perhaps there's something in what you say. My mother couldn't bear the idea of there being two sexes. She wanted everybody to be alike. 'Without the weight of sex, we could all fly,' she used to say. I wanted to please her so I adopted a neutral style. People used to stop me on the streets and say, 'Are you a little boy or a little girl?' 'Neither,' I would tell them."

Kelly: "If you are interested in helping the SAVE THE KANGAROOS FUND, send your contributions to this address." She holds up a hand-lettered sign.

Saul returns with our drinks. "What's happening?" he says.

"Nothing so far. Kelly's telling them about the plight of the kangaroos."

Dennis: "How'd you get interested in men?"

Kelly: "We're not interested in men."

Dennis: "You married one, didn't you?"

Kelly: "Saul's different. Most men are too competitive. They can't bear to be told the truth. I used to live in the Outback. One of my brothers kept mice. He fed his rodents high protein matter, created romantic cages filled with bits of soft carpet he had stolen from people's clotheslines. He piped in love songs. 'I am trying to replicate human society among the rodents,' he told the family.

"What you're really trying to do is get your mice to

reproduce,' I said. 'It is clearly a case of womb envy.' He denied it, but a short time later he let all his mice go."

Jen: "Saul isn't like that."

Dennis: "No?"

Jen: "He never tries to compete with us."

Dennis: "What does he do when he is with you?"

Kelly: "We spend a lot of time eating. The entire family gets together every Sunday afternoon for a long brunch."

Jen: "We usually overeat, and our gluttony fills us with self-disgust. It spills out in confessions, sins against the patriarch, as if our bloated stomachs were burping up evil. 'I spilled coffee on his *Art Digest*,' someone will say. 'I polished my table with a pair of his best undershorts,' someone else will confess. Another wife told how she gave him coffee that she said was decaffeinated and then pretended to be mystified when he couldn't sleep. And on and on. Sometimes we run out of real sins, and then we make up acts of betrayal and deceit."

Kelly (giggling): "Poor Saul. You should see his face during this outpouring. Eventually he cries out, 'No wonder I'm not well!' "

They should see his face now; he is glowering at the screen. "Poor Saul, indeed," he mutters. "Why are they on that disgusting show?"

"To save the kangaroos," I say.

Kelly: "He's a good sport, though."

Jen: "Yes. Considering all the troubles he had as a child. His mother was a lot like mine. She too wanted to wipe out gender. When he was a little boy, she gave him a doll. When his father came home and saw Saul undressing his doll, he let out a roar. 'Are you trying to drive me crazy?' he asked his wife. 'Crazy because I don't want my son to grow up with a coarse and insensitive nature?' she replied. 'I gave him a doll to temper his crude ways.' His father seized the doll and threw it out the window. 'I'll show you crude ways,' he yelled. Saul wept; his mother vowed never to talk to her husband again as long as she

170

lived; his little sister crept downstairs and claimed posses-
sion of the doll. Ever since, Saul has had a craving for
women."

Dennis: "What do you mean?"

Jen: "I mean this single event set up a chain reaction,
a lifelong need to compensate for the lost doll. Women
were his only recourse. Each time he is alone with a wife
he feels compelled to undress her, to complete that action
aborted by his father so long ago. He goes about it slowly,
precisely, as though carrying out a forgotten ritual. For he
has never recovered from that traumatic evening his father
seized the doll and prevented him from ever seeing what
was under her clothes."

Dennis: "Is that what he does with you girls?"

Kelly: "Fuck off."

Jen: "Ours is an intellectual relationship. We spend
our time in illuminating conversations. He knows more
about contemporary life than anybody. He was the first to
notice that decoration had lost its relevance. And he was
also the first to notice that decoration had regained its
relevance."

Dennis (bored and restless): "What do you do for
fun?"

Kelly: "There's always something going on. Life is
very interesting when you live it with a number of people."

Dennis: "I mean bed fun. What part does he play in
your games?"

Jen: "It's none of your business."

Dennis: "Don't be that way. Our audience is always
looking for inspiration. Share some of your sexual insights
with us."

Kelly: "Get lost."

Dennis: "C'mon, fellas, get real. All those lonely in-
somniacs out there are looking for guidance, looking for
inspiration."

Kelly and Jen look at each other and giggle. Dennis
twists and pulls at his black beading.

Dennis: "Give us a break."

Jen: "Our mouths are sealed."

Dennis: "You got a complex? That's the way I hear it. You got a complex, a guilt attitude, a pathology you ain't able to resolve."

Jen: "We don't have a complex."

Dennis: "I sense a bad ambivalence you two girls are suffering from."

Jen: "Not me."

Dennis: "What I'm seeing is a heavy-duty identity crisis."

Jen: "I am proud of our relationship with Saul."

Kelly: "Likewise."

Dennis: "You're unreal. From where I sit, you got this fear thing."

Jen: "You've got to be kidding. Frightened? Us?"

Dennis: "Yes, you. A phobic-panic re: marriage."

Jen: "Not us. Ours is a participatory relationship. Each one of us has a role. Lovers and lovees, if you know what I mean."

Dennis: "I'm sorry, sweetheart, but you'll have to speak up. Stop mumbling words."

Kelly: "He's being deliberately obtuse."

Jen: "It's all that beading."

Dennis: "Bleeding?"

Kelly: "You see what I mean?"

Dennis: "Okay, if that's the way you want to play it, be my guests. But don't blame me when people make judgments. If you want everybody to think shame is the name of the game, it's no skin off my nose."

Jen: "Shame is not the name of the game. It's more like a sacred ritual. First he undresses us. Then he withdraws. He stands in the doorway of the closet and tells us what to do. He orchestrates our pleasure, which is his pleasure too. 'How happy I am,' he says. His presence intensifies our enjoyment. His participation validates our love.

"Afterward, we discuss everything, what it was we liked best, our favorite hold, etc. We describe our fantasies,

172

the key pleasure points on our anatomy. He needs to know these things because he is planning to write a book about women, a history and theory of the aesthetics of pleasure. He intends to devote an entire chapter to us. He has already made many preliminary notes. His interest in us, his pleasure in our pleasure, makes us happy. It is as though we are creating a community of loving women that the world, through Saul, can understand and embrace.

"My mother used to say, 'Someday gender will be banished.' When Saul is with us, that day seems close."

Saul turns off the television and stares at the darkened screen. "What did I do to deserve this?" he says.

"Actually she made the whole thing sound extremely intellectual. . . ."

"Every flake in New York was probably watching."

". . . as though the three of you were engaged in an important research project . . ."

"Watching and salivating."

". . . a project that would ultimately be of benefit to all mankind."

"This is no time for levity. I thought they were my friends," Saul says.

"They are your friends," I say.

"I feel betrayed."

I mutter reassurances, automatic comforts. But as soon as Saul goes to the bathroom, I open up my book.

A grievous punishment is upon me. Now I am in a dark place, a dungeon waiting the will of the King. For I did not heed his edict. Instead, behind our dwelling place I built another dwelling place, a place of beauty, of secret rooms and fenestrations to admit within its walls the midday sun. Bold heights, interiors of noble proportions, recesses wherein a pair could hold a secret discourse. Now it is but a remembered thing, for upon discovery they burned it.

As they might burn me. For they call me a

173

witch. Only one under the spell of the devil would be so wayward, they say. "My work is fairer than a summer day," I say, for I will not be daunted by my inquisitors. It will be done, if not in this life, in the next.

My daughters I will never see again, but their days will be more spacious than mine. That is my solace.

I close the book, haunted by my Lady Jane X, forbidden to do her work, punished for her vision and daring. And all the others through the centuries since—the poets, the architects, the scientists—silenced, exiled to the kitchens and nurseries because of their sex. I think of the mothers imagining always a larger frame, immense changes for their daughters. Always a generation away from the time when gender will be banished, always a generation away from the Promised Land.

13

Gregory, Saul's lawyer, is showing us a video. On the screen, a group of men are emerging from a courthouse. They cover their faces with hats or shield them with their hands. Unable to see where they are going, they stumble as they walk. "You see here the worst aspects of a criminal mentality," Gregory says, "a body language that shrieks guilt." Now the scene switches to another courthouse. The same bunch of criminals are emerging. "Watch closely," Gregory says. The men are smiling. They look straight at the camera and wave. One of the criminals holds up his hands in a V reminiscent of the middle Nixon.

"I want you to note the difference," Gregory says. His voice is solemn, as if he were teaching us a prayer. "In the first scene everything about them is wrong—their posture, the aggression on their faces, their attempts to conceal themselves. Their every gesture screams out to all the world, 'I am guilty!' In the second scene, you get a totally different impression: people who have nothing to hide, who proclaim their innocence in the open, friendly way they face the camera." He tells one of his assistants to run these scenes again. "Pay close attention," he says. And we do as he bids, fastening our eyes on the screen, following the criminals' every move, every gesture.

It is evening. We are gathered in the loft. Everybody except Valery and Josh is here. Valery is in a play and will join us later; Josh is attending a concert of healing sounds with the family of a classmate. Gregory sits in a chair facing the rest of us. He glances from one person to the next, pausing to study each face as if he were memorizing a subject of great complexity.

"Most legal people don't care what a client looks like. All they think about is the law. I happen to have a broader perspective. I believe the persons behind a crime matter, that how they impress the world goes a long way toward affecting the outcome of their case. The Mafia-with-a-human-face campaign is a perfect example. It enabled the public to see organized crime not as an antisocial activity but merely as another way of doing business, alternative methods of competing in our free-market economy. Do you hear what I'm saying? Do you see where this is taking us? Image. That's what we're talking about. Image."

Gregory is the lawyer you hire when you have no case, when all the facts point to illegal acts for which there is no legitimate defense. Gregory conducts his cases less from a legal standpoint than as a public relations campaign. He is counseling us on our behavior, for, as he says, "The entire family is on trial."

Evelyn found Gregory. "He is a master of illusion," she told Saul. "He specializes in hopelessness, cases without argument, people destined to spend years of their lives in jail." She warned Saul not to be overly critical. "If you don't like this one, you're on your own." The trial is less than a month away.

In preparation for Gregory's visit, Saul has strewn academic journals across the long table, a newspaper picture of himself with the Mayor at a dedication of a building we renovated, and a model of a rooftop gazebo for which we won a prize. But it is hard to separate these testimonials to his accomplishments from all the other clutter on the table.

Saul's mania for collecting things has gotten completely out of hand. In addition to the antique tools he is always bringing home, he has bought the collected works of William Borden, an eighteenth-century landscape architect who believed in labyrinths; three miniature copies of the Metropolitan tower that he found at a flea market; a bronze clock in the shape of a bird; a bunch of glass grapes. Danger has unhinged him. He feels the need to replicate his childhood, to build a cocoon out of things.

He has falsified the past. His mother is no longer neglectful, his father no longer dour. Even his cousin, the yo-yo champ, has taken on a new coloration. Now Saul remembers clambering through alleyways with him, rescuing kittens.

Saul's chaos has crept into our living quarters. Like some slimy creature emerging from the deep with the intention of engulfing the earth, his exoneration document is taking over the loft. Scattered over the table are unsorted clippings, unopened mail, pens, scissors, a magnifying glass, scores of periodicals waiting to be carved up. Stacks of unread newspapers climb the walls. A jar of glue has spilled across the floor.

Gregory arrived at the loft with many assistants, young men who take notes, run the video, move chairs, carry equipment. One of them seems to be solely employed as a replenisher; he leaves the loft repeatedly and returns loaded down with goat milk yogurt, blue corn chips, cioccolati biscotti, sushi pizza, all of which disappear down Gregory's gullet as if he had hired himself out as a garbage disposal unit. "I have an abnormal metabolism," he tell us, "a volcano inside that consumes calories faster than I can replenish them." He compares his stomach to an ancient Mayan settlement, each new snack a virgin sacrificed to appease the god of hunger.

Saul doesn't like this comparison. He doesn't like

Gregory. He cannot bear to have smart men hanging around. "The Mayans never sacrificed virgins," he says.

"Well, somebody did," Gregory says.

The rest of us find the contradictions in Gregory reassuring. His custom-made suit, radiant face, numerous assistants, and certitude announce success; his obesity, shortness of breath, gluttony, sweat, some fatal weakness. This combination makes him human and accessible. Watching him is like watching a play in which two opposing forces—his appetites and his achievements—are locked in a mortal struggle.

"There is a single word that sums up the image we are striving to project." Gregory sits before us, solemn and wise, a Buddha, a Socrates. "What is that one word?" he says. We look at one another, wondering whether we are supposed to guess or if Gregory intends to tell us. After a moment he whispers the word: "Identification." He falls silent again to give us time for the information to sink in to our collective consciousness. "Identification," he says. "Repeat that after me."

The entire family mumbles the word once and then again. "Identification. Identification."

"What do I mean by that? Polygamy with a human face, that's what we are striving for—to instill in the public at large a sense of recognition, of familiarity, so that your domestic arrangements will seem ordinary and normal. We want the man in the street to be able to look at you, not as freaks but as people no different from himself. We want to help the public accept the idea that seven wives is not necessarily peculiar. The key is identification, creating a face that people will not only recognize but will be able to empathize with. There are men out there looking for women. We want to make them feel it isn't all that difficult. We want to make them think, If this joker, this ordinary person, can acquire seven wives, anything is possible."

"Believe me, it isn't all that easy," Saul says. "It requires courage, the determination to put the lives of others ahead of your own. It requires—"

178

"I never said it was easy," Gregory says. "I am talking image, I am talking about the impression we mean to convey. Our task is to make both the public and the court see you not as an exploiter of women, but some poor slob who stumbled into illegalities the way people walk into dog poop."

"That is not the impression I am likely to convey," Saul says. Evelyn makes a warning noise in her throat that silences him.

"Not to worry, we'll create you out of little bits and pieces."

While his replenishment assistant hands Gregory a diet sangria and a sour-cream puff dotted with caviar, another mops at his face with a lavender-scented Handi Wipe. He licks at his cream puff solemnly, continuing to study us.

"You're just one factor in this case," he says to Saul. "Everybody in this room is on trial. You, you, and you." As he swallows the last of his cream puff, he stares at each wife in turn. What does he see? I wonder. What kind of image do we project? His scrutiny unnerves me. I stare down at my hands. How could anyone identify with us? The nervousness is widespread. Jen and Kelly clutch at each other, Connie rattles her gold chains, Evelyn clicks her ballpoint pen in and out, Beryl drums on her rounded belly.

"Not to worry," Gregory says again. "I like what I see—the diversity, the cultural variety you represent. A group of women, all collecting together to marry this one man. It is like a public opinion poll with everybody saying yes, implying widespread approval for this particular arrangement. This diversity will help our case, make the court realize that this isn't some freakish cult group getting together to perform abominations, but a bunch of normal, hardworking, tax-paying citizens. Strivers. People who add to the gross national product. We want the court to realize that as long as people like you exist, the system will hold."

Saul says, "The system has already collapsed."

Gregory chides him. "Gloom is counterproductive," he says. "That attitude will go against you. It inspires bleak thoughts in others. We must project an air of cheerful optimism, as if we were telling the world, I have nothing to fear, nothing to hide. We must think good thoughts—about things that make us happy—crusty bread, fresh caviar, strawberries."

"Strawberries." A triumphant look crosses Saul's face. "A perfect example of the system's collapse: the pandering to jaded appetites regardless of the environmental consequences."

A startled Gregory gropes for a glass of Perrier while Saul seizes his exoneration volume and thumbs through it. When he finds what he is looking for, he proceeds to read.

" 'Genetically engineered antifrost in the strawberry fields causes widespread concern among scientists. "They are releasing unknown forms of life into the environment," a leading biologist says.' "

"It is the known forms of life I am concerned with," Gregory says. "The judge and the jury. The fact that they know and we know it is against the law to marry seven women. We cannot deny that seven marriages took place. Therefore, our only hope is to encourage their understanding and sympathy so that they will be compelled to say to themselves, It could happen to me. What we are going for is a love that knows no bounds, a man so bighearted he will jeopardize his very freedom for the sake of his family."

Saul relaxes. A smile crosses his face as he glances from one wife to another like a lion surveying his pride.

Gregory, munching on a veal cutlet, bids one of his assistants take a Polaroid picture of each of us. He deploys a second to go among us and collect our vital statistics—age, height, country of origin, political convictions if any, etc. Each time a Polaroid emerges, a third runs with it to Gregory, who begins to mark it up with yellow crayon even before it has fully developed. All this activity makes one

180

feel that Gregory has divided like a cell into several new Gregorys.

He marks up the Polaroids as if he is editing our essence. Now he is marking up mine. Each time he draws a line, I feel a part of me has been demolished—my face, my body, my feet. Something inside me shrivels. I turn against my flawed self, my unplucked eyebrows, my hair still in its pyramid mode.

Finally Gregory looks up from his task and says, "I have never seen a nicer, healthier bunch of people. To look at you, you would never know you were all engaged in group marriage. Believe me, you are not what the court will expect. And that is in our favor."

On all sides, I hear people inhale, as if only now did any of us dare to breathe. Gregory gives us a brilliant smile.

"If you don't mind my saying so, you, young lady, are gorgeous. Gorgeous." He repeats the word as if it were a morsel, something to chew on and savor between mouthfuls of pâté, sorbet, petits fours, etc. He is addressing Connie. She is wearing a three-piece chintz suit adorned with nineteenth-century flowers, the official Vanguard Vicki uniform. Here and there, in discreet places, she has snipped little pieces of her suit for clients who are considering this particular fabric for curtains and/or slipcovers.

"I like your style. It tells the world something about yourself. That you have old-fashioned values. That you put service to the public ahead of vanity. That you're not afraid to take a few risks. This is the look that will tell the judge, This family is okay; this is a mainstream family that deserves respect."

Connie, looking dazed and ecstatic, nods. "My highest goal in life is to bring a little beauty into people's lives."

"I guessed as much." Gregory turns to one of his assistants. "In the seating plan make sure she has a conspicuous place."

Evelyn too is ecstatic. "He sees things that nobody else sees," she says. "His is the mind of a visionary."

"Why do you think I took this case? Because it's easy, a piece of cake? No! It's a challenge, an opportunity to use all of my skills and talents. For we are not just defending a criminal, we are altering the perceptions of what constitutes a family. Everybody knows the nuclear family has crested, but nobody knows what will take its place. You, my friends, are the wave of the future."

Now he is treading on Saul's territory, the expert on all things new. Saul starts to say something, but Evelyn clutches at his wrist, whispering, "Let him finish. Let him develop his thesis."

"Stand up, darling." Gregory is studying Beryl now like a scientist looking at something rare and puzzling. He asks her to walk across the room. "Is that a pillowcase you're wearing?"

Beryl nods.

"How original." His shining eyes narrow. Sweat pours down his face. "Originality is an admirable quality," he says. "But not for us. The court won't like you if you wear a pillowcase to the trial."

His criticism offends Beryl. "It happens to be a hundred percent cotton," she says.

"Even so, the judge will look upon it as a slur to his dignity."

"My entire birthing class adopted this style."

Her opposition makes Gregory nervous. "Food," he says. He shuts his eyes until the replenishment assistant appears. Gregory gulps down a peach melba. Restored, his face takes on a rapt expression. We watch him thinking. "What about a nice middy blouse and skirt, circa 1900. The kind of outfit that says sweetness, innocence, even a touch of virginity."

"It's not me," Beryl says.

Gregory closes his eyes once more as if he is removing himself from our case.

The room grows quiet. A tragic expression fixes itself on Beryl's face. She glances at each of us in turn as though searching for an ally. Finding no support, she sighs. "All right, I'll wear a middy to the trial. There's nothing I wouldn't do, even if it means sacrificing my integrity, to help Saul's cause."

Since the Beryl doll failed, Beryl has rejoined the family. The toy manufacturer, fearing a boycott by the Religious Right of his war toys line, withdrew the Beryl doll from production. Boxes of dolls lie in our workroom gathering sawdust. "I am no longer subject to the pressures of the marketplace," Beryl says.

The attack on the Beryl dolls intimidated her; the strung-up dolls were like atrocities involving small babies. "I never want to be in a scene like that again," Beryl said.

Whatever the cause—this attack, feelings of guilt over Saul's arrest, or simply hormonal changes—Beryl has changed for the better. She is more sensitive to the feelings and needs of others and less certain that she is the center of the universe. "How are you?" she says each time she appears. "What's new?" She is also learning how to share. She squeezes off little pieces of her carrot cupcakes and offers them to others. The Ding Dongs that she now prefers to Mallomars, she also passes around. "There are plenty more where these came from," she says. For the sake of the baby, she has moderated her diet, adding sometimes an apple and sometimes a pear to her meals.

With the change in Beryl has come a change in Saul. He seems less down on her, more hopeful that she will be able to cope. He is almost reconciled to her having a baby.

Now, at her willingness to sacrifice her integrity, he says, "I appreciate the offer. But I can't let you do it. A middy and skirt would falsify you." He turns to Gregory to explain. "Beryl is post-modern. Everything about her is in a future tense. Her lifestyle, her job, her clothes—all speak of impending disaster. To deny that is to negate her identity."

"The problem is, people don't like that look," Gregory says.

Carried away by his need to establish his credentials, Saul persists. "She lives in a time of scarcity, in a post-abundant world when the entire population will be compelled to forage in garbage cans and dumpsters. To dress her in things of the past is absurd. It denies her prescience, her profound sense of catastrophe."

Saul's description of Beryl dazzles her. She looks from one to another of us to make sure we have fully appreciated his words. Face mournful, arms crossed in front of her, she assumes the pose of Michelangelo's *Pietà*. All she lacks is a dead Christ on her lap. "It's all right," she says. "I'll wear whatever they want me to wear no matter how peculiar I look."

"Never," Saul says. "We cannot let you violate your essence."

Gregory's digestive system grows deranged. He farts, burps, groans. His stomach growls. His replenishment assistant hands him a baby zucchini, a baby potato, a baby eggplant. Dripping oil from the baby vegetables on Beryl's Polaroid, he X's out her photograph with his yellow crayon, as if trying to demolish the original. "Okay, it's your funeral. The court will see a pillowcase and think, irreverence."

"Post-modernism is irreverent . . ." Saul says.

"I'll wear the middy," Beryl says.

"She was with you during the arrest," Gregory says. "They will call her up to testify. If she isn't properly clothed, the case will crumble."

"I know a place on Canal Street where they sell vintage middies," Beryl says.

". . . its excesses stemming from a gallant sense of loss," Saul says.

"You think it was easy for the Mafia to assume a human face?" Gregory says. "You think you're the only one with an integrity problem?"

The arrival of Valery interrupts their argument. She comes bursting in, brimming over with excitement and vitality. "I didn't bother to change," she says. In her costume, an admiral's jacket over a tattered skirt of woven leaves, she looks savage and beautiful. All the men stare at her—Saul, Gregory, his assistants—the same faraway expression on every face.

The play she is appearing in is a post-nuclear-holocaust musical. All the survivors have caught a radiation disease and evolved into women. They are trying to figure out how to reproduce through parthenogenesis so they can be fruitful and multiply. Valery has a song in the play. It goes, "Once I was an admiral, proud and brave."

Saul and I attended a performance together. We had never seen Valery act before, except when she was doing her emoting exercises. "She makes you believe she was an admiral in a former existence," Saul said during the intermission.

"I find the whole thing totally unreal," Jen said later.

"No more unreal than your performance on late-night TV," he said.

"Nobody saw us," Jen said.

"We were merely trying to publicize the plight of the kangaroos," Kelly said.

They both try to minimize the damage, but everyone is mad at them. "It was cheap popularity. . . . Showing off. . . . Trying to act interesting and mysterious."

First remorseful, then full of rationalizations, Jen and Kelly now act put-upon. "Why are you picking on us?" they say.

In the course of the play, Valery sings several songs. A romance with a flower develops, for in this post-holocaust world, species intermingle. The flower was once a neurosurgeon. In his former existence, he moved people's nerves from one place to another in an effort to alleviate their symptoms. The flower sings, "I would like my old life back." Everybody in the audience weeps. At the final curtain, Valery plucks the flower to thunderous applause.

"Tonight was fabulous," Valery says. "When the neurosurgeon tried to pollinate me, the entire audience got to their feet and cheered."

"Valery, this is Gregory," we say.

Gregory looks as if he would like to take a bite out of

her, as he explains to Valery what he is trying to do. "The message we are going for is ordinary people: the man on the street, the family next door, people in trouble who will break the jury's heart, fill the judge's soul with mercy."

He asks Valery to take a walk. "Pretend you are a housewife with a shopping list on her mind, heavy responsibilities. Children with orthodontic problems, a husband who errs."

Valery walks across the floor muttering to herself. "Rice," she says. "Butter. Cilantro." In her admiral's jacket and skirt of leaves, she looks like a hooker trying to play out a client's fantasies.

"Do it again," Gregory says. Although she has studied acting in all its ramifications, as a worried housewife she is totally unconvincing. "It won't do," Gregory says.

"I need to study the part."

"I'll help you. Come to my office tomorrow afternoon." An assistant hands Valery Gregory's card.

"She doesn't have the time," Saul says. "Her part in the play is very demanding. She needs her rest."

"It's all right," Valery says. "It's the least I can do." She abandons triumph for self-blame. "You know, none of this would have happened if I hadn't joined the family," she tells Gregory. We all try to deny it. "There's no denying it," she says. "I was the straw that broke the camel's back. He couldn't cope with the complicated schedules. Ask Evelyn if you doubt me."

"There were other factors," Evelyn says.

"You need your rest," Saul says.

"We'll work it all out later," Gregory says. "It's getting late. Meanwhile, we need to work on your image," he says to Saul.

"My image? What's wrong with my image?" he says, running a hand through his perfect curls, fondling his expensive tweed jacket.

"It's too New York," Gregory says. He stares at Saul, jots something on a note pad, whispers to one of his assistants.

186

Saul grows nervous, defensive. "I have some ideas of my own. I have been working on an exoneration document." He gestures at the mess in front of him. Gregory reaches across the table and pulls some clippings toward him. "I want to be tried in context," Saul says. "I want the world to get a perspective on the charges against me. Compared to the thefts, the murders, the vicious plunder of our resources I've been documenting, my crime is a joke."

Gregory glances at the clippings without really seeing them. After a moment he pushes them back at Saul. "This is the reason a layman cannot have a voice in his own defense," he says.

"If the accused cannot be heard, what point is a trial? Who will speak for the innocent defendant?" Saul, noticing grease smears from Gregory's oily hands all over his clippings, pulls out his pocket handkerchief and rubs at the stains.

"Prejudice is what you will elicit if you try to introduce other crimes," Gregory says. "We have a different strategy entirely."

Saul tosses aside his handkerchief and rises to his feet. He paces back and forth the length of the loft. Gregory beckons an assistant, who stacks the papers and Polaroids and notes scattered in front of him and drops them into a briefcase.

"It's late," Gregory says. "We haven't even had our dinner yet." He shifts in his chair.

"Saul, the trial is less than a month away," Evelyn says. "At least listen to what he has to say."

Saul sits down and sags in his chair. Gregory closes his eyes as if drawing a curtain. After a moment he opens them and stares at Saul. "The women will be center stage. We will group them together in a conspicuous place."

"Whatever you say," Saul says. He looks from one wife to another as if hoping for some show of solidarity.

"In this way, you will be barely visible, a speck on the landscape, just a vague presence."

Saul laughs. "How are you going to make that happen? Absent me from my own trial?" Again he looks around the room, inviting us to share his amusement.

"It can be done." Gregory's somber look silences Saul. "We are going for victim with a capital *V*: a man who blundered into matrimony the way some men blunder into a gambling hall and lose their life savings."

Saul looks disgusted. "I am not an actor," he says. "How could I ever convey such shoddy qualities?"

"We'll put you in an ill-cut suit, a cheap street tie, clothes that fit badly, that clash. Mr. Everyman. What we are going for is a dressed-down look that conveys 'victim' combined with 'sincerity,' the sort of man people would buy something from not because they expect it to work but because they feel sorry for him."

"Jesus," Sauls says. "An ill-fitting suit. You expect me to go to court dressed like that?"

Evelyn takes his hand and strokes it, the rest of us mutter words of comfort. "Ill-fitting is in this season. . . . The baggy look is the next wave. . . . Anyway, whatever you wear you can't help but look nice."

But Gregory isn't finished. "Oh, I know it isn't easy to dress down. It takes guts, a certain raw courage."

"Okay. Okay. I'll turn myself into a cipher—a slob, if that's what it takes. Obviously the entire family seems to want me to look ill-dressed."

"Then the only other thing is your hair."

"My hair?" Saul says.

"It will have to be shorn of curls." A stricken look crosses Saul's face. Gregory holds up a hand as if he is directing traffic. "Nothing drastic. I'm not talking marine recruit. A modified crew will do."

14

Josh presses a button; he fiddles with a dial. Bleaksville leaps upon the screen. We glimpse trees, grass, buildings, buses, hordes of people; they flash before our eyes like a landscape viewed from a fast-moving train.

These scenes were taken the day we arrived in Bleaksville for the trial. Now Josh has edited his tape and we are gathered in the loft to view the proceedings.

The camera pans in on the municipal buildings that border one end of the square. It pauses before the town hall. The sign above the entrance that once read: HOME OF UNDESIRED THINGS. YOUR GARBAGE IS OUR LIVELIHOOD has been altered, the word "undesired" crossed out and replaced by the word "unusual." Ribbons of masking tape have eradicated the second sentence altogether. Behind the municipal buildings a huge structure is rising, dominating the landscape, shadowing the square. Then Bleaksville disappears and Josh stands in the foreground, a paper in his hand. He reads:

"To understand the events of the trial, there is something you must know. Since my father last visited Bleaks-

189

ville, the town has been bought up by a Japanese conglomerate now in the process of converting all home industries to automation. Every household is wired to a terminal. A Japanese monitor has been watching while the housewives weave a place mat out of computer paper margins, his task to figure out not only how to do it cheaper and faster, but also how to make the product more attractive to the sophisticated East. As a result, new place mats that look woven, but are actually stamped out, are replacing the old. Each household has been provided with a little stamping machine, and the handwoven proto place mats are now collector's items, a folk craft that the Japanese send back to Japan and sell for big yen.

"The entire town of Bleaksville has been transformed into an outpost of a modern industrial empire. The building that is going up behind the courthouse is a laboratory designed to research ways of turning disposable items into something else. Even before the lab is completed, work is going on in some of its lower floors. Operating with a three-shift work force, it is open twenty-four hours a day. Researchers have already discovered new ways of recycling the padded mailing envelope. They are currently studying the disposable diaper. The sheriff and his boys are now security guards. Gone are their paunches, and their plaid shirts have been replaced by sober industrial jackets. All street signs are in both Japanese and English. Adjacent to each McDonald's and Wendy's is a sushi bar. The lone movie house, closed for many years, has reopened with a samurai festival. 'Our goal is twofold: not merely to industrialize but also to bring enlightenment to the submerging West,' the Japanese say."

Josh looks up from his paper and smiles brilliantly at the camera. "Now we will return to the scene of the crime."

The scene shifts to the grassy square. It is morning. The sun is shining. [In order to record everything from the moment of our arrival, Josh has leaped out of the still-moving vehicle.] His camera is trained on the huge old trees just coming into leaf that form a corridor to the

190

courthouse. Between the trees are other trees, smaller, more shapely, that have recently been planted by the conglomerate. Birds perch in the trees, local birds in the large old trees, oriental birds in the newer ones. Now the camera leaves the trees and moves over the square jammed with people and then back to the stretch limo that brought us here, where it pauses, waiting for us to emerge.

[It was Gregory who insisted we travel that way. "They like their celebrities to have class," he said. "What about identification?" we said. "Now we are talking beyond identification to aspiration. We are talking about dreams." The stretch limo had a snack bar. We ate peanut butter and sardine sandwiches all the way up. Nobody liked the sandwiches, but we were nervous and there was nothing else to do. Gregory, who traveled in a separate limo with his contingent of assistants, had confiscated all the good snacks: the Brie en croute, the goat cheese, the layered vegetable terrine.]

Now the scene cuts to a flashback of the replenishment assistant running back and forth between limos switching snacks. Suddenly he notices Josh taking footage of the exchange. A dramatic encounter ensues. The assistant runs toward the camera, fists clenched as though to smash it, his posture and expression reminiscent of the emoting once seen in silent movies. [This part of the film wavers, suggesting drunkenness on the part of the operator, for in order to protect his equipment, Josh was forced to run backward, shooting as he retreated.]

While the camera waits for us to emerge, it moves back to the municipal buildings and pauses before the Bleaksville courthouse, built in the thirties: a box made out of glass bricks, a Tudor entryway flanked by two enormous stone animals of an unknown species. At the base of these statues is incised the words THE BLEAKS, and a sign above the Tudor doorway reads BLEAKSVILLE COURT-HOUSE AND DEPARTMENT OF RECORDS. Japanese calligraphy has been superimposed on all these signs. A group of

Japanese businessmen stands in front of the Bleaks while another group takes pictures of them.

The grassy square is filled with people. Josh has captured a kaleidoscopic view of the scene. His camera picks out a group of men wearing leather bomber jackets despite the warmth of the day. Zipped halfway, the jackets reveal bare, hairy chests. Amid this hair, gold teddy-bear pendants dangle from chains. The pendants, selling widely throughout the metropolitan area, signify Saul, now known as the teddy-bear lover. The leather-jacketed men hold signs: GAYS FOR GROUP MARRIAGE. POLYGAMOUS RIGHTS. CONSENTING ADULTS SAY YES. SAVE THE SAUL. POLYGAMISTS ARE AN ENDANGERED SPECIES.

The camera moves on to a contingent from the Religious Right standing at attention in a military line, holding up maimed Beryl dolls on sticks and a banner saying POLYGAMY IS A DISEASE. The entire contingent is munching on hot pretzels.

All over the grassy square signs bob, banners billow. A group of free speech proponents hold up a banner proclaiming FREE SAUL—SUPPORT THE FIRST AMENDMENT. A group called Architects for Appropriate Structures has fashioned signs in the shape of sinister skyscrapers oozing money. Across the skyscrapers are written TRY THE REAL CRIMINALS—DEVELOPERS ARE DESTROYING OUR CITY. People for a Polygamous Future, Widows for Amour—these groups also carry statements in support of Saul; Americans for Monogamy, Citizens for Decency, and Families for a Nuclear Future hold posters denouncing Saul and demanding he be jailed. Japanese photographers circulate among the demonstrators, taking hi-tech three-dimensional pictures which they sell back to the subjects.

Also circulating among the demonstrators is a person in clown makeup. He is selling poster-sized pages of an art calendar depicting erotic Japanese scenes. Josh holds his camera close to one, and we see groups of Japanese figures engaged in intricate erotic holds. Evelyn objects to its inclusion. "It is pornographic," she says.

"When you are going for a harsh naturalism," Josh says, "everything is pornographic."

The Japanese conglomerate has bused scores of street vendors into Bleaksville from the city and rented each of them a space on the grassy lawn. The vendors have set up carts and started charcoal fires or spread their wares out on the grass. Their wares consist of Saul candles and Saul earrings and teddy-bear pendants and glossy photographs of the family. One merchant has propped counterfeit Beryl dolls against a crate. Another is selling an unauthorized biography of the family.

[We bought a copy and read it on the return journey. In this version of our life, Saul lies around the house all day drinking beer and watching Paravision on his VCR while his wives risk their lives cleaning office windows on high floors. He is a crystal freak. Crystals of all sizes and shapes overflow from the shelves and bookcases. In the evening, after work, he forces the wives to polish these crystals. The subtitle of the biography is *Slaves to Love*. Evelyn intends to sue the publisher.]

Near the limo an enormous swordfish dangles above a sushi cart. Each time a customer approaches, the vendor hacks a piece from it and carves it into delicate slices. When the driver opens the limo door, the smell of the dangling swordfish assaults us. "It is the smell of slaughter," Kelly says. Holding her nose, she refuses to get out of the limo.

Connie emerges first. This part of the film is shaky and out of focus, for as soon as she steps out the media converge upon the limo, elbowing Josh out of the way. He fights his way back, pushes to within a dozen yards of the car, and keeps his camera going as, one by one, we emerge.

Connie is wearing custom-made high-heeled chintz boots to match her suit. The camera pans in on her as she stands before the open door, smoothing her clothes. She tucks her shirt into her skirt, tugs at her vest. She has overdone the Vanguard Vicki look, for not only does she have boots in matching chintz but a parasol, too, and a huge floppy hat. A score of photographers and TV crews surround her. They train their cameras on her, thrust microphones in her face, demand a statement. In halting Italian, Connie says, "*Non e possibile*," for we have all agreed that only Evelyn will talk to the media. They press against her, shouting "What?" and insisting that she make a statement. Connie pulls a phrase book from her voluminous purse and turns the pages searching for an appropriate response. "*Arrivederci*," she says. The reporters write this down.

Then, turning from them, she waves and smiles at the waiting crowd. A contingent of widows from her support group rush forward holding a sign. IF LOVE IS A CRIME, WE ARE ALL CRIMINALS, the sign says. The spectators applaud. Gripping her parasol between her legs, Connie raises her arms above her head and clasps her hands like a victorious boxer. Her hat flies away.

Valery emerges next, huddled over herself, looking as if she had developed curvature of the spine. Despite the heat of the day, she is wrapped in a full-length sweater coat, the very one she wore the day we first met her. The post-holocaust musical has closed for political reasons, but Valery blames herself for the play's demise. "My admiral was too tentative," she said. "I should have projected more authority, a person accustomed to giving orders and expecting them to be carried out." We told her she was wrong. We argued that the theme of the play was to question gender roles and that her portrayal of the admiral had struck the right note. It did no good. Determined to reap the blame, Valery turned against herself. Her huddled posture dramatizes her failure. The media surround her, yell questions, demand opinions. Valery gives them a tragic look. "Life is an absurdist joke," she says.

Now Beryl lumbers out of the limo dazed and confused, as if recently wakened from a deep sleep. She is wearing a middy and sailor pants that she found in a secondhand boutique on Canal Street. "It is the first outfit I have bought in many years," she said. The middy, of

194

World War II vintage, is sprinkled with saltwater stains as though it might have been involved in a drowning; a bullet hole pierces its collar, hinting at other sinister events. In order to get the pants over her pregnant stomach, Beryl chose a pair several sizes too large. In these clothes she looks like a street urchin, an orphan from an early Chaplin film. Nevertheless, the crowd lets out a collective sigh when she appears. "Isn't she adorable," people say. They try to break through the circle of media people for her auto-graph, thrust Beryl dolls at her to sign.

The Beryl doll has become a collector's item. Only a few still exist, although counterfeit dolls, made in Vermont kitchens and Chinatown sweatshops, have proliferated. They are nothing like the originals. The workmanship is shoddy, their faces blurred, their clothing made of some inferior fabric, so that the dye rubs off on the person holding the doll. As in the original, the Beryl baby pops out when the mother's stomach is pressed, but it is almost impossible to pop it in again.

Beryl scrutinizes each doll, for she will autograph only the authentic Beryls, and while she stands there signing some, rejecting others, the media shout questions at her. "Is he guilty?" they say. "Do you think the world should be free to make these unholy alliances?"

Beryl glares at the media, then, obviously recalling Gregory's counsel on image, gives them a brilliant smile. "We are all guilty," she says.

Just beyond the circle of her admirers, a lone child sits on the ground popping out the baby Beryl and clicking it back inside while its parents stand over it taking photo-graphs.

Now Evelyn alights, loaded down with documents and papers, among them a statement she has prepared for the media. She stands before the limo door, statement in hand, and starts to read. "If what we have done is criminal, then the meaning of crime must be redefined." She gets no further. The zipper on her skirt breaks and she grabs at it with both hands to keep it from sliding to her ankles.

The statement blows away along with all the other papers she was holding.

Connie and Valery start to run after the papers. I jump out of the limo and join them. Josh follows us with his camera. Like football players charging the opposition, we run through the crowd, hair blowing, eyes feverish. The fierce wind carries the papers aloft, where they hover in the sky like gulls. Some drift down and impale themselves on tree branches, others settle on telephone wires, where they flap like clothes hung out to dry. Still others, I am sure, end up in the pockets of memento seekers. We manage to retrieve just a handful of documents out of the scores we brought with us.

Gone are the depositions testifying to Saul's goodness that we so painstakingly collected: letters affirming his fine character, his probity, his reputable business practices. "He itemized every nail," a client wrote. "His workmanship was impeccable," another said. The lumberyard wrote, "He paid his bills on time." "He is a hands-on parent," the principal of Josh's school said.

Clutching at her skirt, Evelyn is trying to sort through the few remaining papers while the media thrust microphones at her, demanding to hear the rest of the statement. "Later," she mumbles and, thrusting her papers into the limo, she climbs back inside. Kelly and Jen jump out and raise their arms, their thumbs and index fingers joining in a circle. This acts as a signal. Dykes for Dichotomy, Women for a Same-sex Tax Exemption, etc. roar their approval.

"I need a safety pin," Evelyn calls out. She pokes her head out of the limo. "Does anyone have a safety pin?" A ring of pins dangles from Connie's Vanguard Vicki suit, ready for contingencies: a client needing to keep color samples fastened together, a loose valance. Connie hands her in a pin.

Josh pokes his camera inside the limo, shooting his father's clumsy attempts to pin Evelyn's skirt. This part of his video is dim, for the tinted windows filter the light.

Saul struggles to thrust the pin into the band of Evelyn's skirt; he sticks himself and curses. He sucks his bleeding finger while Evelyn attempts to fasten her skirt. Eventually she succeeds. "It was that last sardine," she says.

She climbs out backward, fearful that the crowd will notice the zipper gap. The media close in on her, demanding that she finish her statement. "No comment," Evelyn says, "until the trial is over." The media mutter angry remarks.

Evelyn is trying to soothe them when Saul alights. In his dark glasses, shorn hair, cheap, ill-fitting suit, he looks furtive and sleazy. The media crowd around him like a swarm of angry bees.

Forgotten are all the lessons we were taught about poise and confidence, the open smiles and small gestures of friendship that will win us widespread support. The orderly walk from the limo becomes a rout. We avert our faces, stumble, run, our body language shrieking guilt.

Music is playing everywhere. Rock and classical, jazz and country, they all merge as if the sounds of the world had been let loose in one cacophonic blast. As we fight our way along the walk leading to the courthouse, a street vendor rushes up and hands each of us a tofu hotdog while hordes of Japanese photographers take pictures. Someone hangs a teddy-bear pendant around Saul's neck. A black-suited, angry-looking man thrusts a petition at us supporting nuclear power and demands that we sign. The Religious Right decapitates a Beryl doll.

The camera leaves the family and moves around the grassy square. A section has been set aside for the citizens of Bleaksville. The Bleaksville High School band is playing "Have a Nice Day," while drum majorettes twirl and pirouette in front of them. Local women, wearing paper kimonos recycled from disposable hospital gowns and decorated with hand-painted chrysanthemums, are selling cottage crafts from booths. All the women are wearing three-D glasses. In addition to the neo-woven place mats, they are selling popsicle-stick trivets, toast warmers made out of padded mailing envelopes with cutouts from magazines pasted on, and Chinese takeout containers transformed into miniature greenhouses.

The camera rejoins us at the steps of the courthouse. Above us, flanked by his assistants, Gregory is holding a press conference. He is talking about himself, the cases that he won, the Mafia-with-a-human-face campaign. "This one will be a piece of cake," he says.

While Gregory talks he rubs his stomach. A look of pain crosses his face; his replenishment assistant appears and hands him a glass of Alka-Seltzer. He drinks it down and after a moment he belches. "That's better," he says.

He beams down at us, murmurs encouraging words. "What a day. Acquittal weather. Everybody walks on a day like this."

One by one, he shakes our hands, studies our appearance, fiddles with our outfits. Connie ascends first. He buttons her jacket, tidies her windblown hair, and then, after a moment's hesitation, unbuttons the jacket. Beryl is next, still munching on her tofu hotdog. Gregory wipes mustard from the corners of her mouth. He yanks out her middy bow and reties it; as he does so, he notices the bullet hole in the collar of the middy. He fiddles with it, trying to conceal the hole. He tucks the collar inside the middy, but it bunches into a little hump. He twists it, folds it, but it springs back into its original shape.

His inability to conceal the bullet hole brings on another attack. Groaning, he bangs at his midriff until he elicits a burp; then, dismissing Beryl, he turns his attention on Jen. He fluffs her sausage curls, which instantly collapse into limp spirals. He tightens Kelly's belt, undoes the top button of her shirt, and pulls back Valery's shoulders, each movement accompanied by a little sigh of pain.

Now it is Saul's turn. Gregory's hands are all over him, trying to smooth the wrinkles out of his cheap suit jacket, reknotting his tie, flattening his hair. Nothing helps. In his ill-fitting suit, with his hair erect like new-mown grass, Saul looks like a cheap hood. "I feel as if I am going to my own execution disguised as someone else," he says.

"Not to worry," Gregory says. "The presence of so many people will keep the court honest. They'll all be on their best behavior. And you: they won't even notice you. They'll be too busy playing to the spectators. You'll be lost in the crowd." Gregory swallows another Alka-Seltzer. Then he and Saul enter the courthouse together.

Inside the lobby, a Japanese court attendant sits in a booth selling tickets to the trial. Just beyond, another attendant stands posted beside a ticket collection stand. Saul passes by the booth and, ignoring the ticket taker, starts to walk inside the courtroom. "Stop!" the ticket taker screams. He demands a ticket from Saul.

"I'm the defendant," Saul says. "We're his wives," we say.

The ticket taker blocks our way. "No tickets, no trial," he says.

"That's fine with me," Saul says. He starts to walk out of the building. Gregory blocks his way. "If there's one thing the law hates, it's levity," he says.

"But this is outrageous," Saul says. "Surely there must be a law against making a defendant pay to get into his own trial?"

Gregory shrugs. "The law is a living entity," he says. Saul still refuses to pay. "I'll spring," Gregory says. "Put them all on my Visa." He buys everybody in the family a ticket.

Josh, recording this scene from the entryway, is the last of the family to enter. Gregory hands the attendant a ticket and gestures in Josh's direction. The attendant blocks Josh's way. "No camera in the court," the attendant says.

"But I am the defendant's little boy," Josh says. He has trained the camera on himself. "Without this footage, the record will be incomplete. I have taken pictures of every important event in my father's life. Each time a new wife came on the scene, I was there with my camera. Surely you cannot deny me the opportunity of recording his trial."

The attendant repeats his admonition. He shakes his head, waves a warning finger at Josh. Josh continues to argue. The attendant confers with another attendant. They both say, "No camera in the court."

Josh stands in the doorway pouting while, behind him, the waiting crowd mutters complaints. The court attendants stare at him, press a buzzer, and an official-looking person emerges from the courtroom. The attendants whisper, point at Josh. The official gives him a stern look. "Move," he says, "or else."

"Or else what?" Josh says. The official blows a whistle and two security guards appear. "Help," Josh says. Evelyn appears. "My mother is a lawyer," Josh says. The official threatens to cite him for contempt and obstruction.

"Take your video equipment out to the stretch limo," Evelyn says. "This is the real world."

Josh leaves the building, muttering "Some mother!"

The video ends. We stare at the darkened screen. Nobody moves. Nobody says anything. Finally Josh speaks. "Well?" he says.

"Well what?" we say.

"Say it. Without footage of the trial, my work is nothing."

"Oh, Josh, for heaven's sake, how can you be so self-centered with your poor father in prison?" Evelyn says.

Someone turns on the lights. We look at one another with melancholy faces. "It was a circus," Jen says. "Hopeless from beginning to end."

"I'll never forgive myself for hiring Gregory," Evelyn says.

"How could you know?"

"I should have known."

"We were all taken in by his manner. He seemed so sure of himself. He seemed to know exactly what he was doing."

200

"All theater, no substance," Evelyn says. "It should have been obvious from the start."

"There's no point blaming yourself, Evelyn," I say. "If we'd been able to hire a Supreme Court justice to defend Saul, the outcome would probably have been the same."

"I don't know."

"It was impossible to have a fair trial under such circumstances."

"Then why didn't Saul appeal? He knew what a farce the trial was. Why did he keep saying no?"

"He wanted to get it over with."

"That's not a good reason."

"It was his reason. 'I just want to get this thing behind me,' he kept saying."

"I know. But what does it mean? Why was he so stubborn?"

"You know what I think? I think he's sick of his life. That he wanted to escape from all his responsibilities, all the emotional demands."

"Don't say that."

"I think it's true," Evelyn says. "It wasn't a fair trial, and he knew it. They would never allow those industrial engineers with their stopwatches into a legitimate courtroom. It just would not be permitted. Western law is leisurely. It moves at a very slow pace. But at Saul's trial every time there was an objection or a pause to introduce a piece of evidence, they would click on their watches and start counting."

"Western law. The prosecutor is a product of Western law. But he was worse than anyone. All those speeches about immorality and the American way of life had very little to do with the law. He was using the trial as a political forum. It was disgusting."

"If only we hadn't lost the depositions testifying to Saul's good character. That might have shut him up."

"The jury didn't like us. I heard them criticizing our clothes."

"The whole thing was a farce from beginning to end."

201

"When they introduced the Beryl doll to show how we were cashing in on our immorality, I just wanted to die," Beryl says.

"Our biggest problem was Gregory. How he could have allowed the prosecutor to eject baby Beryl three times without objecting is beyond me."

"His mouth was full. That's why Gregory didn't object. He couldn't. He was eating contraband sausage at the time."

"It serves him right that he nearly choked to death."

When the judge told the prosecutor to stop playing with the Beryl doll, Gregory rose to his feet, chewing hard. He mumbled something with his mouth full, tried to swallow, coughed, choked, and, gripping the edge of the table, slumped to the floor. For a moment, nobody moved. Then the prosecutor leaped to his feet and ran over to the prostrate Gregory. He slid his hands around him in an embrace, employing the Heimlich maneuver. After a moment, a link of sausages popped out of Gregory's mouth. Everybody in the courtroom applauded.

"The prosecutor could have asked for the death penalty after that. He was everybody's hero."

"Still it could have been worse," Evelyn says.

"How?" we say.

"The judge could have sent him up for five years."

"Eighteen months is bad enough," I say.

"It's a lifetime as far as I'm concerned," Connie says.

"By then my baby will be walking and talking," Beryl says.

"By then I'll be a grownup, practically," Josh says.

We all fall silent for a long, sorrowful moment. Then Kelly says, "What would have happened if Saul hadn't made his statement before the sentencing? Would the judge have been more lenient or less?"

"More."

"Less."

"What difference does it make? He was bound and determined to have his say."

"I'm glad he spoke up," Jen says. "It put everything in perspective."

"I wish I had a copy."

"I have a copy," Evelyn says. "He gave it to me during the processing."

"Read it," we say.

She digs in her briefcase and pulls out Saul's statement. She reads:

" 'Even as I speak, this planet is being plundered, peasants killed, rain forests destroyed, magnificent buildings leveled. By criminals? No. None of these deeds of vandalism are crimes. They are economic development, they are in the national interest or in defense of the free world. Never crimes. Never punishable by law. Had I been a polluter, a politician, an exploiter of the environment, I would have been lauded and enriched. But the crime I am charged with is of a different magnitude—small, private, quiet.

" 'In a society where easy conquests and temporary love are everyday events, I chose fidelity. I chose to honor and cherish each of these women. Had I acted differently, toyed with one and then another and then turned aside from them as soon as my lust was satisfied, I would not be here today. Adultery is not a crime. Promiscuity is not a crime. Society tolerates all kinds of sexual activities not sanctified by law or religion as long as they remain hidden and trivial. My crime was to love openly and with all my heart: to be a husband, a father, a man who fixed things, who listened, who cared.' "

"It's wonderful."

"Brilliant."

"A fine statement."

"So true, so on target."

"I'm proud of him."

"It was Saul's finest hour."

Tears roll down our cheeks. "It won't be eighteen months," Evelyn says, but she is weeping too. "It will be more like six, if everything goes right."

"When did anything ever go right?"

"He'll never survive."

We are still bewailing the outcome of the trial when the phone rings. Jen goes to answer it. She listens for a long moment.

"Who's calling?" we say.

"Hollywood. They want to buy our story."

"What story?"

"They want to make a movie about us. They want to call it 'The Story of Saul.' They want to buy our lives."

PART III

15

Saul's letters have been edited and abridged to leave out the boring parts: those dealing with the endless requests for food and other things; instructions regarding the business, the techniques of bidding, what to say to reluctant clients, how to close a deal; also certain philosophical passages that seemed unduly sentimental; and all passages beginning, "This time last year . . . , Had I but known . . . ," etc. Where things are left out, I have indicated it with dots.

Dearest Helen:

. . . There are too many men here, too many hairy faces, deep voices, sweaty bodies. This one-gender world reminds me of the post-holocaust musical Valery was in. But a world populated solely by males is a more truly imagined hell.

The air is foul, thick with tobacco smoke, sweat, flatulence. The noise level is deafening. All the men own ghetto blasters. They play them day and night, each one tuned to a different station. Sound is magnified; it reverberates from the metal bars, bounces off the concrete floors, echoes from the ceilings.

The environment seems deliberately designed to kill the spirit. The world is a gray place—gray walls, a gray cement floor, a gray cement yard outside my window. I try to visualize home, our white-walled loft, spots of red, golden floors, but I can't convince myself that it still exists. I feel like a person in a fairy tale who went to sleep in one world and woke up in another, where all color and beauty had been banished.

Our cell is minuscule, hardly large enough for one person, let alone two. Fortunately, the man I share it with is small. His name is Edgar but everybody calls him Poison. I have no idea why he is here. Most of the men avoid any hint of wrongdoing. To hear them talk, they don't belong here. They were fingered by friends or loved ones, victimized by corrupt judges or ignorant lawyers. A few exaggerate their crimes, claiming for themselves such brilliant thefts, such daring bank heists, they would surely be in a prison sturdier than this one if their claims were true.

Everybody here knows our story. They treat me like a hero, my multiple marriages comparable to the exploits of a godfather or an astronaut. They keep asking me how it works and who is in charge of the money. If I fight with one wife, they want to know, do I move out and live with another? Women have such a jealous nature; they are like animals, they say. How do I keep them from tearing each other apart?

I try to explain how it works, our sharing, our mutual respect, our belief in equality. This concept makes them uneasy. "You can't be equal with a woman," they say. "As soon as you try to be nice, they take advantage."

These discussions go on during meals. The food is eclectic at its worst. You wouldn't believe the menu. Gummy grits, gray meat loaf. Canned carrots and peas. There is no fresh anything. But that is the good meal. At other times we are served a stew with unidentified objects floating around in it.

Send me the following: some nectarines, a small Brie. . . .

I am bored and lonely. There is nothing to do except bedmaking and other menial tasks, for although the men are supposed to be learning vocations, very few prison jobs are available. Every morning a guard comes by to check out our cells. Poison has been showing me how to tuck in corners and smooth out lumps, but even so, the guard doesn't like the way I make my bed. He carries a heavy ledger with him in which he marks things after our names. Mine has one for each day I have been here. What they signify I don't know, for the rules are as arbitrary as those in Wonderland.

Poison spends his days watching game shows. He is preparing to be a contestant when he gets out. He reads almanacs and other books of an informational nature, asks me to test him on his facts.

I think about all of you constantly. Last night I dreamed you had all married other men, small nasty creatures with disgusting habits. You, Helen, had taken up with the seltzer man. When I asked you why, you said, "In order to have unlimited seltzer, that's why." I hope this is not a portent of things to come.

When I think of our life together. . . .

I worry about all of you. Is Beryl getting enough exercise? Has Evelyn had any word from the high schools Josh applied to? Is Jen's toe mending? Has Connie remembered not to overload her circuits? I wish I were there, sitting at the long table, surrounded by my sweet women, each one so charming. . . . I think of the talks we had, the brilliant conversations, the various subjects we touched on—the theater, God, the meaning of life. . . . How little I valued it when I was there.

Some kind of malaise, some spiritual exhaustion, must have taken hold of me. I felt crowded, claustrophobic. There were too many demands on my time, my emotions, too many calls for my assistance and advice, too many emergencies to be dealt with, demanding an inexhaustible supply of patience and sympathy. But now that I am here

and you are all there, how I miss my conjugal responsibilities.

P.S. Send me some all-cotton boxer shorts. . . .

Dear Saul:

Jean has almost finished the crib for Beryl's baby. It is
a work of art. The headboard is a primitive female god, a
replica of the pregnant Venus. The footboard abounds in
mythical images—serpents, ibises, rams' heads—rough-
hewn to suggest artifacts dug up at some archaeological
site. Kangaroos dangle by their tails from the railing that
encircles the crib, each one with a pouch in which things
can be stored: baby powder, oil, cotton balls. All the figures
are carved out of wood. Kelly is painting them in the most
glorious, faded, antique greens and ochers. In a day or
two, when she is finished, we intend to photograph the
crib so you can fully appreciate its qualities.

This crib is a labor of love. Jen has put all her craft in
it, all her imagination, not merely for the baby but for you
too, so you can stop worrying about its intellectual development. The crib is a museum space, uniting mind and
spirit, culture and history. The baby will have an opportunity to absorb the very best of the world from its birth.

Valery lost her lease and has moved in with Connie.
In return for shelter, she is trying to help Connie reorgan-
ize her life. She has cleaned out Connie's refrigerator and
now she is helping her with the dogs.

They found a book on canine behavior, a kind of
therapeutic handbook. It was full of psychological advice.
It told them to repeat certain commands: Sit, Stop, Don't.
They were instructed to say these words first in a gentle
voice and then, as the day progressed, in a sharper and
sharper tone, until by evening they were snarling the
commands. "In this way your canine will know you mean
business," the book said. The book also suggested a name
change to encourage a better outlook on life. It listed a
number of names that inspire happiness and other good
traits in your pet. "You will be pleasantly surprised at the

personality improvement your dogs will undergo." After pondering names, they selected Serena and Joy from the list. Now everybody in the family calls Aster and Belinda by their new names in the hope it will communicate something positive to them.

Last night, the entire family met here with the scriptwriter. His name is Peter. He is twenty-three years old. He has been a major motion picture scriptwriter since he was seventeen and twice was almost nominated for an Academy Award. He intends to immerse himself in our lives.

He wrote down all our names, our ages, our weights, questioned us about our secret anxieties, our goals. Then he had us go around and give the reasons why we'd married you. Everybody said love. "There must be more to it than that," the scriptwriter said. "Because of his sensitive nature," Valery said. "He respected our abilities," Jen and Kelly said. Beryl said you reminded her of her absent father, Connie venerated your outlook on life. "We had the same level of integrity," she said. Evelyn said you helped her keep up with the world out there.

The scriptwriter intends to live with each of us for a while so he can absorb our essence, do justice to our lives. He is starting with me. He has been here ever since.

After the others left, he said, "What dark secrets lie behind your cheerful temperament? What sorrows, what furtive desires?" He needs to know these things in order to get a handle on my part. We talked a long time about you, and he is beginning to have a sense of your personality. The way he sees you now, he thinks Alan Alda might be the man for your part. He intends to suggest this to the producer. How does that strike you?

I know when he is here alone, he goes through everything, studying old bills, take-out menus. This morning when I came back from the bakery, I caught him counting the towels and sheets. He opens drawers, turns out pockets in our jackets and coats. I am not sure what he is looking for. He follows me into the workroom and while I labor

211

over a blueprint or answer the mail, he inquires about my forbidden appetites.

"I have a secret yen for apple pie," I tell him.

"What else?" he says. By the nature of his questions I have a horrible feeling this is going to be another *Jaws,* an X-rated film full of ravenous creatures chewing each other up.

Your loving etc.

Dearest Helen:

The crib worries me. Its primitive details will be confusing to a baby who has had no opportunity to learn to differentiate then from now. I'm afraid he'll be lost in it, disoriented, like a rat in a maze. It is hard enough to know what's real in this world. If we don't learn to distance ourselves from the past, we rewrite history, we falsify our lives.

I'm thinking of Beryl as I write these words. She never knew her father. For all we know, he was a container of sperm purchased at a take-out fertility bank. Her mother has never admitted this, yet it fits in with her style, the belief that you can buy anything for a price. Under these circumstances, how could Beryl say what she did to the scriptwriter, that I reminded her of her absent father? I can't understand why none of you set the record straight. Whatever happened to loyalty? To truth? I have never looked upon myself as a father figure to any of my wives. A guide, perhaps, a helping hand, an instructor in times of confusion. But a father figure implies something else— age, oedipal confusions, misplaced desire.

If I can't depend on the family, how can I sustain myself in this hellhole? It is a daily struggle to hold on to one's identity. Prison vandalizes the personality. It makes men boys, returns us to an earlier stage of our development, encouraging not growth or responsibility but merely obedience. Obedience to the invisible men who make the decisions for us, unquestioning docility toward all the insanity that rules our daily lives, the things that we eat, the hours that we eat them, our early risings, our menial tasks, the lack of privacy, or quiet, our total loss of autonomy.

Because there are so many empty hours, the prisoners talk endlessly about themselves in language picked up from social workers and psychologists. "My problems stem from a mixed personality disorder," one says. Another has a poor self-image; a third, tendencies toward thoughtless decision-making. "Because of an immature personality structure, I act out," a fourth says. He reels off a string of curse words to demonstrate his lack of control. They are all trying to get in touch with the feminine side of their natures, for they have been told that this might help reverse their tendencies.

I am worried about the business. Too many jobs went to someone else. Bidding is a subtle procedure. I suggest. . . .

I don't care who plays me in the movie. I have more important things to worry about. I must admit, though, Alan Alda seemed off-the-wall. Somehow I envisioned a Burt Reynolds or William Hurt, a strong man who is also able to convey something deep and tragic, who is not afraid to take chances with his part. That is closer to the real me.

For although I walk around with a stalwart face, my adjustment is skin deep. The slightest thing threatens to unhinge me: a guard's curses, the smell of stale sweat, the lack of privacy. I visualized a monkish cell, quiet, a time to read and think. I longed for solitude, but solitude is the last thing one gets here.

I haven't been able to read more than a page of a book since I arrived. It's too noisy. Poison is always watching one of his game shows. Each time a question is asked, he screams out the answer. He is trying to develop an outgoing personality. His ultimate goal is to become a celebrity panelist on *Hollywood Squares*. "A high energy level is what they look for," he says.

He would also like to appear on *Love Connection,* but

he is not certain he has the looks for it. "You gotta be tall," he says. Because of his obsession with game shows, he is filled with odds and ends of information about geography and racing cars, famous lovers, events that changed the course of history.

I would like some posters for my wall, a Matisse, an early Jackson Pollock. If you can find it, I have a yearning for a certain still life, a bowl of peaches by Fede Galizia. Also send me some apricots, a country ham. . . .

Dear Saul:

You probably got my wire by now. Beryl is fine. The baby is a beautiful eight-pound boy. His name is Saul II. Everybody says he looks like you. Ramon was supposed to be Beryl's birthing partner, but at the last minute they had a fight. Ramon accused Beryl of a lack of seriousness, Beryl accused Ramon of exploiting women.

Jen and Kelly presided in his stead. Although they hadn't rehearsed any of the procedures, they were very helpful. Beryl had acquired a birthing tape from Samoa, a series of grunts and heavy breathing designed to put her in touch with her natural self. Jen and Kelly kept the tape running the whole time she was in labor. They bathed her face. They sang songs. They fed her Ding Dongs to keep up her strength. A midwife from the shelter presided.

The midwife would not let Josh video the birth, although she allowed the scriptwriter to stand in a corner of the birthing room recording Beryl's dialogue. "Hell, damn, ouch," she kept saying. "It will make a tremendous movie scene," the scriptwriter said. Though he admitted the dialogue needs some work.

Josh spends every minute he can with Peter. I suspect he has been cutting classes so he can hang out with him. He stays wherever Peter happens to be staying, insinuates himself in all the interviews. "Ask me anything," he says. "I am the family historian. I have records of all the important events."

He is trying to interest Peter in some of the footage

he has taken of the family, to be inserted in the film, either as a prologue or epilogue that will establish him as a moviemaker in his own right. But, being Josh, he is also worried about early success. He read an article recently about many millionaires under thirty growing weary of their lives. "We crested too early," they told the writer. "I wouldn't want that to happen to me," he says.

That's all the good news. The bad news is that Joy, formerly Aster, died. He chewed up Connie's Vanguard Vicki order book and an hour later he keeled over. Connie is inconsolable. "He was just beginning to find himself," she says. "Just beginning to get in touch with his inner harmony." We all try to comfort her. "Serena (formerly Belinda) will be better off," we tell her. "She will have a chance to blossom."

"She liked being dominated," Connie says. She'll never forgive herself for leaving the order book within Joy's reach. She broods about her hidden motives—ugly resentments that might have led to this carelessness. "I must have the courage to face the truth," she says. It hasn't sunk in yet what she is going to tell the company. I hope she doesn't lose her job.

I have sent you a crate of comice pears, some muscat grapes. . . .

Dear Helen:

The men threw a little party when they heard about the baby. I am glad everything is okay. Naturally I was pleased that she decided to name him after me. I think Saul II has a nice ring to it. Somebody sent out for a bottle of wine. If you have the money to bribe a guard, you can get just about anything here. We all had a glass. The wine made me dizzy.

Now that I am once more a father, I have been reviewing my life. If I had it to do over again would I do it in this particular way? The answer is sometimes yes and sometimes no, depending on my mood. I wish I hadn't been so good, so law-abiding. I wish I hadn't observed so many rules. I avoided jaywalking, I paid my taxes, I did not try to shelter any of our money. Unlike Josh, I was a good boy in school, never challenging authority. If someone told me the earth was round, I wrote down *round* without feeling compelled to cry out, How do you know?

I was a good boy at home, too. My mother gave me a dollar a day for food, and I never asked for more. I assumed every growing boy received that amount, and I did my best to live on it. I hunted out the cheapest cafeterias. Places where you could eat unlimited bread. I lived the life of a street person when I was young, making do, acquiring survival techniques. I discovered where you could get free lemon so I could make myself a lemonade, and where you could get the biggest sandwich for the least. I was cooperative, uncomplaining, sweet. A model citizen, a good boy.

The effects of my mother's parsimony are still emerging. It is true this society encourages acquisitiveness, but mine seems to take a special form. Each one of my marriages filled some early need that went unmet: a yearning for toys, a hunger for delicacies, a longing for an unexpected treat. And yet the more I married, the more I felt some emptiness, some need that even now continues to nibble away at me. I have accomplished so little. Perhaps that's the price I have had to pay for marrying so often. I think of all the things I might have done, the brilliant insights that have gone unwritten, the spaces that have gone unbuilt. Where is there a monument to my style, my vision, my craft?

Tell Josh not to worry about early success. What should concern him right now is hard work and study. Perhaps that sounds old-fashioned, but this is something he should know. Most of the men here have been poorly educated, and their inability to cope with our complicated world is largely responsible for their troubles. I am trying to teach them a few things: how to write a sentence, how to spell. I have started writing letters for them. "I like your style," they tell me. It would help if we had some books.

Perhaps a primer about the law, a subject that interests them above all others. Also a book of humorous stories for Poison. "A joke is worth a thousand facts," he says.

I have written my condolences to Connie, though just between you and me, I think she is well rid of him. Last time I was there, he ate my shoelaces and mauled an expensive cravat. It's a wonder he didn't die long ago with all the nonedible things he has chewed up and swallowed.

Beryl sent me pictures of Saul II. "He looks just like you," she wrote. Quite frankly I can't see any real resemblance. Perhaps when he grows a little more hair the likeness will emerge.

My own hair is finally growing out. It was a terrible mistake to cut it short before the trial. Certain qualities reinforce a man's sense of himself. With some it may be bulging biceps or a jutting jaw. My identity is tied up with my hair. I know how Samson must have felt shorn of his hair, the terrible sense of loss, the distorted perception that drained him of his strength. I felt so vulnerable until my hair grew out.

Now that I am beginning to get to know some of the other inmates, they seem less strange and threatening to me. Less coarse. Somehow, even less male. They have all had hard lives, disappointments. They search for simple rules, some overall wisdom to guide them safely through life. "Learn to look people in the eye. . . . Don't trust anyone who smiles all the time. . . . A limp handshake means trouble."

They repeat these simple thoughts over and over as though saying a prayer that will guide them through their lives. "Never look back." My cellmate repeats this statement a dozen times a day.

I think I know why they call him Poison. He was an exterminator before he went to prison. "A high-stress occupation," he says. One day, he was called into an apartment in the East Village for an emergency extermination. The occupants, a young couple recently relocated from a small Ohio city, were in a state of hysteria. Giant bugs had invaded their premises. "They must be urban mutants," the young couple said. "You are overreacting to city life," Poison said. He told the couple to be cool. While they cowered in the kitchen doorway, he began to spray. Suddenly bugs came running out of every crevice like soldiers sprayed with fire. They staggered down the kitchen wall and across the kitchen floor, reeling, zigzagging, eventually keeling over.

Poison couldn't believe his eyes. The bugs were two or three inches long, larger than any he had ever seen before. As soon as he saw their size, he demanded more money. When the young couple said no, Poison threatened to turn his spray nozzle on them. They paid him and ordered him to leave. Too late, Poison realized what a challenge this was to his professional skill; he offered to finish the job for the original sum. But by now the couple had turned against him. They claimed he'd dripped insecticide all over the floor. They criticized his pale face, implying he had an industrial disease. Bugs were still staggering out of hidden places when Poison closed the door.

He couldn't get the incident out of his mind. A few weeks later, at a convention for exterminators, he wanted to share his experience with his colleagues. In a workshop entitled Your Public Image, he got up and described the giant bugs. The other exterminators laughed in disbelief. Poison was bitter. "It was then I began to develop my antisocial tendencies," he said.

All the men here have similar rationalizations to explain their inability to function in the world. Their troubles stem from something outside themselves—misunderstandings, malice, scorn. People didn't value them. Their loved ones turned against them. They were dismissed unfairly from a job. It never occurs to them that something might be missing from their own character—patience, understanding, the ability to feel for others.

Am I like that? I can't help wondering if I too suffer from some fatal weakness: too little patience, an inability to empathize. Yet it seems to me I have these virtues in good supply, perhaps even an overabundance of generosity and selflessness. In fact, my strengths might be considered weaknesses by some, for I have never learned to hold back either my body or my soul.

The boxer shorts were too small. I gave them to Poison. Send me some a size larger. It's this damn starchy diet. I'm putting on weight. Send me some kiwis, a carton of Turkish figs. . . .

Dear Saul:

You were right to worry. When they found out Aster had eaten the order book, the Vanguard Vicki people fired Connie. How fortunate that Valery is there to take her mind off her troubles. Connie spends much of her time trying to help Valery overcome her self-doubts. Valery is now conducting a course in knitting at the New School, though she still considers this a sideline until a theatrical breakthrough comes her way. Each time she goes for an audition, Connie helps her prepare for the part. She holds the script, she cues her, and together they analyze the character, work on her mannerisms.

Valery sees herself as a tragic person, so the roles she goes after are filled with torment and dark passions. Yet when she tries to convey these qualities onstage, people don't take her seriously. Instead of weeping, they laugh. "She has distanced herself from pain," Connie says. She is teaching Valery to grieve.

In exchange for all this help, Valery has fixed Connie's vacuum cleaner so that it now sucks in dirt instead of blowing it out.

Connie is considering a career change. When she looked at the New School catalog that Valery brought home, she discovered many interesting courses in sex therapy. She has enrolled in a program and is currently studying the erogenous zones. "There are many more than I realized," she says.

We are handcrafting a series of tables for a gallery owner who displays furniture as art. It happened by accident. We were trying to console Connie. Jen and I were working on a replica of Aster. She sculpted a body out of wood, we added tufts of fake fur, then we mounted a Plexiglas top on the dog and encircled its edge with wire dog tails. This gallery owner had come to our workroom to confer on something else, a job we had bid on but failed to get. When he saw the table, even in its half-finished state, he got all excited. "I have to have it," he said. "Not this one," we told him, but we promised to make him another. Now he has ordered a dozen for his gallery with different animal bases. We have done a cat and are currently working on a monkey, a parrot, etc.

But that isn't all. We showed him a picture of Saul II's crib and he almost fainted. "If I can't have that, I'll die," he said. So we promised him a replica of that too. We have been so busy working on the furniture, we haven't had the time to pursue any new construction jobs. Evelyn is applying for patents so we don't get ripped off the way Beryl did with the Beryl doll.

We have given her the crib, but Saul II is not yet in it. He hovers above it in a net hammock that is supposed to replicate the ripples in the womb, for Beryl is now convinced he was reluctant to be born. This is based upon the fact that he doesn't seem to like the taste of her milk. "He is trying to tell me something," she says. "He is trying to tell you your milk is too sweet for human consumption," we tell her. We suggest she have it analyzed. She and Ramon are friends again. They are trying to market a Saul II doll.

We meet collectively with the scriptwriter to continue the accounts of our lives.

Beryl says: "We used to go walking through the city streets late at night or early in the morning. At every mound of rubble, we would pause, looking for things, useful items we could take home. He taught me to play a game, pretend we were archaeologists at an ancient dig.

"Each time we found a discarded item—a chair, a lampshade, a picture frame—we would stare at it as if we

220

had never seen such a thing before. 'What's this?' we would ask each other. The chair would be the household altar of a god; a lamp, a utensil for grinding grain. As we walked home, the city would begin to wake. Storekeepers would roll up their gates, taxis would screech through the early morning streets, figures would suddenly emerge from doorways and arise from garbage heaps and ask us for change. Saul would say, 'I wish we could do this every night.' 'So do I,' I would answer."

Evelyn says: "Our lives together were extremely intellectual. I would take him to the law library, a high, narrow steel cage, and we would walk among the stacks and I would point out all the books dealing with different aspects of the law. This repository of so many centuries of information thrilled him. 'All the wisdom of the ages is stored here,' he would say. Sometimes another student would be there and I would introduce them. Saul always had a fund of witty stories for occasions like this; he never failed to make the student laugh.

"Saul wouldn't make a move without consulting me first, whether it was business or personal matters. We went over every job he bid on, worked out all the legalities together. When he was considering taking a new wife, 'Sleep on it,' I would tell him. More than one time, I dissuaded him from entering into a hasty marriage."

Jen and Kelly: "We liked to get in the car and race out to this place in Connecticut where they sold ruins. Picture acres and acres of broken birdbaths, twisted railings, smashed lintels. We would spend hours looking for a broken column for one of the spaces we were working on, a Victorian touch in our minimalist spaces. In her designs, Helen always allowed for one extraneous object, so that object had to be just right. She left it to the three of us to pick something out.

"At other times we did unisex things together. We got haircuts, drank beer, worked out at the health club. He worried about health matters. We were always comparing symptoms and swapping medication."

221

Josh: "Nobody liked me in school. My life was totally unlike the lives of my classmates. They have normal, nuclear-type families. They scorned me, called me a communist and a fairy. Picture this. The entire fourth grade chasing me home, hurling javelins at me, jeering, cursing, brandishing a lynch rope. I was a neglected child. My parents never had any good time for me. Whenever my father came over, all he wanted me to do was memorize some geological table."

At this point something happened to Peter's tape recorder and we had to stop. We are going to meet again.

I am still looking for some paisley shorts for you. I can't find your early building codes. The other things you asked for are on the way.

Lovingly,

Dear Helen:

Hurling javelins? Brandishing lynch ropes? How that boy dramatizes himself, exaggerates his suffering! Nobody at the school cared about our marital arrangements. How could they? Hardly a child in school wasn't part of some irregular domestic arrangement. One lived with his father and his father's male lover. Another with a stepmother and a stepfather and, in the long sequence of marriages and divorces, was no longer sure who his true parents were. Several lived with lesbian mothers, aunts, grandmothers, even older siblings. In the entire school there were only five nuclear families, and one of them was interracial.

He usually says these terrible things when he wants something from us: increased pocket money, later hours, more freedom. This kind of badmouthing should not be rewarded. I wonder what sort of adult he will be.

Between Beryl and Josh, I am going crazy. Ramon is bad news. I am sorry they made up. He makes her think she is shrewder, more hardheaded than she really is. I foresee disaster with the Saul II doll. I wish she hadn't gotten involved with him again.

She continues to glorify foraging. I had hoped with the birth of Saul II she would put all that behind her. All I hope is that the baby doesn't catch some disease from the mess in her hovel.

I remember a night we were heading for a movie. It was raining and she couldn't find her boots. We looked through one mound of rubble and then another, unearthed torn lampshades, a broken shopping cart, stacks of magazines, chipped pottery, other things that weren't even in recognizable form. This is the sort of mess that draws rats and disease. I worry about the baby constantly. What if Beryl brings home a garment infected with AIDS? Surely that possibility should make her stop and think.

Reading your letters I feel like a person long dead. All the changes taking place—the animal furniture, Connie's latest career, Valery's job at the New School—they disconnect me from my life.

Please send me some glycerine soap. The prison issue makes me itch. The other day, when I was taking a shower, I noticed one of the men had a message tattoed across his chest. It said, "Help! I am trapped in someone else's body." It's astonishing how many of the men sport tattoos.

Even more surprising is how beautiful some of them are, their primary colors, their naïve forms suggestive of a folk art. There is a resident tattooer here who decorates the bodies of the men. At the moment, patriotism is in. Flags and eagles and pieces of the Bill of Rights are being engraved on people's bodies. Poison is toying with the idea of having ten turning points in history tattooed upon his wrists. "In that way I will be able to beat out all the competitors," he says.

Although tattooing, like most things, is forbidden, our tattooer has set up a studio in a broom closet and the inmates stand on line waiting to be decorated. It's as though two streams run side by side here, two different versions of reality: the real prison with its rules and regulations, its watchful guards, and an alternate place, where all the forbidden things are available.

Actually the guards are a far cry from the guards of my youth, those men in prison movies who snarled and tormented the men in their charge. These guards are neither cruel nor scheming. They are petty bureaucrats. "The rules is the rules," they say a dozen times a day.

Their occupational hazard is boredom. Many of them are trying to better themselves. They listen to language tapes during their watch, practice giving orders in Spanish or Japanese. Others are teaching themselves to tap-dance in the hope of qualifying for a career in show business.

Poison is getting ready to leave. Now that freedom approaches, he is very uneasy. There are so many categories of knowledge he knows nothing about. He is memorizing the *Guinness Book of World Records*—knows the name of the fattest person in history, and the strongest, and the most revered. Each time he encounters a fact that puzzles him, he consults me on its meaning. I think he would like to model himself after me.

Even here, people are dependent on me. They ask questions, they seek my advice. The men treat me like a priest, an empty vessel waiting to be filled with their problems, their questions, their confusions. Everybody likes me.

They try to impress me with their manhood, their sexual performances. Love to them is a question of statistics, size, endurance, etc. Women seem hardly to exist except as instruments on which they can perform.

Nobody here can imagine what it is like to be the lover of seven women. Not just the demands upon my body, but the spiritual and emotional needs I had to meet. If it were a branch of science or art, I would surely warrant a Nobel prize. That I could be the husband of both you and Connie astounds me. To make two such disparate women happy is surely some form of magic. Perhaps happy is not the right word. What we pursued were possibilities, pleasures undreamed of. We tried. We believed in perfection. If not today, tomorrow or next week.

That life seems so remote now, almost as if I had

imagined it. Reality is the prison, the guards, the inmates. Once a week, one of the warden's deputies lines us up in the yard below our window, and the warden lectures us on military bearing. He straightens collars, rearranges jackets, tucks in shirts. He lectures people on badly tied shoelaces. "I am preparing you for the real world," he says. But I wonder how long it is since he left the prison and visited the real world. I would like to tell him how little military bearing is valued out there.

What the men need to know is a trade. I am trying to set up a class in the basic skills of construction. I have applied to the warden for a space and some essential equipment.

Send me some tools and blueprint paper. Send me a salami, a jar of Cheez Whiz, some peanut butter. . . .

Dear Saul:

I am sorry the visit didn't go better. Given only ten minutes each, it was all but impossible to make any real contact. Plus the noise, plus the crowded room, plus the way people stared, and the unfortunate incident involving Kelly. But even so, it was wonderful to see you, to hold your hand. We were all so glad we made the trip. Perhaps you are right, though, and we shouldn't attempt to visit you again. One hundred and fifty miles for such a brief glimpse is a long way to go. We were all so happy at how well you looked, considering the prison fare and the lack of exercise. All I can say is how much it meant to us to be near you even for such a brief time.

All the way home, we discussed the prison environment: the ugly visiting room with its cracked walls, peeling ceiling, stained floor. With all the time on the prisoners' hands, one wonders why they don't assign more cleanup details. It would benefit the men who use the visiting room, make it a more welcome place in which to receive guests. How you have withstood such a grim environment, such coarseness, is a mystery, a miracle, a reason to give thanks. One's sensibility must be totally drained in such an envi-

225

ronment, or, as Jen put it, rubbed smooth like sandpapered wood.

We tried to describe our visit to Peter when we got back to the city. He was waiting for us in the loft. "He's still Saul," we told him, for what mainly concerns him now is the way he should write your part. He keeps asking us questions. "Who is he?" he says. "Why do so many women want to be married to him?"

"It's his avocation," we tell him. "Other men watch ball games or take up self-improvement. They jog, they learn to cook gourmet meals, they read books on geology or other natural sciences, they acquire new skills. They make friends with other men, establish a network, bond. Saul's sole interest is women, the way they smell, the things they say, their worries, their dreams. They are his learning experience in life."

"A loner," Peter says. He goes off to absorb all that we have told him. Each time he comes back, he has a new concept of the way he should write your part. Right now, he has in mind a Clint Eastwood type, cool but violent, gentle but strong. "The kind of man that women love and other men fear," he says.

Of course, with Eastwood in mind, he recognizes a need for action. "No problem," he says. He visualizes a violent confrontation in the women's shelter where you/he would go to avenge the battered women. The scriptwriter is writing a scene in which the hero stalks a wife basher, and when they meet there is a fight, a lesson learned that will not be soon forgotten. Eastwood will wreak vengeance, impose a frontier kind of justice on this urban jungle once and for all.

If there is still a violence gap after that, he has another idea, an even bigger action scene that would take place during your arrest. He has in mind another *Deliverance*, wherein the local sheriff and his boys will rape both you and Beryl. Then, in a flaming act of revenge, Clint Eastwood would draw his hidden weapons and slaughter the entire bunch. He thinks this concept would have a broad appeal. Tomorrow, no doubt, he will try a whole new approach.

The Contemporary Museum of Crafts wants one of our tables for its permanent collection, either a goat or a rabbit. It has to be ready in time for their next show: The Poetry of the Ordinary. In their catalog, they say our work fills a psychological need. "It combines a sense both of the past and the future, allowing the viewer to float in a timeless zone, between nostalgia and modernity. It represents a reaffirmation of aesthetic craving in daily life."

Our dealer can hardly keep up with the orders; everybody wants one of our tables. "They love to spill something on a work of art," he says. Many of the people we did spaces for are on his waiting list. They call us up in the hope of bypassing the gallery owner. "Remember me?" they say.

Beryl keeps adding things to the Saul II doll in the hope that the gallery owner will want to include it among his offerings. Last week she added a tuft of hair; now she is working on a dimple. "What I am going for is a living essence," she says. This infuriates Ramon. He wants the doll to go into production now. He can often be seen pacing up and down Beryl's hovel, muttering "Women," and similar epithets, while she fiddles with the doll.

Connie has lost all interest in the erogenous zones and has dropped out of the New School. She and Valery are working day and night on their act.

They have already tried out at a local club with fantastic success. Gloom apparently is hilarious. Connie is straight man to Valery's sorrowful clown. The way it works is this. Connie gives Valery a lecture on positive thinking. "I can't, I won't be able to," Valery says. As soon as she opens her mouth, the crowd begins to titter. Soon it becomes a roar. If all goes well, they intend to take the act on the road.

Now that Valery is funny in public, we all find her funny. No matter what she says, it is impossible not to laugh. "Nobody likes me. It is my fault. I am an impossible

227

person. My first-grade teacher told me I'd never amount to anything." I don't know what it is, but at the first word we start to laugh.

At the moment she is very angry because the scriptwriter has told her she cannot play herself in the movie. "You wouldn't be right for the part."

"Who knows better than I how to be Valery?" she says, and even though it isn't funny, we start to laugh.

Why is gloom so hilarious? I am trying to make some sense out of it. It never used to be funny. The igloo I conceived as a metaphor for despair did not make people laugh. Neither do the other symptoms of contemporary despair—a love of Jell-O and chocolate pudding, nostalgia, the minimalist movement. Black canvases. Tattered clothes. Unexplained illnesses, pollution, sudden death. People have always treated gloom respectfully, solemnly, to prevent it from inundating their lives.

Valery's gift seems to lie in her absolute conviction that life is horrible and that she is somehow to blame. Her dialogue is an invitation to share in her despair, to surrender hope so completely, everything becomes absurd, funny, laughable.

I sent you the case of canned fruit salad, some Mars Bars, another jar of Cheez Whiz. Your tastes seem to be changing. You never ate things like this before.

I am worried about the tattoos. Don't be swayed by the other prisoners. Remember the actuary who had Nixon's face tattooed on his wrist? This was just before the Watergate scandal broke. He has worn a heavy wrist band ever since. Don't get one. You will regret it if you do.

Lovingly,

Dear Helen:

Clint Eastwood. It would be laughable if it weren't so appalling. The only violence in our lives was internal, inner doubts, self-hatred, the usual conflicts that people are prey to these days. I am appalled at the direction the script is taking. If any rape scenes appear, tell the script-

228

writer we will sue. The truth is bad enough. We don't need invention. Surely Evelyn can protect our interests.

Don't let them portray me as a Don Juan either, a man who used women. I don't want any torrid love scenes between me and any of my wives.

Too bad the scriptwriter isn't a little older, more experienced in the ways of the world. At twenty-three, one reduces everything to a sexual frenzy.

We need a writer who can show us the way we were, everybody helping everybody else, someone who can write a family story filled with mutual respect and understanding. We taught each other skills, we got along; over the dinner table, we held uplifting conversations that often lasted into the night. We were serious people, responsible citizens. Don't let them depict us as flakes, seeking only to satisfy our carnal cravings. It was the last thing we had on our minds.

Here in prison, I am a celibate. I miss having someone to put my arms around, touch, feel. I miss the warmth of another body, the soft sound of breathing. How I longed to be close to you, each one of you, when you came on your visit.

I am sorry Kelly got so upset when Mousie whistled at her. For one thing, he didn't realize she was part of my entourage. For another, these men are somewhat inarticulate, particularly when women are present, so it was his way of paying her a compliment. The men were really shocked at what she said. "We didn't know ladies used such language," they said later. "She's from Australia," I explained.

Despite this incident, they all had nice things to say about all of you, even Beryl, though they were embarrassed when she began to nurse Saul II right there in front of the entire prison. I keep thinking of that day, and how hard it was to bridge the time and space that have separated us all these months. You all seemed like strangers to me, different from the way I remembered you—even, I admit, a little frightening. How opinionated everybody is! I never noticed that before, or the assertive ways you express yourselves, not simply in words but in the things you wear, the way you look. The city look. Each article of clothing a statement, an assertion of who you are. In your oversized sweaters, long skirts, and boots, you looked like a group of refugees from some distant Eastern country.

I am afraid I am out of touch. I no longer understand the restlessness of city life, the constant search for novelty. Each day here is like the day before. There are no surprises.

The city is always in motion, always in a state of flux. Each of you seemed to reflect this movement in your clothes, your choice of words, your opinions. Will I ever bridge the chasm that seems to open wider every day? I worry about it all the time. I wonder what life will be like when I get out.

If I could, I would encase all of you in Lucite in some posture I am familiar with, until my time here is over. I fear change, each of you moving beyond me as if you had all boarded a fast-moving train.

And yet there are some things I would like to change when I get out of here. We are too isolated. We need friends, more of a social life, a larger framework in which to operate. I recognize that not too many people would want to invite the eight of us to dinner, but now that I am getting used to men, I would not mind having a stray male or two over for a meal once in a while. We could also go to an occasional movie and dine out at a pizza parlor. And what I long for the most is all of us going on a trip to a tropical isle.

I dream of Hawaii, the sun, the sea breezes, fresh coconuts and pineapples. Water. We could rent a cottage with housekeeping facilities and seven bedrooms near the water. We could fish and snorkel. I have such a longing for fresh air, an expansive sky, an environment without boundaries. If I survive, I hope the entire family can take

230

this trip. I long for things to be just the way they once were, all of us happy. . . .

The warden has given me permission to start a construction class. We are going to build a greenhouse for him next to his house. I have made some preliminary drawings. The structure will be Victorian with domes and a cast-iron frame. I'll need the following for this project—a book on the structural elements of greenhouses, tools. . . .

The brochure on your furniture arrived, and I read it through several times. I can understand the desire for handcrafted objects in a technological world. But how do these tables transcend time zones? And why are they considered art? I used to know the answers to these things.

Perhaps that's why I am drawn to tattoos. They are a simple art form that doesn't change from one generation to another. The eagles of the father can be seen on the son, the same colors, the same fierce expression on the bird's face: a simple statement, free of ironies, of ambiguities.

Despite my admiration, I assure you I have no intention of getting one. I cannot conceive of choosing a statement today that would continue to have the same force and validity a year from now. At the same time, I keep thinking there must be some lasting truth, some statement of enduring value.

I lie here on my bed and try to imagine what that might be. The phrase "Time is a river" comes to mind. I can almost picture it engraved across my chest in gothic letters, primary colors, a winding stream threading its way through the letters, surrounded by small woodland creatures—chipmunks, squirrels, pheasant—like the animals Valery knits into her sweaters. Perhaps a serpent hidden in a tree, a satyr. . . . But it's all fantasy. I assure you I have no intention of getting myself tattooed.

Poison left last week, and so far they haven't assigned me another cellmate. The warden said my room was too messy. He said I had so many things cluttering the space, there was no room for another person. He was referring to my few pathetic possessions: the books, the trade magazines, the Exercycle, a few crates of fruits, a package of dried apricots, the salamis hanging from the ceiling. Poison never complained, I wanted to say, but one does not argue with the warden.

I wouldn't be sorry if he didn't assign me a cellmate. Poison was okay, but the idea of sharing my space with a stranger unsettles me.

Send me another jar of Cheez Whiz, some marshmallow fluff. I don't see why you say my tastes are changing. I always liked peanut butter.

Dear Saul:

The movie is in trouble. They want to cut two wives from it because of budgetary considerations. Naturally, Peter is furious. He is flying to the Coast to haggle with the producers. If they persist in this creative madness, he says he will refuse to go on with the script.

Beryl has sold the Saul II doll to a manufacturer. In each doll, they are going to insert a tape with the Beryl and Saul song on it. When you press the baby's stomach, the song will play. When you press it again, it will stop. "It makes the Beryl doll look Neanderthal," she says. "This is truly state of the art."

Saul II is thriving. His motor abilities are far beyond his age group. He can grip a spoon and rattle the kangaroos on the side of his crib. He can hurl his bottle to the floor. His early recognition skills are remarkable. Each time he sees any of us, he smiles and stretches out his arms to be picked up. Beryl says this indicates a real mastery of his world.

Beryl is very proud of the baby. "He is just like me," she says. His first solid food was a Famous Amos cookie. He loves to forage. Beryl puts a pile of castoffs in his crib (clean, she assures us), and he spends many happy hours sorting through them. His red hair is streaked with darker hair, shades of his daddy.

The interest in animal tables as art is waning, but Sears is considering one of our pieces for their spring catalog. Either a goat table or a parakeet molded in polyurethane and covered in Astroturf for their indoor/outdoor collection.

In the meantime we are working on another piece of furniture for the gallery, a chair that will embody some of the qualities of pop art. We are going for a cartoon look, crooked legs, a lopsided seat, the entire structure out of perspective as though it might have been constructed by a child.

Our prototype, which we showed the dealer, wobbles because the legs are different lengths; the bright red paint is deliberately streaked as if a child painted it. Jackson Pollock blobs and streaks of color dribble over its seat and back.

The dealer gasped when he saw the prototype. "I don't believe it," he said. He wants us to start production immediately. Instead of each chair being unique, like our tables, they will have a mass-produced look, like Andy Warhol soup cans. Only if you look close will you realize subtle differences in both the brush strokes and the blobs of color. Our work will suggest mass production, but each one will be handcrafted. The chair's name is Kindergarten.

In the meantime, Valery and Connie are getting ready to travel. Their agent has booked them into a club in St. Louis and another in Cincinnati. "Black comedy at its most mordant" is the way the *Voice* described their act. "It makes hopelessness seductive."

The more successful their reception, the more depressed Valery grows. "It isn't me," she says. "I had other goals in mind. I am not a funny person. People shouldn't laugh." Yet she just has to sigh and people fall out of their seats. She is the dark lining of our souls. When she sighs, she is saying, We are all in this together. It is this thrill of recognition that makes people laugh.

Josh has been accepted at three of the best high

schools. He sent each of them a tape of his Bleaksville video to show how broad his interests were, how serious his intent. "As you can see by the enclosed, I am a multi-faceted person," he wrote, "despite the fact that life has been hard." Now he has to choose.

Evelyn took us all out to lunch to celebrate. "What a relief," she said. We went to the Hunan Daisy, where you and Evelyn and I used to meet. That time seems like an eternity ago, the three of us sitting over a long lunch, worrying over costs, juggling schedules. Even the menu has changed. They are now serving Mex/Chinese: tofu chili, burritos filled with fried rice, sesame noodles wrapped in tortillas. It is an interesting transcultural concept.

Our lives have changed drastically since those days, but we ourselves haven't changed as much as you seem to think. Once you are back in our midst, you will see that we are the same people that you married, perhaps more so. We still confer over every decision; every small sorrow is shared. We take turns baby-sitting for Saul II; Josh continues to move from one place to another. Jen and Kelly spend hours over their craft as they always did; Connie continues to analyze our motives, help us improve our characters. Evelyn continues the way she was, working long hours, worrying over Josh, trying always to shed a pound or two, priding herself on her realism, her willingness to face facts.

We talk endlessly of your impending release and the kind of celebration we should have. There is a restaurant in Tribeca, an authentic fifties diner with banquettes in peeling vinyl, chipped tables, a worn linoleum floor. They serve meat loaf, and there is a bottle of ketchup on each table. We thought that might be the place to celebrate your homecoming. It has the tacky, soiled quality of the visiting room and might serve as a kind of bridge between prison and the world, less of a culture shock than other places we might go. But you have to reserve weeks ahead. Naturally, if you've had enough of a prison environment, we can

234

always party at home. Jen and Kelly have learned a lot of free-form dances.

Anyway, we are counting the weeks.

Dear Helen:

Even here things change. Prisoners leave, others arrive. Guess who is in this cellblock? Gregory. It turns out he had heavily invested in prison bonds and was trying singlehandedly to fill the jails with his clients. He was found guilty of a conflict of interest. Obviously, I am one of his victims.

We meet in the corridor and pretend not to know each other. Pass by, with eyes averted, chins lifted, staring at some distant spot. How sweet to see him in this place, sans assistants, poorly dressed, his girth expanding like a balloon about to burst from the sinful appetite he can only satisfy on prison starch.

Despite his reputation for sloth and immorality, the men flock around him asking legal questions. Gregory dispenses information like a pope offering blessings.

Speaking of the Pope, a priest is in the cell with Gregory. His name is Father Daniel, but he tells everybody to call him Danny. He copied stories from the Bible and sent them in to magazines as his own. "I changed all the names," he said. "I added a whole bunch of new details." Nevertheless, he was charged with plagiarism and deprived of his calling.

Or that's what he says. I have a feeling it may be something else. People often admit to a lesser crime. His eyes are shifty. Each time he tells a story, he tells it in a different way. He changes the facts, the place where it happened, even the year. Yet despite his faults, we have become friends.

The reason is we have a lot in common. Both our fathers were gloomy Italians. We have long discussions of how they affected our characters. I told him about the time my father threw my doll out the window and the consequences of that traumatic event. He told me his

235

father wouldn't permit him to bake hot cross buns with his mother and sisters, and as a result he became a priest. We have both had to overcome a distrust of other men, a fear of failing, a need always to comfort and succor. With me it was with women, with Danny his flock. "I was always on call," he says. "So was I," I say.

Now that Danny has been deprived of his vocation, he needs to learn a trade. I have managed to include him on the work crew of the greenhouse. He is a big help to me. He learns fast and can read a blueprint and measure a wall. We have finished pouring the foundation and are currently assembling the frame.

Every day, the warden comes to the construction site and stands at a distance watching us. I have the feeling he would like to catch us in some error or crime. He puts me in mind of some of our clients, who would pop into the loft without warning, as if they hoped to catch us in some illicit act, stealing wire or copulating on their time. I hope we can finish the greenhouse before I leave.

The warden is talking now of having a studio built next to the house. "I need a creative space," he says. In case he's forgotten, I remind him I'm due out of here in a few weeks if the parole board gives its okay. He gives me a thoughtful look and then turns away, whistling the theme from *The Bridge on the River Kwai*.

In the night I wake, seized by a horrible thought. Suppose the warden plans to keep me here indefinitely so I will continue building structures for him? All he has to do is recommend that I not be paroled. Remember the Evelyn Waugh novel where an illiterate chieftain keeps an Englishman in captivity so he can read the collected works of Dickens to him for the rest of his life? I break into a cold sweat. What have I walked into? You'd better alert Evelyn to this problem, just in case.

Don't bother to send me any more books. I haven't made a dent in the ones that I have. Send me some Hershey bars and Reddi Wip. Also some. . . .

The letters get shorter and more perfunctory, filled with orders and requests. He doesn't like anything we send him. The Reddi Wip left an aftertaste, the T-shirts didn't fit, he wanted the grape Kool-Aid, not the strawberry. He distrusts the scriptwriter, sees only disaster for the film. He doesn't like the pop art chair.

He sounds so different from the man we married, coarser, more conventional. We wonder if the male environment has had some lasting effect upon his character, instilling in him a love of baseball and hunting and other male bonding activities. We can imagine him now telling a dirty joke or whistling when an attractive woman walks by. We wonder what his table manners will be like and whether he will continue to bathe every day. What will we do if he makes a sexist remark?

PART IV

16

On the way to Bleaksville, Connie and Valery rehearse their act. They flew in from Vegas for the reunion.

Connie: "I bought some perfume at the airport."

Valery: "So did I. What kind did you buy?"

Connie: "Lust."

Valery: "Me too."

Connie: "It's the first time I've had to sign a release."

Valery: "A release?"

Connie: "Lust drives men crazy. Before they would sell the perfume to me, I had to agree not to hold the perfume company responsible if there were any attacks on my person. You wear it at your own risk. What's the matter? Didn't they make you sign a release?"

Valery: "No." She falls into a gloomy silence.

Connie: "Maybe they forgot."

Valery: "They didn't forget."

Connie: "How can you be sure?"

Valery: "They took one look at me and knew I wouldn't be at risk. Face it. The only man I ever drove crazy was the plumber, the time I dropped my hairbrush down the john."

We sniff the air, trying to experience the perfume's power. Are we supposed to laugh? We are too nervous for anything but a titter.

All the way to Bleaksville, the mood is one of bravado. "This is the day," we keep telling each other. "The happiest day of our lives." But we are all whistling in the dark; it is not the happiest day. We are too nervous for happiness. There are too many questions.

Saul is getting out of prison today. What will he be like? How will we act? What will we say? This is on everybody's mind.

We try to conceal our worries from one another, to avoid negative statements during the drive. But this concealment makes for faltering conversation, long silences, sighs, occasional snatches of song. Ultimately we cannot repress our doubts and worries. Valery starts. "He won't think our act is the least bit funny," she says.

"He has never laughed at anything I say," Connie says.

"He'll be jealous of the baby," Beryl says.

"He won't like my hair," Josh says.

"I'm too thin," Kelly says.

"I'm too fat," Evelyn says.

"Wait until he sees my chipped tooth," Jen says.

We are journeying to Bleaksville in a stretch limo. The prison is about fifty miles north of there. The prisoners are taken to the Bleaksville courthouse, where they are processed and then released.

Everybody seems to have sharpened her character, intensified her essence for the occasion, as though to enable Saul to recognize his wives and make the transition from prison to home easier. Connie's Lust is but one example. She is wearing a tight-bodiced, long-skirted Victorian dress. Valery is in a similar gown, made out of calico and trimmed with bits of lace. They wear these gowns onstage in order to establish a comic tension between

242

nostalgia and latter-day angst. As soon as they appear in this attire, people applaud, stamp their feet, laugh.

Saul II is in a sack, a red corduroy pillowcase, which is attached to Beryl by ropes and belts. He clutches a Saul II doll enclosed in a similar pillowcase. Whenever he squeezes the doll, it starts to play the Saul and Beryl song: "Think of me in my little cell in hell. Cold and damp, like the bottom of a well. . . ." Saul II doesn't like the song. After a line or two, he starts to cry and then Beryl reaches in the sack to squeeze the doll and stop the music.

All the way up we hear snatches of the song.

Evelyn is wearing the same suit she wore to Saul's trial. A pin still holds the waist together. "I intended to get a new zipper put in," she says. "I didn't have the time. As soon as I'm done with this case. . . ." Then she moans. "I'm too fat."

Jen and Kelly have layered themselves in safari gear left over from the big hunts and sold as surplus to aid the endangered animals fund. Over their khaki puttees they wear long khaki skirts, jackets with epaulets, pith helmets, camouflage scarves, and jungle belts. Tiny glass elephants and other endangered animals dangle from their ears.

Josh is wearing one of Saul's tweed jackets over stone-washed jeans. He has grown five inches in the last few months, but the jacket is loose on him. Josh's appro-priation of his father's jacket worries us. "You know your father. He will think you are trying to appropriate his life."

"I wouldn't want his life," he says.

Josh is playing with Saul II. He is dangling an edible human head in front of him. Each time Saul II reaches for the head, Josh breaks off a piece and eats it. Saul II stares at Josh, uncertain whether to laugh or cry. Then Josh breaks off a tiny piece and thrusts it in the baby's mouth. So far they have eaten its nose and part of its skull. Now Josh is pulling out pieces of its brain.

Beryl doesn't like the edible head. "I wish you'd get rid of it," she says.

243

"Why?" Josh says. "We're having fun."

Now that Beryl has a child of her own, her feelings for Josh seem to have undergone a change. She is less friendly and far more critical, seeing him as a bundle of mistakes that she herself will avoid at all costs. "Because it's not a good thing to feed to a baby," she says.

"Why not?" Josh says. "All the ingredients are natural; it says so right here on the label. Take a look."

But Beryl is worried about the effect it will have on Saul II's development. "It encourages cannibalistic tendencies. There are enough of those running around."

"Cannibals? Where?" Josh says. They are still debating the merits of the edible head when our limousine pulls up in front of the Bleaksville courthouse. We are unprepared for all the changes that have taken place since we were last here.

The Japanese conglomerate that owned the town has sold it to the People's Republic of China. Chinese laborers are dismantling the industrial base; they are demolishing the hi-tech building behind the courthouse. On the grassy square, a group of the townswomen are clustered around a Chinese technician who is showing them how to crochet the perforated edges of computer paper into doilies. He is teaching them to revert to hand labor. All the hi-tech industries are being transformed to labor-intensive cottage crafts. The women of Bleaksville are wearing peasant coats in somber colors, surplus garments left over from the Cultural Revolution.

The trees that lined the square have been uprooted and baby ailanthus trees are growing in their place. The Bleaks, those stone animals of an unknown species flanking the courthouse, have been fitted out with tails and snouts and transformed into Chinese dragons.

We stand around the steps of the courthouse waiting for Saul to appear. Some of us hold flowers. Beryl is prepared to squeeze the Saul II doll and start the Beryl and Saul song. Josh, who has recently taken up the flute, stands ready to accompany the song. Connie and Valery

244

are holding a huge cake with a figure perched on top, a miniature Saul, made out of marzipan.

Finally a man emerges from the courthouse. "Is that Saul?" we ask each other. His hair is slicked down with some unguent; he needs a shave. "It can't be Saul," we tell each other. This man's body is encased in a shapeless leisure suit. He looks older, heavier than Saul. He moves as if he were on the deck of an unsteady vessel, his steps mincing and cautious. We watch uncertainly as he comes toward us.

With him is another man, younger, smaller, more shapely. The two of them approach. "It is Saul," we tell each other.

"Hello," we say. "Welcome to the free world." Beryl starts the Beryl and Saul song. Josh plays his flute. The rest of us hand flowers and cake to Saul.

Saul kisses all his wives; he sniffs at Connie's perfume and sneezes. Saul II starts to bawl. Saul takes him in his arms. "What's da matta?" he says. "Don't cwy." All the way to the limo he talks baby talk to Saul II.

When we reach the car, he introduces us to his companion. "This is Danny, the former priest. A cardinal interceded and his sentence has been cut short."

"Hi, Danny," we say.

"Danny is coming home with us. He is going to help."

Help with what? I wonder.